Deadman's Handle

Mark Robinson

First published in 2021

All characters and events in this publication, other than those clearly in the public domain, are fictitious and any resemblance to real persons, living or dead, is purely coincidental.

No part of this publication may be reproduced, stored in a retrieval system, or transmitted, in any form or by any means, without the prior permission in writing of the author, nor be otherwise circulated in any form of binding or cover other than that in which it is published.

Copyright © 2021 Mark Robinson

All rights reserved.

ISBN: 979-8-5953-2040-5

For Claire, Archie and Toby

ACKNOWLEDGMENTS

Special thanks must go to Rob and Ashley at the Lynton & Lynmouth Cliff Railway for their support and encouragement, especially their checks of any technical details relating to the railway operations. Any mistakes are entirely my own. This is of course a work of fiction. The railway is real (and well worth a visit if you're in the area) but all the characters are the product of my imagination and any resemblance to actual persons, living or dead, is entirely coincidental.

As always, thank you also to my writing group buddies Stella, Janet, Nick, Maggie and Marcus for keeping me on track (sorry) and of course for your plot suggestions and invaluable grammar checks. One day I promise to get 'was sat' and 'was sitting' the right way round!

Finally, a huge thank you to Rosa De Carlo for the incredible cover design. I absolutely love what you came up with and only hope the book lives up to its cover.

Prologue

Connor peered out over the lawn from his hiding place beneath the bush. He had no idea what time it was, two, maybe three in the morning. There was no one around, and no sound save for an occasional rustling of leaves. Whether from the breeze or animals he didn't care, so long as it wasn't human.

He'd only been here for a couple of minutes but his legs were already stiffening. The night was cold, though he was pretty certain it wasn't winter anymore. It wasn't summer yet either; there was a frost on the ground that chilled his skeletal body. His chest tingled as he suppressed a shiver, but his arms were starting to go numb and his frozen bare feet made him feel as if his toes had turned to ice. His mind was foggy, and when he closed his eyes for a moment he almost passed out. Shaking his head to clear the drowsiness, he tried to plan his next move. Stick with the stealth, and crawl quietly out, or make a run for it. The former had got him this far, but he felt vulnerable waiting here like this, and the longer he took, the more probable it was his absence would be discovered.

That decided it for him. A swift dash across the garden to the wall opposite. Not to the big wooden door on the left, that was way too obvious and would probably be locked. The other corner then. Through the flowerbed, up onto the birdbath, then a small jump should be all it needed to get his hands on top. From there he could pull himself over and be away. To where, he didn't know yet. He sensed he was somewhere remote, with only fields or maybe a wood on the other side. He wasn't sure how he knew that. There was simply a stillness in the air that convinced him he wasn't near a town.

Either way, he was getting out of here. He took one last look then slid out from under the bush, pushed himself up, and ran. His legs felt weak but he kept going, stumbling a little in the uneven mud around the border. He somehow managed to stay on his feet, and with a huge effort clambered on to the bird bath. It wobbled beneath him as he took a deep breath, crouched, then launched himself at the wall.

One hand gripped it firmly, his other forearm resting along the top and his feet scrabbling for purchase below. He gasped as the garden lit up behind him, the security lights around the building all triggered. His foolish run must have activated sensors, and he swore at his own naivety. There was no going back.

He was dimly aware of some pain in his fingertips; he'd cut them on something. That didn't matter, he had to keep going. In the past he would have effortlessly sprung up and over this simplest of obstacles, but he was much frailer now, his muscles all but gone and his bones showed through his sallow skin. With a strength he didn't think he possessed, he swung a foot up then heaved the rest of himself after it. Exhausted, he rested for a second as he lay prone along the top of the wall. Then he saw the wire. That's what he'd cut himself on. It must be what had set off the lights.

He knew he couldn't waste another second here. The brightness emanating from the house stung his eyes, and looking down the far side of the wall he could see nothing but darkness. It must be the same distance to the ground that side, he thought quickly. Three metres at most, maybe less. He'd have to risk it. Shifting his body over the side, he lowered himself as carefully as he could, clinging to the edge with his frozen fingers. When he could hold it no longer he shut his eyes and let go.

His feet hit the ground with a squelch; he swayed, then

fell backwards, sitting unceremoniously in the wet mud as his arms flailed in the air. I'm okay, Connor thought to himself, that was a soft landing, but as he tried to stand the sodden earth sucked him back down. Rolling onto his hands and knees, he crawled through the thick, cloying dirt. There, clean grass, only a couple of metres away. If he could just make it that far he stood a chance. Caked in mud, his knees sliding away as he pushed onwards, he scrambled his way to the edge of the mire. As his hand reached out for the tantalising meadow beyond, a boot stepped into his view.

'Tut tut Connor,' said a voice above him. 'What have we here?' All hope evaporated and his head dropped, the weight of it almost too much for his sagging shoulders. He sat back meekly on his heels, his filthy hands hanging limply by his sides as he gazed down at the boots in front of him. More bare feet appeared. Connor no longer had the strength to stand, and knew there was no possibility of escape now. As he was surrounded he broke into tears.

'Looks like someone needs to be taught a lesson,' said the same voice. 'Alright, bring him in.' The boots walked away, then Connor felt both his arms being manhandled as he was pulled up and out of the bog. He took one last, longing glance at the fields ahead before he was dragged back through to the garden and the door in the wall was slammed shut behind him.

1

'We could go to the beach again,' Aimee suggested. 'Ryan will be there.'

'No way, man,' replied Courtney. 'I heard he got with Shenelle yesterday, the skank.'

'Ryan and Shenelle?' asked Tia. 'I thought she was tight with Brandon. Wouldn't mind some of that.'

'Man, you're rank too,' laughed Courtney. 'Pass us another creamer would you?' She brushed a blade of grass from her black t-shirt and gazed dismissively at the park as she inflated a balloon from the small canister. 'Alright, not Saunton then. What about Croyde?'

'In July? Are you mental? All them pasty faced grockles thinking they're in Benidorm?' Tia wrinkled her nose at the thought of the crowds down for the summer. 'And those packs of groms with their stupid big foam boards traipsing up and down the beach? Nah thanks. Besides, Liam and Callum are gonna be there today and I haven't got the energy for them two right now.'

Ledasha shook her head, the hint of a smile on her face. The same conversation had been going on every day for a month, ever since they'd finished their GCSEs. It had sounded amazing, the thought of school being over and a summer off before they had to decide what to do next. The trouble was, none of them knew what they wanted to do. The others didn't want to even think about it. A careers advisor had handed out college prospectuses but as Courtney had pointed out, what's the use in doing a course in fashion or beauty when they obviously already knew more than the teachers.

'What about Ilfracombe?' suggested Tia.

'What about Ilfracombe?' Courtney echoed disdainfully as she discarded the empty silver charger on the grass.

'We could get the bus. It's only three quid. Hang out for the day. When I was a kid my dad used to take us there, have fish and chips at the harbour. It was nice. 'Til he left anyway.'

She sat there looking quietly into the distance. They all knew that feeling. Even more so for Ledasha and Courtney. For them foster parents came and went, originally in London, but after a continual cycle of trouble they'd been moved to Devon in a pilot programme to give them the chance of a fresh start.

That had been well over a year ago and they'd each been through a succession of temporary homes since then. Some good, some less so. Most meant well, Ledasha knew, and tried to do their best for the kids they ended up with. Day trips were common, especially early on as the new parents tried to show them a happier way of life. It never lasted. They couldn't distract them forever, then the problems returned. Still, thought Ledasha, they'd usually been nice days while they'd lasted.

'Ilfracombe?' she said. 'Yeah, alright. But I need to be back by four, I'll be in proper trouble if I miss my anger management session.'

'Aw, what. Today?' asked Courtney. She flicked more grass from her denim miniskirt as she talked then ran her fingers subconsciously through the tight curls of her hair, checking how the light brown tints reflected in the sunlight. 'Logan said he saw her the other day, kept asking him what he's planning to do next. Like, how's he supposed to know? Not until he's got his results anyway.'

Here we go again, thought Ledasha. Exams, results, boys. It was all they talked about. What would she say though if Mrs Huxtable asked her about her plans? Courtney was right about one thing, the fashion and beauty courses were definitely not for her. The alternatives were staying in school for A-levels, or getting a job. Technically they weren't allowed to do the latter, not unless they did some kind of part time course as well, but she was pretty sure there'd be ways around that. Aimee was working with her sister at the chip shop over the summer and no one had asked her to prove she was still studying.

Then again, thought Ledasha, who would employ her? In and out of care her whole life, including a stint in a secure centre after one fight too many. That's where she'd met Courtney and Logan, shortly before the three of them were transferred to Devon. Barnstaple, with its sensible kids, quiet families and Iris bloody Huxtable giving her counselling every week. The old lady in her tweed skirt suit and flat shoes always made Ledasha feel as if she was expected to behave like a posh girl at finishing school. 'A lady does not conduct herself like that,' Mrs Huxtable had said once after Ledasha had punched one of the boys at her new school in Barnstaple. 'You won't get anywhere in life lashing out. You need to learn to control your temper or you'll never find happiness.'

The words had resonated briefly with Ledasha, and she'd even listened in class for a couple of days afterwards. But who was she kidding? No money, no job, no prospects. She knew she wanted more than this but couldn't figure out what. Until then she was stuck listening to her friends arguing about boys, day after day.

'Ilfracombe though?' asked Courtney as she lit a roll-up and took a long drag. 'Really? Come on Dash, that's so lame. Full of old biddies waiting to kark it.'

Aimee popped a bubble of pink gum before anyone could answer. "Got any better ideas?' she asked as she pushed the remnants back into her mouth with a long, equally luminescent fingernail. It matched the lurid streak in her otherwise peroxide blonde hair, which in turn mimicked her deep pink crop top and ripped jeans with large turn-ups.

Aimee slowly blew another bubble. Everyone waited for the inevitable pop. It was starting to get on Ledasha's nerves but she bit her tongue. As it finally burst Courtney glared at her and shrugged. 'Nah. Beats here I guess. Sick of this place.'

Ledasha could agree with that much at least. She looked around the Barnstaple park glumly. Rubbish spilled from a nearby bin, almost as much as was scattered along the hedge bordering the grass; two seagulls were fighting over a discarded burger box filled with cold chips, while a third stood flapping its wings, waiting for its chance to pounce. A few small children were running around the playground, their parents glued to their phones in boredom. Ledasha glanced at her own but there were no new notifications. She felt stuck in a rut sat here, a day away from it all wouldn't be so bad.

'Come on then ladies,' she announced, standing and brushing grass from her legs. 'Let's do it.'

Aimee popped another bubble then stood up, quickly followed by Tia who was clearly pleased they'd gone with her suggestion. They looked down at Courtney still sitting on the ground, who huffed and took one last drag of her cigarette before stubbing it out. 'Guess it might not be totally bunk,' she said as she jumped up, slipped her bag over her shoulder and set off across the park.

'I'll let Logan know,' said Aimee, tapping into her phone.

'Logan? Really?' groaned Courtney.

'And I'll let Ryan know,' said Ledasha mischievously, pretending to type a text.

'Don't you dare,' shrieked Courtney, making a grab for her. Ledasha laughed and spun away but Courtney caught her arm, accidentally knocking the phone from her hand. It tumbled to the ground, hitting the path hard.

'Courts! What the hell!' Ledasha yelled as she stooped to pick it up.

'What. It's not my fault,' Courtney declared, crossing

her arms defensively.

'Oh my god, you utter bell end,' said Ledasha, looking horrified as her shattered screen flickered erratically.

'Bite me,' Courtney replied. 'You asked for it, texting Ryan like that.'

'I wasn't texting Ryan dumb ass, I was just messing.'

'Well how am I supposed to know that!' Courtney looked at her feet sheepishly. 'Maybe it'll be alright if you turn it off and on again?'

'Look at it!' shouted Ledasha, holding up the busted phone. 'Now what am I gonna do?'

'Um, Loges will meet us at the bus station,' interrupted Aimee to try to lighten the mood. 'That's okay isn't it? I said I'd tell him what we were up to today.'

'If you have to invite a boy I guess he'll do,' answered Courtney. 'His brother's pretty beat, mind. Don't go inviting him along as well or I'm outta here, I mean it.'

'Just 'cause he turned you down once,' said Tia. 'That was months ago anyways, he won't even remember you.'

'Jesus, what is it with you and boys?' Ledasha asked sulkily, still pressing buttons on the side of her phone in the vain hope it would miraculously repair itself.

'Whatevs,' huffed Courtney. 'Just 'cause you ain't into guys, you don't know what you're missing. Sometimes a girl needs some boo-tay! Ain't that right girls?'

The others laughed and high fived each other. Ledasha scowled at them. Making fun of her friends' obsession with boys was usually more fun. They were pretty much all they talked about. That or bitching about other girls.

'Logan had better not be late,' said Courtney. 'I'm not hanging around waiting for him.'

'Like you've got anything else to do,' Aimee replied. 'Anyway, relax, he said he's leaving the house now, he's only five minutes away.'

As they passed the bookies on the corner they could see the buses waiting at the station. The one at stand G had Ilfracombe on the front and was already letting passengers on.

'Balls, it must be about to leave,' said Tia. They broke into a run, crossed Silver Street and up to the bus stop behind the last two passengers waiting to board.

'Come on Loges,' said Courtney, more to herself than any of the others as she paced nervously on the spot. The other passengers had got on and the driver was looking down at them.

'You getting on girls?'

'Yeah, just a minute. Our friend's coming,' replied Aimee.

'Can't wait more than a minute love, sorry. The next one's in half an hour, okay?'

For a moment Ledasha considered jumping on to try to delay him but decided it wasn't worth it. Logan could easily be another ten minutes, they might as well wait. Although the thought of listening to Courtney for the whole of that ten minutes almost swayed her. If her phone hadn't been out of action she might have gone on alone and met the others there but she knew she'd have to stick close to them now.

'Fine. We'll wait,' she said instead, stepping back. The driver gave a nod and closed the doors. They watched as he pulled out of the station. The girls leaned back against the railings, immediately getting their own phones out. Aimee continued to pop her gum. Ledasha turned and folded her arms on top of the rail, watching the world go by as she dropped her sunglasses down over her eyes.

'Here he comes,' pointed Aimee, as a boy waved from across the street. His dark frizzy hair was tied back with a purple bandana, the only colour in his otherwise black outfit. The huge rings on his fingers glittered in the sunlight as he jogged a couple of steps to cross in front of a passing van.

'Sup ladies,' he said in greeting.

'What's up?' said Courtney. 'I'll tell you what's up. The bus left without us, that's what's up.'

Logan's smile faded.

'Ignore her,' said Ledasha. 'She's just pissed she got fired from her job yesterday.'

'No way man,' Logan said, his eyebrows raised as he looked at Courtney. 'What did you do?'

'Me? I din't do nothing! It was that old bat Sandra on fish. Told the store manager I was late every day last week. She's had it in for me since I started.'

'You were late every day,' pointed out Aimee.

'So what?' asked Courtney, incredulous. 'She didn't need to tell him that, did she? Cow. Whatever, I was gonna quit anyways. That place stinks.'

'The money was good though,' said Tia. 'What are you, like, going to do now?'

'I might be able to get you a couple of shifts at the chip shop,' said Aimee. 'They're always after people this time of year.'

'I'm not doing nuffing else to do with fish,' said Courtney flatly. 'I'm up to here with serving food. Maybe I'll start dealing again, I heard there's this new drug that –'

'Don't even joke about it,' Ledasha cut in, looking at her furiously. 'You know what they'll do when you get caught? And you will get caught, 'cause you're a total idiot sometimes. And if you drag me into it and get us both sent back to –'

'Woah, calm down. I was only kidding.' Courtney turned away from Ledasha. 'Can't take a joke anymore.'

'The offer's there if you get desperate,' said Aimee, looking back and forth between the two of them.

'I'm not *that* desperate. Man, I got to get out of this town, it's driving me crazy. How much longer until the next bus?'

'Twenty-five minutes,' said Tia. 'If it's on time.'

'Aw, shit man, this sucks.' Courtney threw her bag on the floor in frustration. 'Why are we going to Ilfracombe anyway? Let's just go to the beach.'

Ledasha, still leaning over the railings, shook her head.

'We're here now. Look, that bus is off to Lynton, let's do that instead.'

The others turned and looked at it. 'Lynton?' said Logan. 'I've never been there.'

'What?' asked Aimee and Tia at the same time.

'How's that possible?' added Courtney. 'It's the classic day trip when folks wanna get you away from your crew. All wholesome and shit. Come on then. I'm not waiting around for the other one and we'll miss this if you lot keep yapping.' She picked up her bag and ran to the end of the railing.

'Crap, he's leaving!' said Tia, running after her as the bus closed his door and started to indicate to pull away from the stop. Courtney ran in front of him holding out her hand. The driver, who'd started to roll forward slightly, slammed the brake and the bus jolted to a stop. Shaking his head at Courtney, she put her hands together in prayer and mouthed 'Please?' at him. The driver rolled his eyes and opened the doors. Giggling with delight, Courtney and Tia jumped on board.

'Looks like we're going to Lynton then,' said Aimee as they ran to join the others. They paid and ran up the stairs to sit on the top deck. Spreading out, each took a double seat and were still laughing as the bus made its way out of the station.

'Road trip!' shouted Courtney. 'Here we go!'

Ledasha and Tia laughed along with her, while Logan grinned, put in his headphones and looked out of the window. Aimee, chewing away, blew out her biggest bubble of the day so far, the pop satisfyingly spreading most of it on her chin. 'Yay,' she added, deadpan.

2

An hour later the bus drove down the high street through Lynton and pulled into the bus stop by a large car park.

'Finally,' Tia said as they stood there looking around. 'Now what?'

Logan shrugged. 'Don't ask me. I've no idea where we are.'

He looked at Courtney and Ledasha. The sun was dazzling and Ledasha still had her shades on, but Courtney was squinting into the brightness. She turned away and pointed up the hill towards the town. 'That way I guess. We can mooch round here for a bit then head down to Lynmuff.'

'What's Lynmuff?' asked Logan as they started walking up the slope.

'It's another town at the bottom of the cliff,' explained Ledasha. 'Lynton up here, Lynmouth down there. There's a path to get down. It's a pretty steep walk back up though. Or we could get the railway.' She had a flashback to a day trip eighteen months ago with the first foster family she'd been placed with when she'd been moved to Devon from London. What were their names, she wondered. Sarah and Dominic? No, Sara, that was it. They'd been nice, tried their best, but Ledasha was the first to admit she'd made it hard for them. She hadn't adjusted well to the move, kept causing trouble hoping that would get her sent back to London. Always sneaking out, not coming home from school when she was supposed to, getting into fights, shoplifting. Nothing big, chocolate bars and the occasional t-shirt. Stupid, looking back. She got caught more times than she'd got away with it, especially with the clothes. Eventually she'd been put back into care but that had led to more fights and more truancy, neither of which got her back to Jay. 'Should've stayed with them,' she said absent-mindedly.

'You what?' asked Aimee.

'Nothing. There's a train thing, what's it called. Goes up and down the cliff. We could get that back up.'

'Suits me. I'm not walking up a hill in these.' Courtney's heels weren't huge but they weren't exactly practical either. 'My feet are already killing me. Has anyone got a plaster?'

'Yeah, hang on.' Tia rummaged around in her bag and handed one to her. 'I've got some flip flops here too if you need to change.'

Courtney fixed the plaster in place then set off up the slope again. Tia gave Courtney a playful push so that she wobbled into the railings, making them all laugh. It was good to be away from Barnstaple, thought Ledasha, her mood brightening slightly. It had been the same routine for weeks now, ever since their exams. Still five more weeks until they got their results. It had seemed a long way off when they'd finally escaped the last one although time was speeding up. She really was going to have to think about what to do next.

They reached the edge of the shops and peered in the windows as they passed.

'Three hundred quid for that?' exclaimed Aimee as they viewed a sculpture in one. 'I did better than that in art and design last year.'

'Bollocks,' Tia said. 'Your statue of David was lame as. Wouldn't even know what it was if you hadn't told us.'

'The proportions were all wrong too,' said Courtney. 'The real one has a tiny cock.'

'Yeah, well, that was my interpretation wasn't it,' said Aimee defensively. 'Might as well make it something worth looking at.'

'Not sure giving him three legs was quite what Mrs

Baxter had in mind,' laughed Tia. 'Still, it beat my Venus de Milo. I'll be lucky to get a five for that.'

'I'm just saying, we could make shit and sell it,' said Aimee. 'These tourists'll buy anything if you put a big enough price on it. A fiver and they're not interested. Say it's five hundred and they're queuing up. It's artisan.'

'Artisan my arse,' said Courtney. 'They're not gonna pay five hundred quid for a three legged lump of clay however much you call it art.'

'Alright, maybe I can't do sculpture. Painting though, there's money there and I can do that.'

Ledasha had to give her her dues on that one. Aimee had always been able to draw. So long as her David tripod didn't let her down she was pretty much guaranteed a nine for her GCSE. She was the only one who knew she wanted to go on to art college, and her summer job at the chip shop with her sister was filling time until then. Ledasha envied her. Aimee was hopeless at most classes but put a pencil in her hand and they were all in awe of what she could do. Now she could drop all the other subjects Aimee would be able to spend the next two years doing something she loved.

They had a final look in the window then carried on along the high street. It was slow progress as Aimee kept stopping to check out the patterns on bags and dresses hanging in windows, but there was no rush so the others didn't mind. At one point she took out a notebook and quickly sketched a design she liked. Ledasha and Logan loitered nearby while Courtney and Tia lit roll-ups and crossed the road to gaze out over the sea. They ambled back when Aimee finished her drawing and had dropped her sketchbook back into her bag.

'I might pop in here,' said Logan as they passed a gift shop. 'See if I can get something for my mum's birthday on Friday.'

Courtney glanced in the doorway and turned her nose up. 'You go right ahead love, we'll be out here.' She still had the cigarette in her hand and blew out of long stream of smoke to reinforce that she had no intention of going in any of the shops.

'You carry on,' said Aimee. 'I'm gonna wander over to see this cliff train.' She pointed to a metalwork archway across the road with Lynton and Lynmouth Cliff Railway written in large black letters in the ironwork.

'Yeah, cool, you guys head on, I'll catch you up,' said Logan as he ducked inside.

They crossed the road and started walking towards the train. The lane opened out as they approached giving them an uninterrupted view of the wide bay. A couple of people were sitting outside a cafe looking out to sea but otherwise it was quiet. Ominous dark clouds were gathering overhead and Ledasha wondered if a storm was coming.

'Oh yeah, I remember it now,' said Tia as she saw the carriage arriving into the station. Leaning on the railing she stared down at the steep track disappearing down the cliff side. The driver connected a pipe and a torrent of water started pumping into a tank below the carriage.

'What's that for then?' Courtney asked him as she joined Tia, both peering curiously at the water. Ledasha and Aimee caught up and looked down as well.

'It's how we power the railway,' answered the driver. 'Fill it with water up here, fed from the river, then let gravity take over. We're now heavier so we go down and pull the other car up.'

Some water splashed onto Ledasha as she watched them, then realised it wasn't from the pipe as she looked up again at the clouds. A heavy droplet of rain splattered onto her sunglasses.

'And that's it?' asked Tia. 'What, no petrol? No electric?'

'You got it,' said the driver. 'Just free water and gravity. At the bottom we let a bit of water out of this tank so we're lighter again, and the other car fills up. He then pulls me back up. Easy. Well, I mean, we do a lot of maintenance on the cables and brakes and everything but the mechanics of it are simple enough. Coming for the ride down?'

'Nah, you're alright,' said Aimee. 'We'll get it back up later though.'

'It's only an extra pound to go both ways, saves you the long walk down the hill.'

'Sold,' said Courtney quickly, tottering forwards on her heels and stepping down into the car. 'I'm not walking all the way down there in these, my feet are killing me already. And it's starting to rain.'

'What about Logan?' said Aimee. 'We should wait for him.'

'I've already missed a bus waiting for him today,' said Courtney. 'I'm not missing a train as well. He'll be fine, he can catch the next one.'

'And I'm not getting my hair wet for him neither,' Tia said, shielding her long dark locks with one hand as she jumped on board. The rain was already starting to get stronger, turning into a persistent drizzle. 'Come on you two, Logan's a big boy.'

The driver disconnected the pump and closed off the tank. He stepped back on board and rested his hand on the brake. 'I'm not leaving yet. Have to wait for the other car to be ready. Your friend might catch up. If not it's only a few minutes until the next one.'

Aimee and Ledasha looked at each other. 'Up to you,' said Ledasha, pulling her hoodie up. 'I don't mind waiting. My phone's bust though so I'm not staying here on my own, I'll never find you again.'

A bell rang on the carriage, and the driver leaned over and put his hand on the gate as if to close it. 'Last chance ladies, all aboard.'

Aimee looked from the driver to Ledasha, then back up the path leading to the road. The wind had picked up and heavier raindrops were landing now. There was no sign of Logan. 'Bugger it, let's go. I'll text him on the way,' she said, hopping onto the car. Ledasha followed and the driver closed the gate behind her. He rang his own bell to let the driver at the bottom know he was also ready to depart, then raised the brake to start the carriage moving.

'There he is!' shouted Tia, looking back up the path. Logan was running towards them waving a box of Devon fudge in the air.

'Sorry, too late now, I can't go back,' said the driver.

'See ya later loser!' called Courtney as she took a photo of Logan running towards the platform. He reached the wet railing where the carriage had been a few moments before and watched as the car descended rapidly, with the four girls waving back at him.

Logan took out his own phone and quickly took a photo of them. 'Wait for me!' he shouted as they disappeared from view.

'It's two minutes to the next one!' shouted Aimee. 'See you at the bottom!' She turned and looked at the others. 'I'm not sure he heard me.'

'He's fine,' said Ledasha. 'Seemed to take it quite well, considering. If it was Courtney she'd be cursing at us all the way down.'

'If it was me,' said Courtney, 'I wouldn't have been dumb enough to go in that shop in the first place.'

Three phones beeped in tandem. All but Ledasha reached for theirs and giggled as they checked out the picture Logan had just Whatsapp'd them. Tia showed her screen to Ledasha. It was a perfectly timed shot, all four of them waving from the back of the carriage as it set off down the slope. The clouds in the background were lit dramatically by the sun trying to break through and a small rainbow was curling around from the train to one side of the track.

'Wow. That could almost be a postcard,' she said. 'He should Insta that one.' The others continued to stare at their phones, so with nothing else to do Ledasha wandered out to the front of the carriage to look down the track. A

Perspex shelter protected her and the driver from the rain, still falling heavily around them.

'How does that work then?' she asked the driver, pointing at the wheel next to him.

'Ah, well, this is what's known as a deadman's handle,' replied the driver. 'The other car does nothing on the way up, everything's controlled by the one coming down. I have to keep my hand on this lever here to control our speed. If I have a heart attack and collapse, I let go of the handle and it automatically drops back to the brake position, stopping the car. Nice and safe, don't you worry.'

Ledasha looked up and saw people waving down from a footbridge they were about to pass under. She self consciously waved back, and diverted her eyes back down to the cables stretching away below them on the track. The other car appeared, rising steadily towards them. It was even quieter than theirs, she noticed, just a single passenger with a long coat and a wide, grey hat, talking to the driver of the other car. Her driver raised his hand to acknowledge him as they passed.

'How many times a day do you wave at each other?' she asked, grinning.

'Too many,' replied the driver. 'Seems rude not to. That's the first time he hasn't waved back though, dozy sod. Clearly can't talk and move at the same time.'

'Is it always this quiet?' Ledasha asked. 'Guess it must get heaving in summer.'

'Yeah, next week we'll be rammed. The schools break up and this place comes alive. You've picked a good day to visit.'

Ledasha could see the bottom of the track approaching now. Aimee came out to join her as they watched the station get bigger. The driver eased the lever up slowly and brought the car to a smooth stop by the gate.

'There you go ladies. Welcome to Lynmouth. Last ride back up is at seven o'clock this evening.'

'Don't worry, we'll be back long before then,' said

Courtney as she pushed past to get off.

'Thanks,' added Ledasha, as she and the others followed. Two older couples were queuing for the journey back up the cliff, and she heard the driver cheerily saying 'All aboard for the Lynton express,' as she walked down the ramp to the roadside. The other three phones all beeped as they reached the pavement.

'Duh, of course it has,' Courtney said. Ledasha looked at them, one eyebrow raised.

'Logan,' explained Aimee. 'Letting us know the train's arrived and he's got on.'

'Right, okay. We might as well wait here then,' said Ledasha. The shower that had threatened at the top seem to have passed and the sun had come back out. She heard the bell ring behind her on the train and crossed over to the sea wall to look at the shingly beach. Not many people were on it today but like the driver had said, once the schools broke up next week no doubt it would be heaving.

She pushed herself up to sit on the wall with her back to the sea, facing the railway. The train hadn't started moving yet, and Ledasha heard the bell ring a second time. This time it got a response, the faint sound of the other bell coming through. The carriage started moving upwards and the driver, spotting the four girls below, gave them a wave as he disappeared up the cliff to the right, making his way back to Lynton.

'I'm famished,' said Tia. 'Let's get a pie or something.'

'Or a paaasty,' said Courtney, mimicking Tia's strong Devon accent.

The others all laughed and imitated her, repeating the word pasty in ever increasing lengths.

'Yeah, I'm hungry now too,' agreed Ledasha. 'Logan can buy, he's the one making us late.'

'Here he comes,' said Tia, pointing to the train appearing from the trees. They watched as it approached the station then disappeared behind the ticket office. Aimee put a fresh piece of gum in her mouth and started chewing furiously. Courtney leaned back against the sea wall, perfecting her bored 'I've been waiting for hours' look, ready for Logan's arrival.

Ledasha watched as the small queue waiting to go back up shuffled forwards, although the small green gate for the exit remained closed.

'What's he doing?' muttered Courtney, adjusting her bored waiting stance to her other elbow.

'He's probably lost a ring or something,' said Tia. 'His jewellery's always falling off. He'll be in a right foul mood if he can't find it.'

They heard the bell indicating the trains were ready to move. Ledasha sat up a bit straighter on the wall, craning to see any sign of Logan appearing behind the gate.

'What's he playing at,' said Courtney crossly. 'Is he trying to wind us up for leaving him?'

The bell rang again and the car began ascending. 'Something's wrong,' said Aimee quietly. Ledasha hopped down off the wall and walked towards the ticket office. The others fell in behind her. Courtney sighed, annoyed that her uncomfortable waiting position had been for nothing, then tottered forwards to catch up.

Ledasha got to the exit gate first and looked around for Logan but couldn't see anyone other than the lady behind the ticket desk. She walked over to the entrance and approached the window.

'Hello dear,' said the ticket lady. 'Going back up already?'

'No, not yet. We're just waiting for our friend,' said Ledasha. 'Did you see where he went when he got off?'

'Got off dear? No one got off the last car. Your friend must have missed it I'm afraid.'

'But that's not possible,' Ledasha replied, shaking her head. 'He was right there. We saw him at the top and he texted to tell us he'd got on.'

'Well, he must be telling porkies then dear. Jim was on his own coming down on that last run. No one got off I can tell you.'

Ledasha looked at her, confused. 'But,' she started to say again, then couldn't think what else to say. She turned back to the others. 'He's disappeared.'

3

'We need to call the police,' Aimee said an hour later. 'And his parents. Anyone know their number?'

Ledasha shook her head. 'I don't even know their names. He's only been with them a couple of months.' She shrugged. 'Said they seemed alright, live over on Chester Terrace I think. Dunno which number.'

They'd looked everywhere in Lynmouth for Logan, then Ledasha and Aimee had walked up the cliff path back to Lynton in case he'd decided to skip the train and walk down.

'I don't get it,' Aimee had said as they trudged up the path. 'He said he got on. Why would he get off again?'

'Dunno. Maybe he didn't have the fare. Maybe he needed the toilet. Maybe he got scared of heights, who knows. If he jumps out at us round one of these bends I'm gonna kill him.'

It took them half an hour to reach the top of the cliff, criss-crossing the railway as they went. The two train cars passed beneath them several times on their journeys up and down the track. They paused each time to look at the passengers in case Logan was somehow among them but didn't bother returning the waves of the tourists on board. Reaching the top, they set off along the road back to the station. Ledasha started to feel guilty about what she'd said. Logan had not jumped out at them on the way.

As they approached the cafe on the cliff top Courtney and Tia ran up. They'd taken the train up the cliff instead while the other two had walked. There was a look of panic on their faces.

'Right, get this,' said Tia, who reached them first. 'This

is, like, really weird. The driver says he got on at the top, right? No one else on board, just Loges. When it was time to go, they set off. He said he was stood at the front of the train, holding onto his brake handle thingy, looking down the track. Logan was sitting inside.'

'But when they got to the bottom,' cut in Courtney, 'he turned round to let him out and he wasn't there. He'd vanished.'

'That's not possible, surely?' asked Aimee. 'You can't jump out, it's too steep and going way too fast.'

'I know, right? It's well spooky.'

'It's well dodgy, that's what it is,' said Tia. 'He must be lying. I mean, like, he seemed genuinely confused,' she added, starting to doubt herself. 'Muttered something about how he must be going mad, was sure he'd got on. Then he, like, changed his mind and said he must have got it wrong, he must have been on an earlier ride and the car was empty this time. He looked well baffled by it all.'

'I don't think he knows what's goin' on,' said Courtney. 'Probably thinks Logan's disapparated or something but doesn't want to admit it.'

'He's not a wizard, Courtney,' said Aimee exasperatedly. 'Next you'll be saying he flew out the window on a broomstick.'

'Can you get out of the windows?' asked Ledasha.

'Maybe, just,' answered Tia. 'It's tight though, and they're high up. Why would he anyways?'

'There must be a mistake,' Aimee said. 'Maybe he's right, maybe Loges didn't get on and he's getting mixed up with an earlier ride?'

'Alright, let's say he didn't,' said Ledasha, thinking it through. 'Let's say he got to the top as we were leaving, pissed at us for going off without him. He sent that photo, pretended he was coming, but decided to sack us off and go somewhere else.'

'Yeah, yeah, that must be right,' said Courtney. 'He's probably hiding in that hedge over there laughing at us.'

They all looked at the hedge but when Logan didn't jump out they went back to their scenario.

'Maybe he told the driver what we'd done,' continued Ledasha. 'Got him to go along with it. Make us think he vanished somewhere between the top and the bottom, trying to freak us out.'

'It's working,' said Aimee.

'Where would he have gone?' asked Ledasha, ignoring her. 'Somewhere close so he could watch us, right?' They all looked up and around them, searching for some sign of Logan hiding nearby. 'Okay, let's split up. Don't wander off too far, I don't want to lose another one of you. Just have a look and meet back here in five minutes.'

Aimee went to check the cafe again while Tia, more of a gymnast than the others, pulled herself up onto the high wall alongside the path and started hunting through the bushes. Ledasha and Courtney walked a bit further back up the path, leaning over the cliff wall for any sign of Logan hiding below.

'He's not here,' called Tia from the top of the wall when they regrouped a few minutes later. 'We should go back to that shop he went in, see if they remember him.'

No one could think of anything better so they traipsed back up the lane and crossed to the shop. Ledasha took the lead and went up to the woman behind the counter.

'We're looking for our friend, he was in here earlier?'

'What does he look like, hon? We get a lot of people in here.'

'He's sixteen, darkish skin, a bit darker than mine maybe. Um, he had a purple headband on.'

'Oh yeah, yeah, I remember. A ton of rings, right?'

'Yes! You saw him then?'

The lady reached past to take a toy monkey and a twenty pound note from an old lady with a toddler. She bagged the cuddly toy and rang it through the till, handing the bag and change to the customer. 'Yes, he was in here, about an hour or so ago. Bought some chocolates and left.

Haven't seen him since I'm afraid.'

'This is a waste of time,' muttered Courtney. 'He's not here.'

Ledasha ignored her. 'If you see him again could you let him know we're looking for him?'

'Sure, no problem. Hope you find him.'

The girls wandered outside and stood looking back across to the Cliff Railway arch.

'Where can he be?' asked Tia.

It was then that Aimee voiced the suggestion that Ledasha had been avoiding; that they should call the police.

'They won't believe us,' said Courtney. 'They'll think we're mucking about.'

Ledasha considered it for a moment. 'Go on then, let's call them. If he turns up in the meantime then fine. If the police think we're mucking about I don't care. But if something has happened to him we'll be in trouble for not telling them. Go on, give them a call.'

'I'm not doing it,' said Courtney. 'I'm in enough trouble for losing my job yesterday. Jan will go mental if she thinks I'm caught up with the police again. Tia can do it.'

'Me? Why me? Aimee invited him.'

'What's that got to do with it? We're all his friends, I just sent the text telling him what we were doing.'

'Oh stop it, all of you,' said Ledasha, getting annoyed with them. 'I'll do it. Give me a phone.' She held her hand out. Reluctantly Tia handed hers over.

Ledasha looked at it. 'Um. What do I call? I can't do 999 can I? Is this an emergency?'

The others stared at her blankly. 'Hang on,' said Courtney, getting her own phone out. She searched for the Devon police website 'Okay, it says here to call 999 if someone's seriously hurt or the road is blocked. We should call 101 if someone's only hurt a bit or if they're driving badly. Oh, no, this is for traffic problems. Um, wait a minute.'

'Don't bother, 101 will do,' said Ledasha, typing the number. Putting the receiver to her ear she held up a finger when Courtney started to say something. She listened for a minute then rolled her eyes. 'I'm on hold.'

She looked at the empty road and crossed back to the quieter path leading to the railway, still listening to the message on the phone. 'It says we can email 101 somehow. At DC dot police dot uk. Got that?'

'We can't wait for them to read an email, surely?' said Aimee.

'No, guess not. I'll give it another minute then – hello? Oh, hi. Yeah, my friend's gone missing, we're all really worried.' She gave a thumbs up to the others. 'No, what? Oh, yeah, my name's Ledasha Hadley. Ledasha. L. E. Then a dash. Then A. No, a dash. A hyphen, like a double barrelled name. Yeah, Le, then a hyphen, then an A. A! Look, why does it matter what my name is, I'm not the one who's gone missing. My number? Why?'

She looked at the others despairingly as she continued to talk. 'Okay. My phone's broke though. I'm using a friend's. Yeah, you can call this number, it's, hold on.' She looked at Tia who huffed but said her number so Ledasha could repeat it to the operator. 'Got it? What? Oh, her name's Tia. T. I. A. Webber. Yeah, two Bs. Yeah, that's it.'

It was quiet for a minute while she listened to the person on the other end then Ledasha started talking again. 'Yeah, his name's Logan Reeves. Yeah, that's right. Fifteen. No, wait, sixteen. His birthday was a couple of weeks ago. I dunno, normal. Five foot eight I guess. Dark skin. Well, not, like, really dark, light brown really. Black hair. Uh-huh. Yeah. Yeah. Um. Black top and shirt, black jeans. He had a purple headband on. And lots of rings. Yeah. Yep. Um, I dunno. Yeah of course we've tried phoning him, we're not idiots. It goes straight to voicemail.'

'Tell her about disappearing from the train,' urged Tia.

'I will, shh. No, not you. Okay. Yeah. Right, yeah, we're

in Lynton. North Devon yeah. I'm, like, here with my friends, we all got the bus from Barnstaple. Five of us. Yeah. Well, we got split up. Four of us got the train down the cliff. We saw Logan waving at us just as we left so he was there then. About half eleven. Yeah, he'd been in a shop. No. No. Well we weren't supposed to know that were we? It's not our fault. Well, we got to the bottom and he texted to say he'd got on at the top, but when the train got to the bottom he'd vanished. Yeah, like totally disappeared. The driver's really confused about it apparently. Well, no, I didn't speak to him myself but one of my friends did. He definitely got on at the top, and he disappeared by the time it got to the bottom. Yeah, I know, but that's what happened.'

She shook her head at the others in annoyance. 'Say that again? Yeah, we've looked everywhere. He's not here and he's not answering his phone. We're really worried. Okay, thanks.' She put the phone down to her chest and spoke to the others quietly. 'She's logging it and will give me a reference number, can one of you write it down?' She lifted the phone back to her ear and listened for a minute. When the operator gave her the number she repeated it back and Courtney typed it into her phone. 'Yeah, got it. What happens now? Really? Yeah, I know, but. Alright. Bye.' She hung up and handed the phone back to Tia.

'She said there's probably some simple explanation, there usually is, so not to worry too much. But she'll make sure it's assigned to someone today and an officer will be in touch with us. If we don't hear anything we can phone and give them that crime reference, or call into the police station in Barnstaple.'

'Sod that,' said Courtney. 'I'm not going in there. Gives me the creeps just walking past.'

'Well I don't want to go in there either,' Ledasha pointed out. 'I'm the one with a record remember so they're hardly gonna believe anything I say. I was already in enough trouble for getting caught breaking into them garages then they did me good and proper for punching Beyonce.'

4

'So what do we do now then?' asked Courtney.

'I want to go and talk to that driver,' said Ledasha. 'See if he's remembered anything else since you spoke to him. Then get the bus back I guess.'

'I need to be at the chippy by five,' said Aimee. 'So we need to leave by three.'

Tia checked her phone. 'That gives us an hour. Can we get some food first, I'm starving. We never did get that pasty.'

It seemed so long ago they'd been joking about that but Ledasha realised how hungry she felt too. They each got a bag of chips from a nearby takeaway, except Aimee who bought a cheese sandwich, saying she wasn't paying for chips when she got them for free every night. They ate them as they walked back to the railway. Looking over the cliff wall, with a clear blue sky and the view of the sea, Ledasha couldn't help thinking how unnatural it felt to be so wrought with worry about Logan while everything else about the day felt so peaceful. There were more people now, the sunny afternoon drawing out visitors who hadn't been around earlier in the day.

They watched the train come and go a couple of times while they finished their chips then wandered over to wait for the carriage Logan had caught. Aimee popped a fresh piece of gum into her mouth while they waited. It didn't take long – a minute later the car arrived and a handful of passengers disembarked. The driver set the water running to refill the tank and welcomed his new customers on board for the downhill journey. The sun was shining brightly now and he lifted his cap to wipe his balding forehead with his sleeve. The girls grouped around the railing next to the track.

'Oh, hello again,' the driver said when he recognised Courtney and Tia. 'Found your friends I see.'

'Er, no,' Courtney replied. 'Logan's, like, still missing. These two were looking for him on the path.'

'Oh. Right.' He turned to welcome another passenger on board. Ledasha checked his name badge while he was chatting and tried to get his attention again.

'Um. Excuse me. Jim? We were wondering if you, like, remembered anything strange about the ride earlier?' asked Ledasha. 'The one with Logan?'

Jim took off his cap and scratched his head. 'The whole thing's peculiar if you ask me,' he said finally. 'I definitely remember him getting on. He said how his friends had abandoned him.' Courtney pulled a face as he said this but if the driver noticed he didn't mention it. 'Then,' he paused and stared into the distance for a few moments. 'Well, then I must have locked the door and come up here to the front then set off when we were ready. Don't rightly remember. Not feeling a hundred percent to be honest, bit dizzy today. Could've sworn he was still sitting there behind me when we left.'

'What makes you think he was still there?' asked Ledasha.

'Well.' He stopped and thought about it, scratching his chin this time. 'We were chatting. He was saying he'd never been here before and I was telling him a bit about the railway. We're the highest and steepest fully water powered railway in the world you know. Then we set off, and when we get to the bottom I turn round and he's not there. It's not possible to get off this thing without me noticing though, I can tell you. The door's locked, the gate's closed. And once it's moving there's no way you can jump out. Like I said, it's right peculiar.'

'So he definitely got on then,' Tia said to the others.

'But couldn't get off without being seen,' pointed out

Aimee. They were interrupted by the bell ringing.

'Sorry, can't help you any more than that I'm afraid. Need to get on,' Jim said as he disconnected the water supply and closed the gate. The girls watched him close and lock the back door, preventing the current passengers alighting, then he walked up and stepped onto the driver's platform at the front of the carriage, rang his own bell then released the brake. The train carriage immediately picked up speed and had soon vanished from view.

'What was he playing at then?' asked Ledasha, more to herself than anything. 'How did he get off?'

'Why did he get off more like,' asked Tia.

'And where,' added Aimee. 'At the top or the bottom? Seems unlikely he'd have climbed out the window. Does it have a trapdoor?'

'Don't be mental,' said Courtney. 'Why would he climb through a trap door? Especially while the train's already moving. He must have jumped off at the last second and Jimmy Boy didn't notice. He's either wandering around here somewhere or he's got the bus back to town.'

'Why hasn't he told us then?' said Aimee.

'Because his phone died, obviously. Or he dropped it and it broke, like Dash's.' Ledasha gave her a withering look but Courtney continued unabashed. 'There must be a simple explanation, like the copper said. He's probably at home waiting for us to turn up.'

'Yeah, that must be it,' said Tia. 'Come on, let's head back. We should call in at his place to check if he's there.'

Something at the back of Ledasha's mind made her uneasy, but without any better ideas she nodded and followed the others back along the path and down the hill to the bus stop. No one said anything as they walked. Courtney and Tia were glued to their phones, while Ledasha and Aimee continued to look in all directions for some indication that Logan was nearby. They reached the bus stop with no sighting, and ten minutes later were on their way back to Barnstaple.

'What d'you reckon the coppers will do then?' asked Tia as she took in the North Devon countryside passing by.

'Nuffing' snorted Courtney. 'They're not gonna bother about some poor black kid in care who's gone missing, they'll just think he's run off somewhere.'

'You reckon?'

'Course. People like us don't matter to them. They need to keep the tourists sweet, that's all.'

Ledasha had been gazing absentmindedly at the trees along the side of the road but turned to Courtney. 'We're going to have to solve this ourselves.'

'Yeah, right. What do we know about finding someone what's gone missing?'

'We know Logan. That's a start. And we can go places the police can't.'

'Like where,' asked Aimee.

'Like onto the railway,' answered Ledasha. 'We could come back at night after they've closed, check out the tracks. Get into the carriage he was in and have a closer look. The cops won't do that. Not until they think there's a body to find.'

They all went quiet as she said that. 'Sorry, I didn't mean,' Ledasha said quietly. 'He'll be at home, we'll be laughing about it later.'

5

But Logan wasn't at home. When they got back to Barnstaple they walked straight over to his road and found the house he was currently living in. The row of terraced houses looked the same, all with net curtains in the bay windows obscuring anything going on inside. The upstairs brickwork of Logan's house was in need of some repair, and was damp from the earlier rain, but the garden was well cared for and someone had built a neat wooden storage area to keep the recycling bins in. The four girls walked up the path, and after a moment's hesitation knocked on the door.

Logan's foster father looked surprised to see them on the doorstep. 'Dash, isn't it?' he said, when he recognised Ledasha. 'Oh, yeah, and Aimee. Hi girls, everything alright?'

'Yeah,' replied Ledasha, distracted by the early evening sun glinting on his head. The grey tufts on either side, matching his full beard, did nothing to distract from the baldness. 'Well, no actually. We wondered, have you seen Logan today?'

'No, sorry. He was in bed when I left this morning and hasn't got back yet. Not sure where he's got to.'

'Oh. Okay.' Ledasha paused, wondering whether to say anything. She didn't want to create a fuss, or worry him, but at the same time she knew she probably ought to say something. Aimee leaned forward and spared her.

'He was with us, Mr, um?' Ledasha realised she couldn't remember his name and looked at him hopefully.

'Tozer. Call me Jeff. He's with you then?'

'Yeah,' said Ledasha. 'Well, no. He was but we got split

up. His phone might have died and we couldn't get hold of him. We thought he might have come back here.'

'Not yet, but I expect he'll turn up later. We try to be easy going here. His brother stays round his girlfriend's most of the time, and Logan's usually pretty reliable, so they come and go as they please.'

'Wish my carers were that laid back,' grumbled Courtney.

'You're not reliable,' Tia said. 'She knows you'd be off chasing Brandon Kay if you had half a chance.'

Ledasha shook her head and turned back to Mr Tozer. 'Can you get him to text us when he's back? It's just weirding us out a bit that he disappeared like that.'

'Yes, of course. Thanks for popping by though girls.' He closed the door and they stepped back onto the pavement.

'Should we have said more?' asked Aimee. 'Something feels really wrong about this.'

'What can we have said?' asked Tia. 'Dash is right, his phone must have died. And we did get split up. That doesn't mean something bad's happened.'

'Yeah, but still. We told the police and everything. Should we warn him?'

'Crap, I forgot about that,' said Ledasha. 'Maybe, although that woman I spoke to said we probably wouldn't hear from them until tomorrow. Someone isn't classed as missing until twenty four hours have passed.'

'What, so they're gonna do nothing?' asked Aimee. 'This is all wrong. Anything could be happening to him. We gotta find him, Dash.'

'Yeah, right,' Courtney replied dubiously. 'What can we do? We looked everywhere. He either wandered off and it's all a mistake, or he's doing this deliberately 'cause he's pissed at us.'

'Or he's been taken by someone,' pointed out Aimee. Courtney pulled a face which showed what she thought of that suggestion. 'I'm just saying,' Aimee continued. 'It's possible.'

'You watch too much telly,' said Courtney.

'Aim's right,' said Ledasha.

'What?' Courtney turned to her. 'You don't think he's been kidnapped an' all?'

'No. Well, maybe. I don't know. He's not a kid, it's not like someone could have like, grabbed him and run off. But I do think we need to find him. The police won't do anything, they haven't got enough people to do a search, and even if they did they're not going to bother are they? One look at us and they'll just see teenagers messing about. Especially as it's Logan. They'll see his record and move him straight to the bottom of the pile.'

Tia shrugged. 'Maybe. We need to try them again though. We can't find him can we? Wouldn't know where to begin.'

Ledasha thought about it. She knew Logan's best hope was if they got to him quickly. The longer they left it the harder it would be. Tia was right though, she didn't know where to start.

'Let's go to Barnstaple Police station,' she decided. 'If we can talk to someone there maybe we'll be able to get them to do something. If that doesn't work then we can work out a plan for what to do next. Agreed?'

'Aw, Dash, I want to, you know I do. I gotta get to work though,' Aimee answered, checking her watch nervously.

'And I'm not going in no pigsty,' Courtney said, folding her arms. 'No way, hos-ay.'

Ledasha shook her head and turned to Tia. 'What about you, Ti? Going to abandon me as well?'

Tia stared at her feet and shuffled uncomfortably. 'Alright, I'll come.'

Courtney looked sullenly at them. 'Look, I could, you know –' she faltered.

'Don't bother,' Ledasha answered. 'It don't need all of us. Just keep trying to get hold of Logan.' Courtney nodded, avoiding her eye. 'You get on Aims, you need to get to work. We'll call round later, let you know how it went.'

'Thanks Dash. It won't be busy tonight, I should be able to have a break.'

Ledasha looked at Tia. 'Come on then, let's go check out the cop shop.'

6

'Are you, um.' The policeman standing before them squinted at the name on the form. 'Leia?' It was now early evening and the two girls had been waiting in reception for twenty minutes after leaving their details with the duty officer.

'It's Ledasha, but yeah, that's me. Everyone just calls me Dash though.'

'Dash, right. Hyphen taken was it?'

'Eh?'

'Never mind, come on, follow me,' he said wearily, then walked back towards the door he'd appeared from. He typed in a code and stepped through, holding it open for them to follow, then led them down an empty corridor to a small room on the same floor. In his late forties, with short grey hair and a neatly trimmed moustache, he looked tired as he sat down behind a table and gestured for the girls to take the seats opposite. Ledasha peered around the room nervously. There wasn't much to see, just the simple wooden table with two chairs either side, and a Crimestoppers poster blu-tacked to the wall. She glanced behind her at the white door. It had a small window looking out onto the corridor, and another similar keypad beside it. She had the uncomfortable feeling of being trapped and had to take a few deep breaths to calm her nerves.

'Okay Miss, er, Hadley,' he said, checking his notebook. 'Dash. My name's Sergeant Wilson, I'll be helping you with your enquiry. I see you phoned earlier about a missing friend in Lynton. Logan Reeves, is that right?'

'Yeah, we got split up, see, and then he vanished.'

'Vanished, right.' He said the second word slowly with what seemed to Ledasha like an unnecessary degree of scepticism. 'Okay,' he sighed. 'Let's get some details. Is this your number? 07967 –'

'No, that's mine,' cut in Tia.

The policeman looked at her witheringly. 'Yours? It says Leia, sorry, Le-*dash*-a here.' He emphasised the dash condescendingly.

'Mine broke,' explained Ledasha, trying to ignore his superciliousness. 'I had to borrow that one to call you.'

'Fair enough, what's your name then?' asked the sergeant, the resigned look on his face already giving the impression he was facing a wasted evening.

'I'm Tia.'

'Full name?'

Tia took a deep breath. 'Tia Maria Webber.' She waited for the sarcastic comment. The sergeant paused with his pen over the paper, raised his eyes at her briefly, then looked back down and wrote it on the notes.

'Age?'

'Sixteen. We all are.'

'All? What both of you?'

'No, the five of us,' Ledasha answered, and went on to explain how they'd all taken the bus to Lynton, got separated at the railway, then not seen Logan again when the carriage arrived in Lynmouth. She started to describe him but the policeman stopped her; he read out the details Ledasha had given when she'd phoned earlier and asked her if there was anything to add. She shook her head.

'Has he ever run off like this before?' asked Sergeant Wilson.

Ledasha and Tia looked at each other awkwardly. Wilson waited patiently for one of them to answer.

'Well, yeah, a couple of times,' admitted Ledasha finally. 'He's not had it easy, okay? His parents, well, his mum's not in a good way, permanently out of it on drugs, and he don't know who his dad is, so he's been in care pretty much his whole life. We was in London but they moved us down here a year ago on a pilot programme. Sometimes it gets too much, alright? He might have run off once or twice. Not like this though. And he's happy now, he's with a nice family.'

'Once or twice,' Wilson repeated as he made a note in his book. 'Was he a drug user himself? Now or in the past when he was still living with his mother?'

Ledasha shifted uncomfortably in her seat. 'Does smoking pot count?'

'Is cannabis a drug?' asked Wilson.

'Well, yeah, but –' started Ledasha.

'Then it counts.'

'Fine, when we was back in London we sometimes had a joint or two. But nothing stronger, we're not idiots.'

Wilson raised an eyebrow and made another note. 'He's nothing to do with this new drug that's doing the rounds then?'

'No,' replied Ledasha. 'He's clean.'

'Okay. You said he's with a nice family. Do you know their details?'

Ledasha nodded and gave him the address of Mr and Mrs Tozer.

'Phone number?' asked Wilson hopefully.

The girls shook their heads. 'Never mind. I'll pay them a visit, see if he's turned up there.'

'He hasn't,' said Tia. 'We already checked.'

Sergeant Wilson made a note. 'That might change later,' he observed. 'Runaway kids often come back when it gets dark.'

'He hasn't run away,' Ledasha said, the frustration starting to creep into her voice.

'No, maybe not. It's possible though, isn't it?'

Ledasha kept her eyes on the table, scratching a line along it with her fingernail. ''spose.'

'Look, in my experience sixteen year old boys don't go missing unless they want to. I know you're worried. I would be too if it was one of my friends.' Ledasha looked up at him hopefully, the warmth in his voice catching her by surprise. 'He'll turn up though,' Wilson continued. 'They always do. Now, I think I have all I need for the time being. Why don't you two go home and get some rest, and I'll call you if he turns up.'

'Okay,' she said quietly.

'And likewise, you let me know if you hear from him, right?'

'Yeah, will do,' mumbled Ledasha. She suddenly had a desperate need to get out of there, the small room closing in on her with a claustrophobic intensity. She realised the policeman was watching her.

'Are you okay love?' he asked gently. 'Do you want a cup of tea?'

Ledasha nearly snorted. How British, she thought. A cup of tea would make everything better. Although now he said it, she did really want one.

'Nah, I'm alright.' She stood up. Tia and Sergeant Wilson did the same and the policeman walked round and opened the door, holding his arm out for them to leave first. He followed them back down the corridor and punched the code into the keypad to let them out into the reception area.

'Like I said, try not to worry. Nine times out of ten these cases are closed the same day, the person just got lost.'

'And the other one out of ten?' asked Ledasha belligerently.

'Well, we have to wait twenty four hours. If they haven't turned up by then it becomes an official missing persons case,' answered Wilson calmly. 'At that point we send his details round to other forces in the area, start putting together a more detailed profile. After forty eight hours we'll release the details to the media, see if that generates any leads. It'll go on our Twitter feed and the Facebook, they're the most effective these days at getting the word out. Within a day or so he'll either be spotted somewhere or he'll have come back of his own accord.'

'And if not?'

Wilson sighed. 'Well, we'll cross that one when it comes to it. For now let's hope he turns up safe and sound. I'll be in touch.' He turned and let himself back in through the secure door, leaving them standing in the empty reception.

'That was a waste of time,' muttered Ledasha as they left the building.

'Not entirely,' grinned Tia. 'I saw the code he typed in so if we ever need to break out of there we'll be sorted.'

Ledasha couldn't help laughing for the first time since that morning.

'Come on, let's go and seem Aims.'

7

As Tia and Ledasha approached the Cod Almighty they could see Aimee leaning against the brightly lit counter inside, her distinctive pink hair shining under the intense lighting. Courtney was sitting looking at her phone at one of the two tables off to one side but otherwise no other customers were about. She didn't notice the two girls arrive until they were standing right in front of her.

'You allowed on a break Aims?' asked Tia as they dumped their bags on the table.

'Gimme two minutes.' She looked round to her older sister standing further back by the deep fryer, who glanced at the empty shop and shrugged. Aimee filled a box with chips, slathered them in salt and vinegar and brought them over to the table where the others dove in immediately. Aimee, claiming she was sick of chips, settled for fresh bubblegum instead. In between mouthfuls Ledasha and Tia filled the other two in on their trip to the police station.

'Sounds like a right useless pillock,' Courtney said when they'd described the sergeant's apparent lack of interest.

Tia shrugged. 'He was a bit of a cock at the start, but he was nice by the end. Made me feel a bit better about it all.'

'He was just trying to get us out of there,' said Ledasha angrily, rubbing one of her chips in a pool of vinegar in the corner of the box. 'Calming us down so we'd leave him alone. Man said The Facebook for God's sake, he wouldn't know how to use social media if bit him on the arse.'

Tia considered this for a second. 'Cock,' she said again as she realised there was probably some truth it. 'They're not going to look for him are they?'

'You heard him. They'll wait a couple of days, then post a photo on Twitter.'

'Whoopie do,' said Courtney. 'We could do that.'

Ledasha looked at her. 'Yeah, we could do that. Should we?'

'I dunno Dash,' said Aimee. 'It might end up making a lot of people worried, and if he does turn up later we'll look right mugs.'

'They should be worried!' Ledasha exclaimed. 'And I don't care what we look like. If he turns up safe then I couldn't give a toss what people think about us. I'm gonna do it. Aw, shit, my phone. I need to get another one from somewhere, this is driving me nuts. Can one of you do it? Find a nice photo of him and post it saying he's missing, last seen in Lynton around lunchtime today.'

The others looked at each other. Finally Courtney sighed. 'Fine, I'll do it.' They watched her scrolling through her phone for a minute. 'What about this one?' she asked, holding up her phone. The photo showed Logan in his school uniform, chatting to Ryan and Theo, two of the other boys from their class.

'I dunno,' said Aimee, taking the phone and zooming in on Logan. 'Should it have the uniform? People might look at that and it's all they'll see. They'll be searching for any black kid in a white shirt and school tie. Reckon we need to go for something more like he had on today.'

'What was he wearing today?' asked Courtney.

'I dunno,' Tia replied. 'Black wannit?'

'You lot'd be no use with a line-up would you?' said Ledasha. 'Yeah, he was wearing black jeans and plain back t-shirt, but had a purple headband –'

'Oh yeah,' said Tia absently.

' – a purple headband,' continued Ledasha, 'and he had all them rings on his fingers. The silver one with the cross. What is it, some kind of Celtic thing? What?' she asked defensively as she became aware of the others looking at her.

'Alright Sherlock,' said Courtney. 'Just 'cause we haven't got your photographic memory.'

'It's not photographic,' Ledasha said sulkily. 'I remember what he was wearing, that's all.'

Courtney shrugged, and Aimee popped a bubble. 'Anything else?' asked Tia. No one answered. 'Come on Dash, ignore her. What else did Logan have on?'

'He was wearing white Converse trainers,' Ledasha added reluctantly. 'The ones with a thin red and blue stripe. And his belt had a silver clasp. You'd better mention his hair too. Big, but with tight curls.'

'You should let that copper know all that,' said Tia. 'We didn't give that many details earlier.'

'If they need to put out a description I'll tell them then,' replied Ledasha. 'I'm not calling them again now.'

'You're not normal,' said Courtney, typing it all into her phone. 'Okay, Twitter's done. Where else?'

'Everywhere,' Ledasha answered. 'Facebook, Insta, Snap. And tag the local papers too. And the cops. And the BBC.'

'The BBC? Seriously?' asked Tia.

'Why not? They'll either ignore us, or publicise it which would be a-mazing. Mental, but amazing. Or at the very least they might check in with the police, then that knobhead will have to do something.'

Courtney tapped away on her phone for couple of minutes. 'Now what?' she asked once she'd finished.

'I'd better get back to the shop,' said Aimee, nodding towards her sister. 'She's already looking for any excuse to make me clean out the fat tray on the grill. Take it easy.'

'Yeah, see ya later Aims,' said Tia. She looked at the empty chip box. 'Guess we ought to go.'

They wandered over to a bench across the road. Courtney stood up on the seat and sat on the back. 'Now what?' she repeated.

'I'm knackered,' said Ledasha. 'I'm heading home, maybe do some searching around on the internet.'

'What for?'

She shrugged. 'Anything unusual I s'pose. Someone knows where Logan is, we just need to find out who.'

8

It was gone nine o'clock when Ledasha let herself into the house. The driveway was wet from where Ben had recently washed his van so she was extra careful not to tread damp footprints into the house. Shivani had a strict rule about taking shoes off in the hallway but otherwise Ledasha had found her pretty laid back. Certainly more so than some of her other carers. Ledasha liked her, and her husband Ben, a carpenter. After two months with them she was starting to feel settled, although she was wary of letting herself get too comfortable. It never lasted.

'Ledasha? Is that you?' came a voice from the front room.

'Yeah,' she called back.

Her foster mum appeared in the doorway. 'Mrs Huxtable called. You missed your appointment with her this afternoon.'

'Oh, sh–.' Ledasha caught herself. Shivani did not approve of swearing. 'Sugar. Sorry, I totally forgot. It's been a crazy day.'

'Look, I'm not going to lecture you Dash, you're not a child anymore. You do understand how important it is that you go to these sessions, don't you? It's a condition of you being allowed out that you attend. Do you want to end up back in a juvenile detention centre?'

'No, of course not! I like it here, I'm doing okay aren't I? I forgot, that's all.'

'Well, that's nice to hear, and Mrs Huxtable said that as this the first one you've missed, and because you worked so hard for your exams recently, then it shouldn't be an issue. But you need to call her first thing tomorrow to reschedule.'

Ledasha nodded, avoiding eye contact. She really did like living here but it felt like weakness to have admitted it.

'Are you hungry? There's some leftover chicken pie if you want it?'

'No thanks, had some chips at Aimee's place.' Ledasha looked down at her feet, suddenly overwhelmed with everything that had happened that day.

'Are you okay?' asked Shivani. 'You look upset.'

For a moment Ledasha thought about telling her the whole thing. About the trip to Lynton, Logan's disappearance, and the visit to the police station. She wasn't sure why she held back, she knew Shivani would want her to be open, but right now she felt exhausted and didn't want to get drawn into a long conversation.

'Broke my phone,' she mumbled. 'It's totally dead. Courtney was messing about and it got smashed. Don't suppose you have an old one I could borrow do you 'til I can get it replaced?'

'Oh, I'll have a look. My last one kept freezing, it's probably not much use. Ben might have something.'

Ledasha sensed Shivani might be on the verge of telling her she should look after her things and couldn't face two tellings off in one night. 'Don't worry, I'll get one from somewhere. Thanks.' She moved past her and went up the stairs hurriedly, keen to steer clear of any further confrontations this evening. She lay down on her bed and picked up her laptop. It was old, a freebie from some charity when she'd needed one to do her GCSE coursework, but it worked well enough and would be fine for what she wanted right now. She blew on it then brushed the screen with her sleeve; three weeks of no use since her exams meant a fair amount of dust had built up. Switching it on, she adjusted the angle until the display didn't show quite as many fingerprints, then opened a web browser. She stared at it for a few seconds wondering where to start, then typed 'Missing teenager'. Several suggestions presented themselves to her in a drop down list, from lost people around the world, to 'Missing teenager found' to 'Missing teenage movie'. She added Devon then hit enter. Two million results came back. Ledasha sighed. It was going to be a long night.

Two hours later she had several pages of scribbled notes and a dozen tabs open on different websites. She could feel her eyes glazing over as she went back to the search results. She'd been sidetracked for half an hour by a Wikipedia page listing people who had disappeared mysteriously since 1970. Ledasha was pretty sure none of it was relevant but she'd found a lot of the cases fascinating and kept wanting to find out more about them. She only had two more articles to go on this page so resolved to finish those then call it a night.

She clicked on the penultimate link on the search page. Teenager disappears from ghost train – Westcountry News. Something about the unusual sounding headline made her sit up.

Connor Derrington, aged 16 from South Molton, was reported missing on Tuesday by his parents Jennifer and Jonathan Derrington. The teenager had left school as usual at 4pm and set off for his home, a twenty minute walk away. En route he passed the small fairground currently set up on the green next to Raleigh Park. Comprising a carousel, some prize stalls and a ghost train, it was the latter where Connor was last seen at around 4.15pm. Police are appealing for any information leading to Connor's whereabouts. He is described as being a white male, short dark brown hair with three lines shaved into the right hand side. Slim and of medium height. He was last seen wearing school uniform and carrying a blue rucksack. If you have seen Connor please telephone 101 and quote log reference 191022-EX176.

Ledasha made a note of Connor's name and South Molton on her notepad then opened a new tab and searched for more details. For a missing teenage boy she was surprised at how little came up. The first page was an appeal from his parents for any sighting. The next was a report from the local paper with pretty much exactly the same information as the first article. It was the third link that really made her pulse quicken.

Concern deepens for missing teenager. Police are appealing for any information on the possible whereabouts of Connor Derrington, the schoolboy from South Molton who disappeared on Tuesday afternoon.

'The facts of the case are unclear at the present time,' said a police spokesperson. 'Connor was seen leaving school as normal – several friends have attested to that. He then walked past the fairground on Raleigh Park and, we think, had a ride on the ghost train. The owner of the ride, when shown a picture of the missing boy, reported that he looked like a boy who paid for a ticket around that time. However, there appears to be some confusion as he did not come back out again. The operator of the ride says the car the boy had sat in reappeared but there was no sign of Connor himself. It seems likely that he did not actually go on the ride and instead something made him change his mind and run away. However, we are keeping an open mind at this time and the investigation continues.'

Ledasha re-read the article three times. She clicked back and looked at other articles on the disappearance but there was nothing else of interest. One article a week later implied Connor had run away, and there was a rumoured sighting in London, but other than that there had been no further developments.

'Weird,' she murmured out loud. There were definite similarities to Logan's vanishing act, if the report was anything to go by. Assuming Connor had actually got on the ride, Ledasha wondered how he had got off again without being seen. She spent another half an hour looking for any more details on the case but could find nothing useful. Maybe he'd reappeared and it wasn't exciting enough to get reported. But what if he was still missing? She closed the lid of her laptop and lay back on the bed, a hundred thoughts running through her head.

9

Ledasha was woken early the next morning by Shivani knocking on her door.

'Dash, dear? Are you up? There's someone here to see you.'

'Just a minute!' Rolling over she peered at the digital alarm clock beside her bed. 6.30am? Who on earth would be calling this early she wondered groggily. Like an electric shock the events of the previous day suddenly flashed through her mind and jolted her awake. Was it Logan, reappeared safe and sound? Not likely. He'd hardly be up at this time. Shit, maybe it was the police. Had they found him? Ledasha didn't want to dwell on what that might mean. 'Please be okay, Loges,' she muttered to herself as she quickly pulled on a dressing gown and went downstairs.

Mr Tozer, Logan's foster parent, was waiting in the hallway with Shivani. Ledasha stopped a couple of stairs short of the bottom and looked down at him expectantly. He wasn't a tall man, not much bigger than Shivani, but Ledasha felt more in control of herself if she remained higher. She thought he was acting a bit shifty, turning a cap round and round in his hands and pacing nervously on the spot.

'Dash,' he said. 'Sorry to wake you. Look, Logan didn't come home last night, and Becky and I didn't have any of your numbers. Have you heard from him?'

Ledasha's hopes sank slightly. Logan was still missing. Almost instantly the opposite thought popped into her head. He's still missing. Maybe nothing bad had happened to him. Yet.

'No. My phone's broke anyways. He might've tried one of the others.'

'Right. Yes. It doesn't seem like him to do this. I mean, we know he's had his issues in the past, and has run away a few times, but we thought he was doing alright with us. He seemed happy. Well, you know, for a, for a –'

'For a teenager?' prompted Ledasha. Tozer gave a small awkward nod. 'Honestly,' she said with an exasperated voice as she sat down on the stairs. 'And you lot wonder why. Fine, I get it. We're troubled. I've heard it before. That's not why he's missing. Least, I don't think it is.'

'Well where is he then?'

'I don't know, do I? I'm worried sick about him. We think something's happened to him and no one believes us. Not even the police. One minute he was there, waving at us. Then he didn't come down. He got on, but he wasn't there. The train was empty. It doesn't make sense.'

Tozer and Shivani both looked at her with confused expressions. 'Um, what police?' asked Mr Tozer. 'What train?' said Shivani at the same time.

Ledasha took a deep breath and gazed up at the ceiling. She noticed a crack in the artex that she'd not seen before. 'It's a long story,' she said at last.

Shivani put her arm round Ledasha's shoulders and gave her a squeeze. 'It's okay, dear. Take your time. Tell you what, let's go in the kitchen and I'll put the kettle on. Tea?' she asked, looking at Mr Tozer.

'Milk and two sugars, ta.' Ledasha followed them down the hallway to the kitchen at the back of the house. There was a small table with four seats behind the door, and floor to ceiling patio windows with a cat flap on the left leading into the garden. Ledasha noticed Ben's van wasn't parked on the gravel at the side of the house. He must have already left for work, although she hadn't heard him go. Mornings were definitely not her thing. She sat down wearily at the table and buried her head in her hands. Tozer sat opposite her, while Shivani bustled about in the galley kitchen.

'How did you know to find me here, Mr Tozer?' asked Ledasha looking up at him.

'Call me Jeff,' he said. 'I know Shivvers from way back. There aren't that many foster families in the area, and you get to meet each other at support groups and so on. I remembered when I woke this morning that Logan said you were here.' He shrugged slightly. 'Should've done somethin' last night, I know. He's stayed out late before though. We've told him off of course but it's not always easy telling kids what to do.' He nodded a thanks as Shivani placed a hot mug of tea in front of him. 'He's old enough now, can't keep them wrapped up in cotton wool forever, isn't that right Shivvers.'

'You said it,' she replied as she sat down next to him. Ledasha locked her fingers around the mug. The heat scalded her but she held onto it as long as she could to give herself some sort of a boost before releasing it abruptly. She glanced up, feeling the brief wave of adrenalin pass. They were waiting for her to speak.

'We were fed up dicking about in the park all day,' she began. 'Sorry,' she added, when she saw Shivani wince slightly at her language. 'It's been boring as f–. Um. Boring as anything, you know. Nothing to do all day, just waiting, waiting, waiting. It was meant to be fun, now the exams are all over. Anyway, whatever, we was bored, so we decided to go to Lynton for the day.'

'Lynton?' asked Jeff. 'Not been there for a while. What made you go there?'

So Ledasha told them, all about how they'd meant to go to Ilfracombe but ended up catching the different bus, about getting split up in the shops. 'He wanted to get something to send to his mum for her birthday,' she said, slightly embarrassed. 'Not that she'd have noticed, but he still tries to make an effort.'

'Oh. Right,' said Jeff. He looked at Shivani who had a questioning expression on her face. 'Logan's mother, she's not in a good way. He was first taken into care when he was nine, and has been back and forth ever since. We get a lot of support, you know. Try and help Logan keep in contact with her. He can go to see her if she's having one of her rare lucid spells, if he's accompanied by his social worker, but he's not allowed to say where he's living. She'd only turn up asking for money when she needs her next fix. You know how it is.' Shivani nodded sympathetically. Ledasha knew too. How many times had she tried to connect with her own mum and little brother. So many wasted days. She was over that now, for her mother at least. The image of Jay being taken away still haunted her but it was ancient history that she didn't want to dwell on. The past was best left in the past.

'Yeah, well, that's when we went to the train. You know, the one that goes up and down the cliff.'

'Oh yeah, I know the one you mean,' Jeff replied. 'Down to the seafront.'

Ledasha nodded. 'We'd got on. We shouldn't have done it, I know. We should have waited but it was starting to rain. We were just messing about. Logan came running towards us but the train was already moving, and we couldn't stop. So we left him. That's the last we saw him.'

10

'You can't blame yourself for that,' said Jeff. 'Christ, we used to do a lot worse than that to our mates when I was your age.'

Ledasha stared at her mug. He was right, she knew that, but it didn't make her feel any better. She'd still gone off and left Logan. It was like losing Jay all over again, only this time she was older and could have done more to prevent it. Should have done more. Whatever Tozer might say, she was responsible. This was all her fault. Unexpectedly it all felt overwhelming and she was unable to hold back the tears.

'Aw, love,' said Shivani, reaching behind for a box of tissues. She took one out and handed it to Ledasha, then left the box in front of her. Ledasha blew her nose, angry with herself for crying in front of the adults, then scrunched the tissue into the pocket of her dressing gown. She was beginning to feel uncomfortably hot. The sun was still low in the sky, shining directly into Ledasha's eyes, adding to her unease.

'Let me pull the blind down,' said Shivani, noticing Ledasha's discomfort. 'Always gets too bright in here at this time of day.' She got up, opening the back door slightly while she adjusted the blind. 'Who wants some toast?' Ledasha was grateful for the cool breeze now wafting over her. She drained her mug and put it back down on the table. Shivani picked it and Jeff's up and, without asking, took them to the kettle to make another round. They waited in silence while the kettle boiled and Shivani scraped butter and raspberry jam onto several slices of toast. She placed the plate on the table and handed Ledasha her mug then returned to get her own and Jeff's. Sitting back down, she looked to make sure Ledasha had perked up before speaking.

'So that's when the police got involved?'

'Not right away, no. We searched everywhere first. Me and Aims walked back up the long way, in case he decided to come down on the path. Courtney and Tia got the train back up. The driver was all confused apparently. Reckoned Logan definitely got on and sat inside. There's no other way out except past him, and he didn't do that. So he was there on the train, but when they got to the bottom he'd disappeared.'

'He must have changed his mind and got off, dear,' said Shivani. 'Easy for the driver to miss something like that on a busy day.'

'It wasn't busy though,' Ledasha replied. 'He was the only one on it. It might be a mix up, it must be, but there's something weird about it. He's changed his tune now anyway. Must've realised how mad he sounded, so Courts said he changed his mind and reckons Logan didn't get on after all.'

'And that's when you called the police?' asked Jeff. 'At least that's something, if they're looking into it.'

Ledasha snorted. 'You reckon? No, we hadn't called them yet. We looked round the town, checked out the shop he'd gone in. We was getting really worried by now so that's when I phoned the cops. They can't do anything yet though, he's not a minor anymore and he's not been missing long enough. So after we got back to Barnstaple, and checked he wasn't at yours, Ti and me went to the police station to try and get them to do something. They said the same, nothing they can do until two days has passed. They're hoping he'll turn up before then.'

'We'll see about that,' said Jeff, standing up. 'Look, don't worry. I'm sure it'll turn out okay and it's not your fault you got split up. I'm gonna go and speak to the police though, see if we can move things along a bit. Thanks for the tea Shivvers, I'll catch you later.'

Shivani got up to see him out. Ledasha could hear them talking quietly for a minute or two on the doorstep, then the front door closed and her foster mum reappeared in the kitchen.

'More toast dear?' she asked, picking up the plate.

'No thanks, I'm okay.' She hastily downed the remains of her tea. 'I'll go and get dressed. I need to find the others, see if they've heard anything.'

Shivani looked at her hesitantly. 'I'm not sure that's a good idea Dash, maybe you ought to wait here. They'll find you if there's any news.'

'I can't, I'll go crazy if I stay here. I'm alright, honest. I just need to do something.'

Shivani weighed it up, and eventually nodded in agreement. 'Thanks,' mumbled Ledasha, hurrying out before Shivani could change her mind. She ran up to her room and quickly threw on a tracksuit, grabbed her notes from the night before and dropped them in a backpack, then ran back downstairs. Shivani was standing at the bottom.'

'Look, I'm sorry I had a go at you last night about missing your therapy appointment. I didn't appreciate what was going on.'

'It's okay,' Ledasha said, pulling on her trainers. 'I'll call you from Tia's phone if I hear anything.'

'You go careful.'

'Will do. See you later.' Ledasha felt a sense of relief as she closed the door behind her. She walked briskly up the road, urging herself not to look back. Why was she in such a rush to get out, she wondered. It was still very early, the others wouldn't even be up yet. What was she supposed to do now?

She turned the first corner she came to and stopped. 'Bollocks!' she exclaimed, leaning back against the wall and gazing up at the sky. An old lady walking her dog on the other side of the road shook her head. Ledasha wasn't in the mood to apologise and stared at her until she moved away.

'Now what?' she said quietly to herself. She looked in her bag. Just the notepad, a couple of pens, lip balm and half a bag of skittles. Checking her pockets she found a few pounds in small coins and a couple of used tissues. She should have asked Shivani if she could borrow a tenner. Too late now. She wasn't sure what she could do but had to try something. And thinking back to the articles she'd read the previous night she knew where to start.

11

An hour later she stepped off the bus in the centre of South Molton. The single ticket had cost her £1.80, almost half her money, leaving her with just enough to get home again. Without a phone it had been a boring start to the journey, until she resolved to make use of the time and plan what she was going to do when she got there. All she knew was Connor's name and the school he went to. Or used to go to, if he really was still missing. It was still early and all being well she could get there before school started. If she was really lucky she might be able to ask some of the other kids about him, and maybe even find out where he lived.

She turned back to the bus driver before he could close the door and asked him if he knew where the high school was.

'About a five minute walk down that way,' he replied, pointing. 'Follow those kids, you can't miss it.' The door hissed closed and he pulled away, leaving Ledasha standing on the pavement. She was suddenly uneasy. Getting the bus here and having a wander round was one thing. Actually speaking to people about Connor was totally different.

'Don't be a coward, get on with it,' she said to herself, running up to the children the driver had indicated. There were four of them, three girls and a boy, chatting away, oblivious to her approach.

'Scuse me?' she asked, coming up behind them. They turned as one to face her. 'Um, I'm a reporter, can I ask you a few questions? I'm going that way anyway,' she added, nodding towards the direction they'd been walking.

The children looked at each other and shrugged. They appeared to be a year or two behind her, probably years nine or ten she decided. 'You nearly at the end of term then?' she asked as they started walking again.

'Another week, yeah,' said one of the girls. 'Not much going on, finished exams last week so we're just watching films and shit.'

'Aren't you a bit young?' asked another girl. 'To be a reporter I mean?'

'First day,' answered Ledasha quickly. 'Bit nervous actually. They've sent me here to do a follow up on that lad that went missing last year. Connor Derrington, you know him?'

The girls all shook their head but the boy replied. 'Yeah. I mean like, not much, but my sister was pretty tight with him.'

'Really?' asked Ledasha, trying not to come across as too excited. 'What, was he like her boyfriend? Is she still at the school?'

'Nah, she's into girls. They were just mates but she's finished already this year. Had her GCSEs so hasn't been in for a month. She's still in bed, lucky cow.'

Ledasha smiled at him. 'So, do you know if Connor turned up again?'

He shook his head. 'No one knows what happened to him. The police think he ran away, something about problems at home, but Chels says that isn't right.'

'And Chels is your sister? Short for Chelsea, right?'

He nodded. 'And can I ask your name?' Ledasha continued. 'I won't put it in the paper or anything, it's only for my notes.'

'Yeah, whatever. It's Ocean.'

'Wiv a big C,' said one of the girls, and they all started laughing. Ocean gave the girl a push.

'Big –, oh, I get it. Sea,' said Ledasha, grinning at them. 'Look, don't suppose you can tell me where Chels is could you, I'd really like to talk to her and it'll really help my article.'

They'd reached the school gates. The girls went straight in but Ocean stayed to keep talking to Ledasha.

'You going round now? Good, wake her up.' He gave Ledasha his address. 'Look, I didn't really know Connor but he seemed alright. No one talks about him, they think he's run off with someone, but they're kidding themselves. He's gone, man.'

He turned and followed the others into the playground. Ledasha watched him go but hurriedly walked away when she realised a teacher was watching her suspiciously. She didn't know where the address was Ocean had given her but figured it had to be back past where she'd first seem him. Retracing her steps, it took a further half an hour of exploring the area before she found the right road.

She walked up the street and found the right number, but nerves got the better of her and after a slight hesitation she kept walking to the far end of the road. Standing on the corner she took a few deep breaths. Would Chelsea fall for the same reporter line she wondered? Doubtful, given they were the same age. She ought to try a different approach but couldn't figure out what might work. She finally decided not to put it off any further, but to play it by ear once she got there.

Determined not to bottle it again, Ledasha strode back to the house and up the short path. She couldn't see a bell so gave three purposeful thuds on the knocker, then took a step back and waited. Nothing happened. She glanced up and down the street but there was no sign of anyone. She leaned forwards and gave the knocker two more goes, as loud as she could. She cringed each time but knew she had to give it her best shot or she'd end up heading back to Barnstaple annoyed at the wasted morning.

She was debating whether to give it a third and final try when she saw movement behind a frosted glass window pane in the door, then a moment later a girl opened it. Wearing a hoodie and pyjama bottoms, her short blonde hair sticking out at all angles, it was clear she'd just woken up.

'What?' asked the girl staring aggressively at Ledasha.

'Sorry, didn't mean to wake you. I need your help. Are you Chelsea?'

The girl's face changed slightly to a puzzled but marginally less hostile look.

'Might be. Who are you?'

'My name's Dash, I've just got the bus over from Barnstaple. My friend went missing yesterday. I think something bad's happened to him but no one believes us. I wondered maybe if it might have something to do with your mate.'

'Connor? Shit,' replied Chelsea slowly. 'You'd better come in.' She disappeared into the house. Ledasha remained on the doorstep, distracted by the way Chelsea's bottom moved beneath her pyjamas. Not now, she told herself, ashamed of her reaction when so much else was at stake. Stepping inside, she closed the door behind her and followed Chelsea down the hallway.

The layout was similar to so many that she'd lived in as she'd moved from home to home growing up. A staircase on her right and a small lounge on the left. The cupboard under the stairs had been converted into a small cloakroom, the door slightly ajar. She wondered if she should have taken her trainers off; Shivani would not be pleased. Chelsea hadn't said anything so she kept walking, finding her host in the kitchen filling up a kettle. Ledasha looked her up and down appraisingly. She found the way Chelsea didn't care one bit about her appearance appealing. So different to her friends in Barnstaple. The scruffy hair, the lack of makeup, the hoodie thrown on to answer the door. She couldn't help wondering what she might have on beneath, and looked away, her cheeks becoming flushed as she told herself not to get carried away.

'They reckon he ran off,' Chelsea said, putting the

kettle on its base and flicking the switch, apparently oblivious to the turmoil in Ledasha's head. 'Nah way, man. He didn't run. Someone took him.' She took two mugs out of the cupboard and reached for the tea bags. 'Tea?'

'Thanks,' Ledasha replied, glancing round. It was a nice place, clean and with various reminders and notices pinned to a cork board on the wall. She wasn't sure what else to say, or even how to react to the normalcy of the situation. Here was a girl, a similar age to herself, one second saying her friend had been taken, and the next offering her a hot drink as if this was a typical Thursday morning. 'Um. Milk and one sugar, thanks.'

Chelsea sorted out the mugs then leaned her back against the counter and folded her arms. 'What did you say your name was again?'

'Dash. Well, Ledasha really but it's a stupid spelling so everyone calls me Dash.'

'I like it. What do you wanna know then?'

Ledasha blushed slightly. She'd come here on a whim, more in hope that she could rule out any connection to Logan's disappearance. She certainly hadn't come to hook up with someone. But now she knew Connor was still missing she didn't know what else there was to ask.

'Um. I dunno really,' she admitted. 'I don't know what I'm doing to be honest, just feels like I have to try something.'

Chelsea watched her. 'Sit down,' she said eventually, pointing to a table. 'And tell me about your mate then. What happened?'

Relieved to have something to say Ledasha filled her in on everything that had happened the previous day, finishing with her being woken by Logan's foster dad that morning and her decision to visit South Molton. Chelsea listened carefully, making the tea as she did so. She sat down opposite Ledasha and continued listening without interrupting.

'Doesn't sound good, man,' she said as Ledasha

finished her tale. 'Don't bank on the cops doing anything either, they never bothered with Con. Loadsa teenagers run off they said. He'll turn up, they said. We was frantic to start with, putting up notices, knocking on doors, searching the fields. No one took us seriously. In the end we just ran out of energy. Couldn't think what else we could do.' She shrugged. 'Maybe they're right, maybe he's having a blast in London while we're all still stuck here.'

'You don't believe that though,' Ledasha said quietly.

Chelsea stared at the tea in her mug. 'No,' she replied quietly. She sat in silence for a moment. 'Sorry. Thought I was past all this.'

'What about his family?' asked Ledasha. 'Surely they're still looking?'

'Yeah, 'course they are. What can they do though? They haven't got any money to hire private detectives so it's just the two of them. Connor's mum doesn't leave the house no more, they say she's given up. You still see his dad sometimes but he's not looking too good neither. Everyone thought it was something to do with that fairground, and for a month after like, Con's dad would follow them round. There was no sign of him though. I'm not even sure he went near that place, it's probably nothing to do with them. Waste of time going after them.'

'That's the last place he was seen though, wasn't it?'

'Apparently, yeah. Guy who worked on the ghost train thought he saw someone that looked like Con anyways. He wasn't sure though, kept changing his mind. He must be simple or something. I mean, either he saw him or he didn't. That story about him going in but not coming out again, can't see how that's possible. I suppose it was 'cause of his being vague and all that the cops lost interest. They say the case is still open but there aren't no new leads so what can they do? He just disappeared. Running off with some girl he met online is what they reckon.'

'But he was only sixteen wasn't he? When he went missing?'

'Yeah, I know, right? You'd think they'd try a bit harder. A few months younger they probably would have. If he'd been fifteen they'd have pulled out all the stops, but I guess once you're sixteen it don't matter so much. You seen it yourself, they ain't got the time or the people to go chasing ghosts.'

Ledasha sat there, thinking. If Chelsea was right, and it sounded like she might be, then finding Logan would be up to her and the others. If anything it was worse this time round. Logan had run away before so it would be an open and shut case as far as the police were concerned.

'We'll have to find him then,' she said, almost to herself.

'Good luck with that. That's what we said last year but it's hard, man. Then there was a rumour he'd been seen in London and some of the others stopped helping. Pretty soon it was just me and Kayden, that's his best mate, but after about six months he started seeing someone and that was that. We'd run out of ideas by then anyway.' She looked at Ledasha and could see that wasn't what she wanted to hear. 'Still, you never know, might be different this time. Do you know what you're going to do? To find him I mean?'

Ledasha shrugged. 'I hadn't really thought much past coming here to be honest. Go back to Lynton I guess and see if anything turns up there. Not sure what else I can do.'

'Look, don't give up. I haven't. I might not be out there knocking on doors but I'm still hoping. That he's out there somewhere, doing alright. Or that he'll be found safe at least.' She reached across the table and put her hand over Ledasha's, giving it a small squeeze and sending a jolt right through her. 'Listen, I'm here if you need to talk to someone. I mean it. There's gonna be times when no one's listening. Not the police, not your parents, not your friends. That's when I got pretty low. When that happens, call me, okay?'

12

After leaving Chelsea's place Ledasha strolled back in the vague direction of the town centre. Her mind was in a whirl, worried about Logan, wondering about Connor, feeling guilty for fancying Chelsea, confused about whether there might be a link between the two disappearances or if she was becoming distracted by a completely separate case. Passing a bus stop, she sat down to decide what to do next.

The sun was bright, causing her eyes to water, so she took out her sunglasses and sat back, enjoying the heat on her face. Was Logan somewhere nearby, that same sun warming his skin? From nowhere the tears welled up but she didn't fight it this time. No one was around, and with her glasses on it wasn't obvious anyway. So she cried. And cried. Finally the sobbing petered out. Ledasha took out a tissue and blew her nose, then used another to wipe under her eyes.

Taking a deep breath and blowing it out, she realised she felt a great deal better. It's true what they say, she thought, letting it out does help. Her self-pity had evaporated, and been replaced with a cold determination. She was going to find Logan, whatever it took. She wasn't going to lose him the way she'd lost Jay. The certainty of it surprised her, having never really achieved anything in her life so far, and not having any idea what she wanted to do with her future. Now she had a purpose. Logan. That was all that mattered, and if no one else was going to find him then it was up to her.

The hiss of a bus coming to a stop in front of her made her jump. An elderly man stepped gingerly onto the pavement then, still holding onto the side, assisted his wife off. They thanked the driver who looked enquiringly at Ledasha. She waved no, conscious that she had no clue where the bus was going. She knew where she needed to be now though. Logan had disappeared in Lynton. The answer was there. As the bus drove away, she stood to check the timetable in the shelter behind her head. There was nothing familiar was on the list of stops. Looking around to get her bearings, she set off back towards the high street where she'd arrived two hours earlier.

She found the right stop and checked her purse. Two pounds nine pence. Ledasha shook her head in frustration. Enough to get back to Barnstaple, or to Lynton, but not both. 'Sod it,' she said under her breath. She'd find a way to get back somehow she thought, as she marched decisively towards the Lynton bus stop.

An hour later, with only 29p to her name, she arrived at the same stop she'd come to the previous day with the others. It felt such a long time ago. She stood gazing down at the car park below. Maybe she could blag the remainder of someone's ticket then sell it on to someone else. No, no time for that, she could waste ages trying to make the fare she needed. Spotting an abandoned plastic chair in one corner, she had an idea. All she needed now was – yes, there. She walked across and picked up some abandoned tarpaulin, then collected the chair and went to the pay and display machine. There was no one else in the area, it was now or never. Quickly, she lifted the tarpaulin over the machine, then sat down next to it and took out her notebook.

She didn't have to wait long. A few minutes later a car pulled in and a middle aged lady came over, clutching her handbag.

'Machine's out of order,' Ledasha said in as bored a voice as she could manage. 'How long do you want?'

'What do you mean?' asked the lady in a plummy accent.

Ledasha lifted her sunglasses and fixed her with a glare. 'Do I look like an electrician? I'm just paid to take the parking money. How – Long – Do – You – Want?'

The lady made no attempt to hide her disapproval of Ledasha's attitude but didn't want to cause a scene.

'Oh. Um. Two hours should do it.'

'That's two pounds,' replied Ledasha, checking her watch and writing the time on her notepad. She added £2 paid, then for good measure put the time the ticket would run out underneath. She tore it off and held it out to the lady.

As the woman looked at it warily another man arrived and queued up behind her. That seemed to convince the lady who took the change from her purse and handed it to Ledasha in return for the scribbled ticket. 'Thanks,' she said as she took it, peering at it doubtfully as she did.

Ledasha ignored her and moved straight on to the man instead. 'Machine's out of order, how long do you want?'

Seeing the man reach for his own money satisfied the first woman, who took the note back to her car then walked off into town. Ledasha gave it another ten minutes, collecting £15, before deciding not to push her luck. With no new arrivals in sight, she pulled the tarpaulin off the meter and moved the chair behind it, then hurried off to the far side of the car park to take the longer route round to the bottom end of town. If she bumped into any of the people she'd served, and if they questioned what she was up to, she'd tell them her shift was over or that the machine had been fixed. Wouldn't hurt to disguise herself a bit though. She removed a hair band from her bag and tied back her voluminous hair, then removed her tracksuit top and stuffed it in her bag. There was a light wind but it was warm enough in her white t-shirt. Finally, she removed her sunglasses, tucking them away alongside her top. An observant person would know she was the same girl who'd conned them out of their parking money but she figured she now appeared sufficiently different that most people wouldn't look twice.

The money meant she could not only get home, and buy some lunch, but also that she could ride the cliff railway. That's where it had all started, and where it had all gone wrong. Ledasha knew that's where she had to go. Walking up through the town, she reached the main road by the gift shop Logan had bought the present for his mum. She couldn't think of any reason to go back in there so, checking both ways for traffic, made to cross the road. Out of the corner of her eye she caught something and stopped in her tracks. Stepping back onto the pavement she looked again. There was a camera pointing down at the pavement from above one of the shops.

'CCTV,' she muttered under her breath. 'I wonder.' She filed it away in her mind and crossed the road, heading down the path to the Cliff Railway. A few market stalls were set up along the lane but Ledasha only gave them a passing glance as they hadn't been there the previous day. Instead she looked intently around her, at the people she passed, at the wall running beside the path, at the bushes ahead. Searching for something, anything, a spark that might give her some kind of clue for what to do next. As the lane opened out at the top, with the viewing area over the sea, she paused. There was no rush to go on the railway. Right here, this was where Logan had last been seen.

The cool breeze coming in from the sea made her shiver. Rubbing the goose bumps prickling her arms, Ledasha moved into the sheltered corner and sat down on the pavement. The sun felt luxurious, and she had the ideal view back the way she'd come in one direction and down to the cafe and station in the other. She took out her jacket and propped it behind her against the rough wall, then opened her notebook at a blank page. If Aimee were here now she would already be starting a sketch, maybe of the view out over the bay, or the railway carriage at the top of the cliff, perhaps even the people sat having a snack at the cafe. She was always amazed at Aimee's talent for drawing people as well as landscapes and objects. Ledasha was hoping for a 5, maybe even a 6 in her own art GCSE, a strong pass which would do for most college courses, but knew she'd never come close to Aimee's natural talent.

For want of anything else to do she started drawing the scene in front of her. The lane opened out wider as it sloped down towards the top of the cliff railway. A tall stone wall along the left hand side, at least three metres high, had colourful baskets of flowers hanging from it and large plant pots placed along the length leading to the train. Opposite, several picnic tables and benches belonged to the cafe, their big umbrellas swaying slightly in the wind. At the end sat a little hut, possibly once the ticket office figured Ledasha, then just out of view she knew there was the carriage itself, coming and going every few minutes.

As her sketch took shape, several questions popped into her mind and she regularly turned to the next page of her book to jot them down. Could Logan have climbed that wall? Unlikely, given how visible it was to anyone in the cafe. The windows may have been steamed up during the downpour but still, someone would have seen him. How about the hut at the end though? Could he have hidden in there? Ledasha resisted the temptation to go and check, realising it was even less likely there'd be anything to find this morning than there would have been the previous day. Was there any way he could have got onto the track itself? She couldn't see it from here but knew from yesterday that would be crazy, even if he had been able to get on it without someone stopping him, and whatever else she might have thought of Logan she was fairly sure he wasn't that mental. The track fell away so steeply it would be suicidal, especially with the oncoming carriage heading rapidly back up the cliff.

She put a cross next to that in her notebook and went back to her sketch. The cafe seemed the most likely hiding place but they'd checked that yesterday. She put down her pen and continued to watch the scene. People ambled around, browsing market stalls on her left, or perusing the postcards outside the cafe. Others gazed out over the cliff top at the sea beyond. A few glanced down at Ledasha with an initial look of disdain until they saw she was drawing, at which point she could see their impressions of her visibly change. The reaction made her cross, that people could be so shallow and assume they knew anything about her. They had no idea what was happening, what she was going through.

She took a deep breath. No sense getting worked up over these idiots. That wouldn't help her find Logan. Think, she told herself. He probably didn't go down or they'd have seen him at the bottom. He couldn't have stayed by the top station or they'd have found him when they came back up. The cafe, the little hut, the wall, they were all red herrings. Logan must have come back this way, into Lynton town centre itself. That was the only explanation. Or if she was wrong then maybe into Lynmouth at the bottom of the cliff, if he'd somehow managed to sneak past them. She could always try that later. For now, Lynton was her best bet. And that CCTV above the shop opposite would be able to tell her.

13

Ledasha put her notebook and jacket back in her bag and stood up. She walked past the market stalls, down the lane and under the Cliff Railway sign back to the main road where she paused to study the camera above the shop a little further along the high street. Looking more closely she realised it was a small cafe. The camera itself didn't move, and was pointing more at the pavement on the other side of the road. Not ideal but still, there was a possibility it might have picked up something.

How to get at it though. She knew full well she had no authority to go demanding to see it. Pretending to be a reporter didn't feel right for this, and Ledasha was doubtful it would work with grown-ups anyway. Again, the truth seemed to be the most likely winner. If she came across someone sympathetic. No harm in trying, she figured. At worst the camera was just a fake prop to act as a deterrent. And if it did work but they wouldn't let her see the footage she'd still have something to tell the police.

She crossed the road and approached the cafe. It looked busy inside. A couple of notices were on the door – a copy of the menu, an advert for part-time work as a waitress, and an Open sign. Steeling herself, she pushed the door and went in. An older man, probably nearly forty thought Ledasha, was serving two plates of fish and chips to an ancient couple sat by the window.

'Take a seat,' he called, nodding towards the corner. 'You're lucky, there's a table free over there.'

Ledasha scanned the small cafe. It was half past one and the place was full. She hadn't planned to eat but now she was here, with the smell of food coming from a kitchen doorway at the back of the room, she realised how hungry she was. The toast at Shivani's felt like a very long time ago, especially after her adventures in South Molton and her short-lived spell as a parking attendant. That thought reminded her she could afford it so sat down, deciding if she was able to access the camera she'd also stay for some food.

The cafe owner walked over and handed her a menu. 'Can I ask a strange question?' she asked, smiling shyly.

'Of course,' he replied. 'Allergy?'

'Oh, no, nothing like that. It's just, the camera you've got outside, I was wondering, does it work?'

He tilted his head quizzically. 'The camera? Sure, it works. Now why would you want to know about that?'

Ledasha glanced around but the other customers all seemed to be absorbed in their own conversations. 'It's a long shot really,' she admitted, 'and I know I have no right to ask. It's just, our friend went missing yesterday and well, the police say they can't do anything yet. He's not been gone long enough. I'm really worried about him, it's not right. And I know he was at the top of the cliff railway at half past eleven. No one's seen him since. I was wondering if your camera might have picked anything up?'

The man looked at her for a long time, then noticed a customer waving at him. 'Hang on,' he said. 'I need to see to these people first.'

Ledasha opened the menu but couldn't concentrate so put it down and reached into her bag for her notebook. The cafe owner came over a few minutes later.

'Look, we're really busy right now, and I'm not sure about all this anyway. Maybe try the police again?'

Ledasha had been half expecting this, and managed to control her frustration and disappointment. Politeness, she decided, was the best approach. 'I get it. I'm just really worried, trying to do what I can, that's all. Um, I'll still have some food though if that's okay? A chicken mayo sandwich?'

'Right-ho,' replied the man. 'Anything to drink?'

Ledasha picked up the menu again. 'A chocolate milkshake please.' She flinched slightly as she noticed the price but really wanted to make a good impression and right now the camera here was her best hope. Still, it was extravagant and she couldn't rely on scamming car park money every day. This detective work was going to need funding. If it carried on like this she'd have to get a job. Maybe she should ask Aimee if there was any work going at the chippie.

The man had already walked off to clear another table so Ledasha read through all the notes she'd made so far, mostly on Connor Derrington's disappearance. The Westcountry News article was another possible lead. If she could speak to the same reporter who'd covered that disappearance maybe she'd be able to get them to write something about Logan's. Or to speed things along, maybe she could even draft the article herself. That way if the reporter was busy they might be more willing to take it on if they could just copy what Ledasha had already written.

The more she thought about it, the more that approach appealed. Even if the original reporter wasn't interested she'd be able to send it to other local papers who might print it. Plus it would help her get her thoughts straight. Turning to a new page, she tapped the page a few times with her pen then started writing. Pretty soon the words were tumbling out, and she could barely keep up with her thoughts. Her English language GCSE paper had included an exercise reporting on the visit of a famous adventurer to the local fete, and in the back of her mind she dimly remembered finding it easy to write lots that day too.

She was so absorbed in her work that she barely registered the sandwich and milkshake being placed on the table. She ignored the food and carried on writing, wanting to ensure she didn't miss any potentially crucial detail. Her exceptional memory replayed the events, enabling her to describe everything from Logan's clothing and belongings to the setting of the cliff top station. She paused as she had a sudden flashback of the other carriage heading up the cliff while she and the others were on their way down without Logan. Only one passenger, dressed in a hat and a long coat, talking to the driver. Hadn't there been something odd about that? Ledasha absent-mindedly picked up the sandwich and took a bite as she tried to remember. The passenger had been standing with his back to her. What was it that was bothering her about it?

'Our driver,' she muttered out loud as it came back to her. Of course. He'd said that was the first time the other guy hadn't waved back. Ledasha wasn't a detective but she knew it was unusual, possibly even suspicious, when someone did something out of the ordinary for the first time. Or didn't do something as in this case. She flicked back a couple of pages and made a note about the driver and his mysterious passenger. That would have been the one they'd spoken to after searching for Logan. He'd been a bit confused about it all yesterday. Would he remember this other guy, she wondered.

She took a sip of her milkshake to wash down the first half of her sandwich. It tasted good. Really good. Looking around the cafe she saw it was emptying out a bit. Half the tables were still occupied but the lunch rush was over. She put down the drink, needing to make it last until the shop was quieter. If she could get the cafe owner on his own then maybe there was still a chance he'd help her.

Ledasha picked up her fork and slowly ate some of the salad. Normally she'd have left it but it all added to the delaying tactics. That tasted amazing too, she noticed, slightly surprised at herself. Shivani was a great cook but Ledasha's diet mostly consisted of junk food when she was out with her mates. This was delicious.

Swapping her fork to her right hand, she picked up her pen in her left and continued writing the draft of her newspaper report. Her handwriting had always looked identical whichever hand she used, a useful skill when racing to get down essays during her exams. She hesitated when she got to the police involvement. Should she include it? And if so, should she paint them in a positive light or negative? As frustrating as it had been, she had some sympathy for Sergeant Wilson. The majority of missing people most likely did turn up a day or two later, and there probably wasn't a lot he could do anyway. Still, he could have taken them a bit more seriously. She decided to stick to the facts and write down what had happened, trying to leave emotion out of it, so at least it was on record. She could always take this bit out or change it before sending it to the paper.

The very act of writing was beginning to straighten everything out in her own mind. In a way it was a distraction. There was always so much going on in her head it made things clearer to get them down on paper, and meant she could stop thinking about something once it was written. She was up to the morning's drawing session when she realised the cafe owner was hovering over her.

'Shall I take that?' he asked, pointing to her plate. Ledasha looked down and saw she still had the second half of her chicken sandwich there.

'Oh, no, not yet,' she answered, picking it up and taking a bite. 'Lost in thought,' she continued with a mouthful of food. She swallowed quickly and offered an apologetic smile. 'Writing a piece for the papers.'

The man sighed. 'About your friend? Look, I want to help, I'm just not sure I should. Privacy rules and all that.'

'I won't tell,' promised Ledasha, sensing his conflict. 'Honestly. I only wondered if there's any sign of him, and if he's alone or if someone's forcing him to go off. I don't even need to see it myself, if you'd prefer. I could describe him then you could check the footage and tell me if there's anything worth going to the police with.'

The man looked around the room. Only two older couples remained. 'Alright,' he sighed. 'Finish your sandwich, I'll go and get the footage ready. Half eleven you said, right?'

14

Ledasha beamed at him. 'Thank you so much, I mean it.'

'Don't sweat it. Just don't get your hopes up. There's probably nothing on there.' He walked off and Ledasha quickly ate the rest of her lunch. She downed what remained of the milkshake then picked at the last bits of salad while she waited for him to return. A minute later he beckoned her over to the doorway leading out the back. Putting her notebook in her bag, she hoisted it onto her shoulder and picked up her plate and glass. Best behaviour, she told herself. She didn't want to mess this up.

'Ta,' he said, leaving them on a desk behind the counter. 'Come on, it's in here.' He led her to a tiny office behind the shop floor. The screen showed a reasonable view of the street, slightly smeary but better than the average footage she'd seen on the news. 'Lens must need a wipe,' he said as he gestured for her to take a seat. 'It's clear enough though, hopefully. Here, you might as well drive. Pretty self-explanatory, just use the mouse to press play and click forwards or backwards.'

Ledasha dropped her bag on the floor next to her as she sat down. She was aware of the cafe owner standing behind her as she clicked on the play triangle. The time at the bottom of the frame showed 11.28. They must have been setting off on the train around then. Logan would have been running towards them as they waved at her. This all felt very surreal. The footage wasn't a continuous video but jumped from frame to frame as a sequence of photos.

'Saves space on the hard drive,' commented the cafe

owner. 'Doesn't need hundreds of frames per second, not for a security camera. A picture every two seconds does the job. Don't think we've ever even looked at it before. Not since it was first installed.'

'That's okay. Should be plenty, I only need to see if he left,' Ledasha replied as she watched people casually walking along. Some were more purposeful but many were ambling slowly, stopping to look in shop windows. The lane leading up to the station was in the distant background. If Logan came this way she'd have a direct view of him.

The cafe owner hovered in the doorway, one eye on Ledasha, the other checking his few remaining customers were happy. Ledasha had noticed all were halfway through their meals so were unlikely to need him any time soon. She kept glancing down at the time on the footage. 11.33. Still no sign of Logan but that was no surprise. He was unlikely to have come back yet. Their train had probably taken a couple of minutes to reach the bottom, then it would be another few minutes to fill the tank with water. His text had said he'd got on, so even if he'd got off straight away he would only have got back to the main road around now at the earliest. Ledasha sat forward, scanning the street intently.

A big silver car went past, followed by a red sports car. An old lady in a bright pink coat pushing a trolley made her way slowly up the right hand pavement. A man in a long coat and wide brimmed hat crossed the road by the lane. Wait. Ledasha hit pause and leaned in closer to the screen. She couldn't tell if it was shadow, or a trick of the light, but it looked like there might be someone else walking beside the man. It was hard to see at this distance; the lane was a long way off and the smeary camera didn't show a very clean image. The person's head and body were obscured by the man's coat but a foot was visible. She moved the footage on a couple of frames. Yes. It wasn't a shadow, the shadowy legs behind were definitely out of time with the man's.

'Do you see that?' Ledasha asked, pointing to the man on the screen. 'There's someone else behind him isn't there?'

The cafe owner leaned in a bit closer. 'Might be. Hard to tell from here.'

Ledasha frowned and pressed play again. The man with the hat was walking diagonally across the street, taking him further away from the camera. In a couple of seconds he was gone, the bend of the road taking him out of view. She rewound the footage, watching the man backstepping until he disappeared up the lane. She pressed play and shuffled forwards in her seat. There! She clicked pause as soon as he came into frame. A tiny flash of dark, frizzy hair was visible just behind his hat.

'That's him,' she murmured. Something wasn't right about it though. Logan's headband, that was it. Ledasha squinted at the screen but there was no sign of any purple. Odd that he wasn't wearing it. She moved slowly through the footage, frame by frame, hoping for a better view. Logan, if it was him, was obscured behind the man's large trench coat and it was impossible to make out from this distance whether the person's hair in the image matched Logan's spiky dreadlocks. She skipped back to the first frame again but it was no clearer the second time round. 'Is there any way you could send this to me?'

The owner looked at the screen thoughtfully. 'I guess there's nothing sensitive in the picture.' He handed Ledasha a notepad and pen. 'Here, write down your name and email address and I'll send it to you.'

Ledasha scribbled her details and handed it back.

'Um. Leia?' he asked, looking confused at the name Le-A.

'No. Mental parents. Called me Le-dash-A. I know, don't start, I've had it my whole life. Most people just call me Dash.'

'Cool. Well, I'll get this over to you later. I need to get

back to the customers now.'

'Yeah, okay,' replied Ledasha, turning back to the screen.

'No, I mean, I can't leave you in here unsupervised. I know you'd be fine, you seem like a nice girl, but –.' He left the sentence hanging.

'Oh, of course. I still owe you for the food too, seven fifty-five, right?' She reached into her pocket and counted out eight pounds. 'Here, keep the change, and thanks ever so much for your help.'

The man gave a small smile then took the money. Ledasha stepped past him to head back to the front of the shop then stopped. She really did need more money if she was going to keep trying to find Logan. She turned back to the cafe owner. 'Um, just wondered, I noticed the advert in your window. For the job? Are you still looking?'

'The job? Yeah, it's still available. It's a temporary thing, a few hours a day over the summer. Taking orders, serving food, loading the dishwasher. You interested?'

It wasn't ideal being in Lynton, she'd have to pay bus fare to get here every day and it would take time away from her search efforts, but if she was going to be coming here anyway she might as well get paid for it. 'What's the pay?'

'Six pounds an hour. Plus a share of the tips. That's above minimum wage for teenagers,' he added when he saw a flicker of disappointment on Ledasha's face. 'How old are you?'

'Sixteen,' she admitted. 'And I know minimum's only four twenty before you say. Alright, I'll take it. Thanks. When do I start?'

The owner looked at his watch. 'Tell you what, if you're free now then you can do an hour while it's quiet to learn the ropes, sort out all the washing from lunch. Then start properly from tomorrow. That work for you?'

15

At the end of her shift Ledasha stepped outside, squinting into the bright sun. She felt pleased with herself. She'd never had a job before. She was fairly happy she'd mastered the dishwasher, and had memorised the menu before Marcus, the cafe owner, had even asked her to take her first order from two mums who'd come in for tea and a cake. He'd still made her write it down. There was no need, Ledasha knew she could remember the orders of everyone in here even if the place was full, but she didn't want to argue. Not on her first day anyway.

The job was fun but she had proper work to do now. The whole point of this was to find Logan. Reaching for her sunglasses she walked over to the spot where she'd seen 'hat man', as she'd taken to thinking of him, on Marcus's camera footage.

She stood by the lane, looking across the road in the direction he'd headed. There were no obvious cameras here she could try getting access to. Following the route he'd taken, she scanned lampposts and buildings as she went, until she reached the car park where she'd worked earlier. Well, sort of worked, she told herself. No cameras here either but given what she'd done that morning that was probably just as well.

Not wanting to loiter any longer than necessary, Ledasha wandered back up to the high street. There was nothing here to give her any clues or answers. She checked her finances. Lunch had been more than she'd planned but she still had seven pounds. Marcus had said she'd get her pay packet every Friday. A pain having to wait another week but she wasn't going to complain. At this moment she could afford a return ticket on the cliff railway then her bus home. She wasn't sure what a trip on the railway might achieve but she was here now and something told her she had to go on.

Walking back up the lane, past the market stalls, she arrived at the top station to find a small queue waiting for the train to arrive. She joined them, and shuffled forwards once the arriving passengers had alighted and the driver beckoned the line forward. It was the same driver from the previous day when she'd first taken the train down with the other girls. A nice guy but not the one she wanted to talk to.

When she got to the front of the queue the driver recognised her. 'Hello again,' he greeted her cheerfully. 'Back again already? You got separated from your friend didn't you? Find him alright?'

'Um, no,' Ledasha replied. 'He's still missing. I was hoping to talk to your friend in the other train, Jim wasn't it? See if he remembers anything new?'

'Oh. Right. Oh dear. Well, he's not here today I'm afraid. Phoned in sick this morning.'

'Oh,' repeated Ledasha. 'Is he okay?'

'Don't know the details, but was told it's nothing serious. He should be back tomorrow I'd have thought.' He glanced down at the water filling up the car then back at Ledasha. 'Have you told the police about your friend?'

'Yeah, but they can't do anything yet. They have to wait, like, twenty four hours or something.'

'Oh. Yeah, 'course. Well, it must be more than that now isn't it? Might be worth giving them another try.' The bell rang from the other car, and the driver disconnected the water. 'Are you coming down?'

Ledasha looked at the carriage. She did still want to work out if there was any way Logan could have got off without the driver noticing. 'Yeah, go on then.'

'It's a car by the way,' said the driver smiling as she stepped through the gate.

'Eh?'

'This,' he said, closing the gate behind him and pointing to the green cabin she was now standing in. 'You called it a train earlier.' He shook his head slowly. 'Trains have lots of carriages. This here is a car.'

He winked then shut the door Ledasha had used and walked down the outside. He stepped onto his control platform at the front and rang his own bell. The other passengers had all crowded around at the front, jostling for the best view.

Ledasha remained standing at the back. She tried the door quietly before they started moving. It was locked. She looked up at the two open windows, high up on the back wall of the cabin. With a jolt the car launched forwards and started its journey down the steep cliff side. If they'd been stationary she could maybe have climbed up and through one of them but there was no way anyone would attempt it while moving. They probably weren't going that fast, not that it felt it from inside anyway, but she figured you'd need have a death wish to try jumping. Racing down the cliff at this speed he wouldn't have stood a chance. No, Logan didn't jump out once the car had started moving. He must have got off before it had even left the station. The timing on the surveillance camera backed that up, if the grainy image she'd seen had indeed been Logan. She was starting to doubt herself now she was away from the screen. Either way, she was now more confident he hadn't left the train halfway through the journey.

The carriage pulled into the bottom station and the other passengers filed out. The driver turned to look at her but she shook her head. There was nothing for her here. Several passengers boarded for the return journey but Ledasha let them fill up the front of the carriage and stayed where she was. Five minutes later, she was standing by the back window watching the top station come into view. The car glided to a halt, and a moment later the driver appeared by the door to let her out.

'Can I ask you something?' she asked him.

He moved to one side and switched on the pump to refill the water tanks. 'Of course,' he replied, saying goodbye to each passenger as they stepped past.

'While we were going down yesterday, your mate was coming up in the other train. Car,' she corrected herself quickly.

'That's right,' he said. 'Can't get very far without the other. We'd soon notice if he wasn't coming up!' He laughed at his own joke. Ledasha pressed on.

'He didn't wave at you though. Jim that is. You said that was the first time that'd ever happened.'

The driver scratched his chin as he thought about it. 'Yeah, I remember. He was miles away wasn't he? Chatting to one of the punters.'

'Yes. Can you remember anything about that other man? The one who was talking to your friend?'

He shook his head slowly. 'Didn't notice to be honest, love. You'd have to ask Jim. He'll be back tomorrow, I'm sure.'

'And these cars. Once you're moving, there's no way to get off them is there?'

He gave a loud laugh. 'No chance. You've seen how steep it is. No, once you're in and the car's moving you're on it for the duration.'

'But Jim said Logan got on yesterday. He was convinced he got on and they set off, but then he wasn't there when they got to the bottom.'

'Reckon he's pulling your leg then,' replied the driver. 'There's no way you could get off this car mid-journey. No way. He either didn't get on, or Jim let him off at the bottom and he hid from you. Like I said though, you'll have to ask him tomorrow.'

Oh, don't you worry, thought Ledasha, I will.

16

Ledasha woke with a start as the bus was pulling into Barnstaple station. She must have dozed off and felt disorientated as she found her bearings. It had been an exhausting day, especially after the early start that morning. She wiped some drool from her mouth, but no one seemed to have noticed her asleep. As the bus came to a stop, she jumped up and ran down the stairs and out onto the pavement.

What to do next, she wondered. She hadn't really missed having her phone today, she'd been too busy. Now though all she wanted to do was talk to the others. Checking her watch she saw it was gone five, so Aimee would probably be at the chip shop. Letting out a big yawn she set off down the road.

Courtney and Tia were sitting on the back of a bench opposite the chip shop, with their feet on the seat. They were talking to a boy but he had his back to her and Ledasha couldn't tell who it was. Tia spotted her first and called out. The guy turned to see what was going on and Ledasha realised it was Reece, Logan's brother.

'Where've you been?' asked Tia accusingly. 'We've been, like, looking everywhere for you.'

Courtney acknowledged Ledasha's arrival but remained seated on the top of the bench. 'You know Reece, right?' asked Tia.

'Alright,' nodded Ledasha. 'Any news this end?'

They all shook their heads. 'There've been some shares of the messages we put out last night,' said Courtney. 'But not loads. A few people have commented to say hope he turns up. Like, what use is that? No one with anything useful though. What about you? Where you been all day?'

'It's a long story,' said Ledasha. 'Come on, let's see if Aims can get out for a bit.'

They crossed the road and, after a reluctant agreement from her sister, Aimee brought out two big bags of chips. They walked round the corner and sat on a bench. The sun was right in her eyes so Ledasha kept her shades on as she filled in the others on her trip to South Molton.

'Bloody hell,' Reece said as Ledasha described Connor's disappearance.

'It might be coincidence,' warned Ledasha. 'I don't wanna scare anyone. This could all still be a massive mistake.'

'Yeah?' said Courtney. 'Where is he then?' They all went quiet at that. 'So you spent all day in South Molten then?' she continued.

'No, I went back to Lynton. Thought I might as well have another look around.'

'Oh.' Tia looked taken aback. 'We should've done that. Did you find anything?'

Ledasha wasn't sure what to say. She knew Marcus had been reluctant to let her see the CCTV footage and didn't want to draw attention to it yet in case it gave them false hope. 'The driver who was on Logan's carriage didn't come into work today. Phoned in sick apparently.'

'That's a bit weird isn't?' asked Aimee. 'What if he's done something with him?'

'What, like, done him in and bundled him out the window halfway down?' said Courtney. They all stared at her in disbelief. 'What? You're all thinking it.'

'Shit man, we gotta tell that policeman about this,' said Tia.

'What's the point?' asked Courtney. 'They won't do anything. Not yet, it's still too soon.'

'Jeff then,' suggested Reece. 'He's doing his nut. If we tell him all this the police are bound take more notice.'

Ledasha thought about it. Logan's foster dad had

seemed okay earlier. He hadn't blamed her at least which a lot of other adults would have done. And she begrudgingly admitted he probably did deserve to know what was going on. And Reece was right, the police were more likely to listen to him.

'Alright,' she agreed. 'Tell him about the boy in South Molton. The police should look into both in case there's a link we can't find. I don't think the other driver's in on it though. He seemed nice enough when we spoke to him. Besides,' she added, looking pointedly at Courtney. 'He couldn't have hidden a body halfway down that cliff without being seen, surely? He wouldn't have been able to stop without the other driver knowing, and if he'd somehow thrown Logan out someone's bound to have seen it.'

'It's always the quiet ones,' said Courtney ominously. 'And maybe he knows a good spot to hide it if you time it right.'

They all went silent while they pictured it. 'Maybe,' said Ledasha reluctantly. She was thinking of the camera footage which may have shown Logan walking away, but it was so blurry she really couldn't be sure. 'Doesn't feel right to me but it's possible, I guess.'

'We should check it out,' Reece suggested.

'What, go climbing around on the track? We'd never be able to do that, the trains are going up and down every five minutes,' said Tia.

'Not during the day you prat,' replied Reece. 'We need to go back at night. Have a look while no one's there.'

'Have you seen that cliff?' asked Courtney. 'It's mental steep. I'm not climbing down that.'

'I'll do it,' said Tia. 'Can't be any harder than the balance beam or the vault. It's just a slope.'

'I'm in,' Reece added. 'And I might be able to borrow Ryan's car to get us there.'

'I dunno,' Ledasha said. 'I'm pretty beat already. It's been a long day.'

'Fine,' said Courtney. 'You sleep, we'll look for Logan.'

'I didn't mean that. Okay, I'll come.'

'You'd better not fake on us now,' Courtney said accusingly. 'You're, like, the one with the brains, we'll need you.'

'I'll be there,' replied Ledasha. 'I need some rest first though. Pick me up at 1am?'

17

Ledasha let herself into the house and found Shivani and Ben sitting in the kitchen. For a second she thought she might be in trouble but then noticed the worried looks and sensed their relief when she walked in.

'Good timing,' said Ben, getting up. 'We've just cooked some pizzas. Come and join us.'

She was about to decline and say she was going up to bed but she was hungry and had the feeling the pizzas had been ready for a while. 'Thanks,' she muttered, dropping her bag and sitting at the small table. Ben busied himself laying out plates while Shivani leant over and gave Ledasha's hand a small squeeze.

'So,' Ben said as he placed two pizzas in the middle of the table. 'What have you been up to today?' Shivani was a vegetarian but the other had chicken and peppers. Ledasha stalled for time by reaching for the latter and pulling a slice onto her plate.

'It's a long story,' she replied, taking a bite of her pizza. She chewed for as long as she could while she considered how much she should say. Reece was going to tell his foster parents about the possible link to Connor so that was okay. 'I'm worried about Logan, obviously. I think something's happened to him but the police aren't taking it seriously. So I went on the internet and did some searching. I read about a boy who went missing last year. Connor. He just disappeared one day and no one can explain it. Sounded similar to what happened yesterday.'

She took another bite of pizza. Ben looked a bit surprised but didn't say anything, waiting for Ledasha to go on. 'He lived in South Molton so not far away. I got the bus over there this morning.'

'You went to South Molton?' asked Ben, astonished.

'Yeah. Dunno why really, felt like I had to do something. Anyway, I managed to find a friend of his who told me all about it. Everyone thinks Connor ran away but she says that never would have happened. Same as Logan. He wouldn't run. Why would he?' Ledasha swallowed another bite of food. 'Well, that was it really. Connor's still missing. Logan's still missing. I didn't know what else to do, so thought I'd go back to Lynton for another look around.'

'Lynton as well,' commented Ben as Ledasha took another slice. 'This is getting out of hand Ledasha, you can't go gallivanting off all over the place looking for Logan. Leave it to the authorities, this isn't your responsibility.'

'It is my responsibility!' Ledasha shouted back. 'He went missing when he was meant to be with me. And why can't I go off to Lynton anyway, I'm not a child.'

'It's okay Ledasha,' Shivani replied, glaring at Ben. 'We understand. Did you have any luck in Lynton?'

Ledasha shook her head. She was cross, and although she trusted her foster parents she didn't want to tell them about the camera footage yet. Marcus probably shouldn't have shown it to her and she didn't want to get him in trouble. For now it would remain her secret. 'Not really. I sat on the cliff top and did a sketch, then went on the railway again. I wanted to talk to the driver who last saw Logan but he was off sick today. I had a good look at the train though. Can't see how he would've jumped off halfway down, not without killing himself. And not without being seen either.'

'Look Dash,' Ben began, then paused to check with Shivani. She nodded and he went on . 'I know you want to find Logan. We all do. But you need to leave it to the police. Mr Tozer has been to see them and they are taking it seriously. We just don't think it's healthy for you to get too closely involved. I know it's worrying, and you feel responsible for Logan, but he's not Jay. What happened with your brother is completely different. We don't want you getting into trouble again.'

Ledasha stared down at her plate, not wanting to look them in the eye. She knew this wasn't like when her brother had been taken from her, although she felt just as powerless now as she had then. Why did they think she was going to do something that could get her into trouble though. It was almost as if they knew she was planning to go back to the railway that night.

'We've been thinking,' continued Ben when Ledasha didn't respond. 'You don't get your results for another month, and college won't start until another few weeks after that. You've got all summer, with nothing planned except hanging out with your friends. It's time you got a job. Something to give you a bit of spending money. Why don't you come in to work with me tomorrow morning? We might be able to find you something.'

'No need,' said Ledasha, taking another bite of pizza. 'I got a job today.'

She tried not to look pleased at the surprise on both their faces. 'Oh. Where?' asked Ben.

'When I was in Lynton there was this advert in a cafe. It's only part time over the summer holidays, and it'll take me an hour to get there on the bus every day, but I can manage that. You're right though, I need spending money and when I saw the advert I popped in and asked. I spent an hour working there this afternoon learning the ropes.'

'Well, that's brilliant,' Shivani said, smiling at her. 'Well done you.'

'Yeah, well done Dash. I'm proud of you,' echoed Ben. 'That'll take your mind off things while the police do their job. Logan will be back any minute, don't you worry. In the meantime that's great that you're keeping busy. When do you start?'

'Tomorrow,' answered Ledasha through a mouthful of food. 'Twelve o'clock, ready for the lunchtime rush. I checked, there's a bus at 10.15 that'll get me there just after eleven so plenty of time. Might even go in early, make a good impression.'

They were clearly taken aback by her announcement. That was lucky, Ledasha thought to herself. The job had been an impulse thing and she still hadn't been sure whether she was actually going to go through with it, but now it had proved useful in getting them off her back and given her an excuse to get out of the house every day. 'Actually,' she said hesitantly. 'This is a bit awkward. I haven't been paid yet and I'm really short of cash. I don't like to ask but don't suppose I could borrow a couple of quid for the bus fare could I?'

'Of course,' said Ben, reaching for his wallet. 'Here, take a tenner.'

'Thanks Ben.' Ledasha took the money gratefully. 'Pay you back, promise. I'll call it a night if that's okay? Gonna chill in my room with some music. Big day tomorrow.'

'You go,' said Shivani. 'We'll clear up. And well done again.'

Ledasha shut the bedroom door and dropped onto her bed. Now she was on her own the conversation played over and over in her mind. She started to feel cross that Ben had brought up Jay. The day they'd taken her brother away had been the worst of her life. In her fury she'd punched and scratched at the social workers, and when one had pushed her away she'd grabbed a saucepan, the first thing that had come to hand. The sound it had made as it connected with the back of the man's head still made her wince. She knew that had been wrong and had only made things worse but she'd been beside herself, screaming hysterically at the people forcibly taking her helpless little brother away while he cried and tried desperately to reach out for her. She'd been managing up to then, looking after him despite everything. They should have taken their mother away. She and her druggie friends were the danger, not Ledasha. That move with the pan had led to her being taken into care as well, and she hadn't seen Jay since. One day she would track him down, make sure he was alright. That would have to wait though, Logan was more urgent right now.

She pulled her laptop towards her and tried to put thoughts of her own family out of her mind. Marcus had sent through three photos from the camera footage. She zoomed in to the first, trying to get a closer view of the man blocking what she was convinced was Logan walking beside him. The grainy quality deteriorated at that magnification and didn't tell her anything new. The man had a wide-brimmed grey hat and big sunglasses, and a long, grey coat. Apparently he'd been better prepared for the downpour than they'd been.

Ledasha zoomed in closer. He had gloves on too. Black ones, possibly leather. And black shoes. Very smart, but unusually overdressed for the time of year she thought, despite the turn in the weather. She scrolled the image back up to his face. Very little was visible but there was no hiding the nose. Definitely white, although it barely filled a pixel at this distance and could be unreliable. The photo showed what Ledasha was convinced was Logan's hair level with the man's hat. Logan wasn't tall, about the same as Ledasha, which meant the man must be quite short too. Ledasha made a note in her book then went back to the other two photos.

The next was from a few seconds later as the man was crossing the road. She stared at it for a few seconds but it didn't tell her anything new. The third was different though. The timestamp was eight minutes later, and showed a white van coming towards the camera. Sun was glinting off the windscreen and it was hard to make out the occupant but it looked like it might be the same man in the driver's seat, still wearing the grey coat and hat. The passenger seat was empty though, that much was clear. Maybe he was tied up in the back, or had gone off with someone else. Or maybe it hadn't been Logan she'd seen after all. Ledasha memorised the number plate and went back to checking the rest of the photo but the more she looked the less convinced she became. There were too many possibilities.

Her mind was buzzing but she was aware it was already nine o'clock and she was starting to regret agreeing to go on the late night visit to the railway. It was a stupid idea but it was too late to back out now, Reece would be picking her up in four hours. With the journey there and back, and time exploring the railway itself it was unlikely she'd be back before four in the morning. She had to get some sleep if she was going to make it through a day of work tomorrow. Closing the lid of her laptop, she set the alarm by her bed for quarter to one then lay back and closed her eyes.

18

The beeping made her jump. Despite all the thoughts going round her head she must have fallen asleep within a few minutes of lying down. Hitting the button quickly she lay still for a few seconds, her pulse racing, worried the noise might have disturbed Shivani and Ben. The novelty of being woken at this hour, and the immediate recollection of what they had planned, made her instantly alert, way more than she normally was in the morning.

She was still wearing her dark tracksuit from the day before. Swinging her feet onto the floor, she stood up slowly, pausing self-consciously as the bed creaked.

She left her room and tiptoed down the stairs in darkness, acutely aware of every sound being amplified in the stillness of the night. Once on the ground floor she almost walked into a small table by the front door with a plant pot and various keys and bits of post on, managing to stop herself crashing into it just in time. As she was about to open the door she remembered Ben kept a torch in the kitchen. Creeping down the hallway, she silently rummaged around in the drawer until she found it, zipped it in her tracksuit pocket then padded softly back to the porch.

She slipped her trainers on, checked to make sure she had her key, then quietly opened the door, slowly pulling it closed behind her. She froze on the spot for a few seconds as it clicked shut, then hurried to the end of the path. It was five to one and no one was about.

She didn't want the sound of the car stopping to wake Ben or Shivani so walked to the end of the street and waited in the shadows, hoping she wasn't seen by any of the neighbours who might still be up at this hour. She shivered as she waited. It was a cloudless night, colder than she'd expected. Putting her hands in her pockets she jogged on the spot a couple of times. Fifteen minutes later a red Polo approached with Reece at the wheel. She stepped forward and waved him down, running up to jump in the back next to Aimee and Tia. Courtney was in the front looking excited about their adventure.

'This is well hype,' she said, turning to face the three girls in the back. 'Honestly man, I'm jacked up here. Breaking into the railway to look for clues. Mental innit!'

Ledasha sighed. This was a waste of time and she knew it. They'd be better off spreading the word on social media and pressuring the police to search the cliff. Still, Courtney had a point. It did feel exciting to be doing something, even if it was foolish. 'We should plan what to do,' she said as they left Barnstaple and set off towards Lynton. 'Tia, Reece, you two are the most sporty. You'll be best at climbing up the railway from the bottom. Check the bushes by the side as you climb. Logan would've been in the car on the right as you look up so if he did jump out, or get pushed, I guess that's the side he'd be on. Courtney and Aims, you two need to keep a lookout.'

'You what?' asked Courtney. 'Look out for what?'

'Anything. Security, late night strollers, anyone. If someone comes, you need to distract them. Make sure no one sees the others up on the tracks.'

'What about you?' asked Reece.

Ledasha bit her lip. She didn't like the thought of what she was about to say. 'Drop me off at the top, I'll work my way down 'til I reach you.'

'You sure babes?' asked Aimee. 'It's pretty steep.'

Ledasha knew it was insane to go climbing on the railway in the middle of the night but if she was going to do it she'd rather be alone, taking her time and focussing on what she was doing rather than risk being distracted by one of the others. Much as she liked Courtney she could be annoying at times, and she couldn't see Aimee being cut out for this.

'It's dark, right?' replied Ledasha. 'Doesn't matter how far down it is, I won't be able to see it. I'll be fine, don't worry. I'll sit on the track and shuffle down slowly. Just don't hang around at the bottom alright?'

19

With no traffic on the road the journey to Lynton only took half an hour. Reece pulled over for Ledasha to jump out, then carried on to the turning down the hill into Lynmouth. Even though the road was empty she didn't want to hang about so rapidly walked along the lane towards the cliff. Rounding the bend she cautiously checked for any sign of life but needn't have worried. No one else was crazy enough to be out here at this hour.

She reached the railings at the top of the railway. One of the cars was parked there, the other presumably waiting at the bottom station. Gripping onto the railings she peered down into the gloom, shuddering as a strong breeze gusted unexpectedly. 'What am I doing,' she muttered to herself. Taking one last look around for witnesses, she breathed deeply then climbed up and straddled the railing, holding on tightly as fear gripped her. 'Get on with it,' she whispered. The others should be down at the car park in Lynmouth by now and would already be making their way towards the bottom of the track. The sooner she got moving the more ground she'd be able to cover before they reached her.

She swung her other leg over the railing and, still gripping tightly to the top, eased her feet down. Lowering her whole body until she was sitting on the floor, she twisted so that her hands remained glued to the railings. The train car next to her looked oppressively large from where Ledasha was sitting. 'Shit shit shit shit,' she swore, glancing down. The track disappeared into the darkness. From here it felt almost vertical, and if she let go she was sure she'd go tumbling to her death.

Inspecting the layout ahead of her, Ledasha figured it would be safer to be on the train track. From here they were like two ladders descending into the murkiness below, each with two cables running down their centre which she assumed connected somehow to the dead man's brake handles on the cars, or whatever it was the driver had called them. As dizzy as it made her feel, the ladder-like track was still preferable to the gravel at the side of the rail. If she slipped and starting sliding out of control she'd be able to grab onto the sleepers, which might just save her. She shuffled her bottom downwards, holding on to the railing behind her with one hand until her feet reached the reassuringly solid bar. Taking a deep breath, she pushed her left hand more firmly into the ground, counted to three, then let go of the railing.

Nothing happened. Slowly letting out her breath, she awkwardly turned onto her knees and slid one palm down a few centimetres, then the other. Carefully, she lifted a foot and stretched it down to the next sleeper. They were spaced widely apart and she had to let both feet skid down in the darkness until she felt a firm contact. One down, at least a hundred to go, thought Ledasha.

She lowered herself to the next rung on her makeshift ladder, then the third. She eased past the top wheel of the car beside her and moved down one more sleeper before stopping. There was clearly no way Logan could have dropped down through any hatch in the floor of the car. Not that she'd noticed one inside, but from here Ledasha could now see more clearly why not. The design of the carriage was a solid wedge with the passengers sat on top. The uphill set of wheels directly beneath the cabin, with the lower wheels at the far end of the wedge down the slope. The acute angle gave the whole thing a very strange shape but however it might look it was clearly not something Logan could have climbed underneath.

The sound of voices made her jump. Gazing down the track there was nothing to see in the darkness, then she realised it was the others talking below. 'Idiots,' muttered Ledasha. They clearly didn't appreciate how much their voices carried in the still night. She unzipped her pocket and took out the torch, then flashed it three times in their direction. The voices stopped abruptly. Ledasha felt uneasy that they were drawing so much attention, mixed with a feeling of reassurance. It still felt like a long way but knowing they were coming up to meet her made the task seem a little less daunting.

She set off again. One, two, three, four, five rungs. Stop, turn on the torch and check the undergrowth on both sides of the track. Zip the torch away in her pocket, five more rungs, stop, search. Five more rungs. Five more. The constant zipping and unzipping of her pocket was getting annoying so Ledasha put the torch between her teeth instead as she moved down the next set of five. Halting, she gripped the track with one hand and took hold of the torch in the other. She quickly scanned the dark scrub beside her, then panned across and waved the light around the far side. It was becoming a well practiced movement, and Ledasha flicked the torch off, about to put it back between her teeth, when something registered at the back of her mind. She switched the torch back on and aimed it to the other side of the track. A fluttering of something caught her eye. It was hard to make out in the gloom but as her vision adjusted she gasped. Logan's headband was snagged on a bush growing out of the rock face.

She put the torch back between her teeth and reached across to the other track. Stretching her left leg she managed to get her weight onto the rung, and keeping flat to the ground she shuffled over. She clambered over the cables running down the middle of the track, taking extra care not to touch them. The heavy railway car looming above her in the darkness looked ominously precarious. She knew it was locked securely in place but didn't want to do anything which might accidentally release the brakes.

Its water tanks were probably empty, so it would be counter-balanced by the other car below, but she wasn't taking any chances. In her mind she imagined the cables as being electrified and eased herself over, keeping a safe gap between them and every part of her body.

She paused for a closer look when she got to the outer rail. The headband was high up on the side of the stonework which had been carved out of the rock to build the railway. Ledasha extended her arm but couldn't reach it. She straddled the rail, her right hand and foot still gripping rungs but most of her body now lying on the verge. Pulling herself up onto her left knee, she leaned further out. She could almost touch it. A slight breeze caused it to waft agonisingly away from her, then as it floated back down she lunged and caught it. In the same moment her right foot slipped and she was sent sprawling to the floor. The torch fell from between her teeth and clattered off below her, the beam of light spinning wildly in all directions.

Her heart pounding, she lay there, still gripping one of the rungs with her right hand and clutching the bandana in the other. She took a few deep breaths, stuffed it in her jacket pocket then slowly edged back over the rail and onto the relative safety of the track. The railway car above still looked threatening and she made her way swiftly across the cables and onto the other track.

Although it was dark, the night was clear with a bright moon and her eyes soon adjusted. She was annoyed with herself for dropping the torch but she was starting to think it had been more of a hindrance than a help. Keen to get going again, she moved down five more rungs before pausing to look around. Finding no sign of Logan or anything else suspicious she moved on. The slip had made her more cautious and she was painstakingly careful each time she placed her foot on a sleeper. Despite that she made good progress and was soon passing beneath the path which snaked up the cliff, criss-crossing the railway a couple of times on its way between the two towns.

Ledasha shivered as the shadow of the footbridge passed over her. The moonlight faded and it became much harder to see anything, but she didn't break her routine as she continued her controlled slide down the track. Even so, she was relieved when she reversed out on the far side of the bridge into the brighter moonlit section.

A voice whispered up to her from close by. 'Dash. It's us.' She recognised it as Tia's and turned her head to look down the slope. She and Reece were already two thirds of the way up the track.

'Man, am I pleased to see you,' Ledasha replied, just loudly enough for her voice to carry. 'My fingers have gone numb on here and my feet keep slipping. It's hard work going downhill.'

'You find anything?' asked Reece. 'Cause there's frig all down here.'

'Yeah, I did. I'll show yas later though. Let's get down first.'

'Why don't you two go back up if that's easier. I'll scoot down and pick you up at the top.'

Ledasha glanced down the slope at what seemed like never ending darkness then up at the much lighter view above. 'Reece, I love you dude.'

'No sweat. See you on the main road.' He started descending, while Tia shrugged and carried on up to Ledasha.

'Looks like I'm the only one who gets to do it all then. Race ya to the top.'

Ledasha grinned and started climbing back up. She soon discovered it was much easier going this way, helped in no small part by the streetlights further up by the cafe giving her something to aim for. In what felt like no time they were clambering back over the railings and onto the safety of the path. Ledasha lay on her back, relieved to be back on flat ground. 'Oh man, I'm filthy,' she moaned, looking at her hands and clothing in the streetlights. The knees of her tracksuit were both black and greasy, and her palms were covered in oil and brake dust. 'I ain't never doing that again,' she said as Tia rolled up next to her.

'Aw, come on. There's a bit of your left cheek which isn't covered in oil. Let's do it again.'

Ledasha couldn't stifle a small snort, and when Tia did the same they both soon found themselves laughing. 'Come on,' said Ledasha. 'We ought to get moving or Reece'll be sat waiting for us.'

Tia rocked backwards onto her shoulders then flicked her legs away, somehow flipping herself up to a standing position.

'How do you do that?' asked Ledasha as Tia pulled her to her feet.

Tia grinned. 'It's easy. I'll teach you tomorrow.'

20

A knock on the door confused Ledasha, until she heard Shivani's voice.

'Morning Dash. You ought to get up if you're going to catch that bus.'

'I'm up,' she called back, rolling to look at the clock by her bedside. Nine thirty, bollocks. She'd snuck back in the house just after 4am but her mind had been reeling and she'd not been able to get to sleep. On the journey home she'd shown the headband to the others but none of them had been able to come up with a plausible explanation.

They'd stopped talking after a while after that and sat in silence while Reece drove. Ledasha, her eyes heavy in the hot car, had resolved to devote her commute to work thinking about how it had come to be tangled up in a bush partway down the track, but once she'd made it back to her bedroom she felt alert again with dozens of ever more ludicrous scenarios repeating themselves in her head.

Realising she still looked a state after clambering around the railway she jumped out of bed and nearly knocked Shivani over as she ran for the shower. As she closed the bathroom door she shouted back a 'yeah thanks' to Shivani's offer of a cup of tea. The steamy water cleared her mind a little but the oily smudges on her hands and face were harder to remedy. Once dressed she quickly threw on some highlighter and a subtle lipstick. Her eyes were puffy but the makeup did a good job of covering them up. It helped that her naturally long, dark lashes always stood out, but she viewed her eyebrows critically in the mirror. They needed some work. There was no time for that now, it was already five to ten.

Running down the stairs, she found the mug of tea and a plate of toast waiting for her on the kitchen table.

'Nervous?' asked Shivani, who stood by the sink wiping a plate with a tea towel.

Ledasha took a big bite of toast and chewed it hurriedly, shaking her head as she swallowed a gulp of tea. 'No, it's fine. Just overslept.'

'You'll be great I'm sure. I'll cook something special for dinner tonight to celebrate.'

'Sounds good, thanks,' Ledasha managed, her mouth full of food. She took another big swig of tea then dumped the half full mug back on the table and picked up the other slice of toast. 'I'd better run.'

She pulled on her trainers and grabbed her bag, then ran all the way to the bus station. The bus was already waiting at the stop and she waved franticly at him as she ran up in case he drove off.

'You're alright love, two minutes to spare,' smiled the driver as Ledasha dove on board. She was so out of breath it took her a moment to get the word Lynton out, and she collapsed gratefully onto a downstairs seat next to the window. The bus was well on its way before she could take a bite of toast without wanting to be sick.

She snoozed on and off as the bus wound its way to Lynton, and by the time they arrived she was feeling particularly dozy. There was still plenty of time before her shift so she popped into a corner shop and bought a can of coke, then walked to the cliff top to drink it. The fresh breeze helped and, throwing the empty can in a bin, she set off towards the cafe with a renewed energy.

As she walked back down the lane from the cliff railway, a white van passed along the main road in front of her. Ledasha jumped. She couldn't see the number plate but it looked exactly the same as the one Marcus had found the previous day. Running to the end of the lane, she saw it disappear round the corner. She chased after it, hopeful that it might get held up somewhere, but when she reached the turning it had gone.

'Dammit,' Ledasha muttered. She closed her eyes and tried to recall the image of the van. The driver hadn't been visible, the glare from the sun reflecting off the passenger window. Was there anything about the van itself? It was similar to Ben's, tall and white, like a thousand others on the road, although this one was newer looking from what she could tell. She replayed the van driving past. There was a black stripe between the wheel arches, and another black stripe higher up over the back wheel. Was that unusual? She wasn't sure but filed it away in her mind. She'd have to chat to Ben later, try to make it sound like she was showing a casual interest in his van to see if there was anything distinctive about the one she'd seen.

That would have to wait. It was still twenty minutes until she was due at the cafe but she wanted to make a good impression. Heading back up the road, she pushed open the door causing the little bell to tinkle above her. Marcus stuck his head out from the doorway at the back of the room.

'Ah, you're early. Come in, you can leave your bag in the office. Here's your apron, notebook, pen. Go and wash your hands then we'll run through the menu.'

Ledasha nodded and took the items. The previous day had gone well but she was suddenly apprehensive about what was to come. As if sensing her doubts, Marcus gave her a friendly smile. 'Don't worry, you'll be fine. Go on, go and get yourself ready.'

Ledasha went to the small bathroom and looked in the mirror. There were still bags under her eyes but another dab of blusher hid the worst of it. She put on the apron and patted it down. I'll do, she decided, and went back to the dining room where Marcus was straightening a chair behind one of the tables.

'The cutlery and paper napkins are in the unit over there,' he pointed. 'Can you roll up a set in one of the napkins and leave them on that tray on top. You'll need to keep an eye on them throughout your shift and top them up as they run low. It's a handy job if you find yourself a few quiet minutes.'

Half a dozen completed sets were already on the tray. Ledasha took a knife and fork and wrapped a napkin around it, placing it with the others. She reached down for the next set but the one she'd already done started unravelling itself. She picked it up again and examined the ones Marcus had already done more closely, trying to copy the tautness of the napkin. Her next attempt was an improvement but it was now creased. She took it off, stuffed it in her apron and started again from scratch. This one was just right and blended in perfectly with the others.

'That's it, you've got it,' Marcus said approvingly. 'Well done for getting rid of the first one, we want it all to look right. A word of warning though. Don't put everything that goes wrong in your apron. I made that mistake on my first day and it was overflowing by the end of the day.'

Ledasha returned his grin, grateful for the kind words. It was rare for an adult to praise her, and it was a strange feeling. She went back to her task and was soon stacking up the cutlery efficiently. Marcus chatted to her about the menu as she worked, letting her know the soup of the day and pointing out the specials on a blackboard. The rest of it was the same as the previous day though and Ledasha was comfortable she could remember the whole menu.

'If someone asks for a sandwich?' asked Marcus.

'I ask brown or white, and if they want spread,' Ledasha replied confidently.

'And if they want the pie?'

'Would they like chips or boiled potatoes with it.'

'And if you were eating here, what would you recommend?'

'Me?' Ledasha looked worried. What was the right answer, she thought. 'Um. The special?' she asked tentatively.

Marcus laughed. 'Clever girl. Yeah, good answer,

although it can depend a bit on what's selling well on the day. If we have a lot of something we want to shift I'll let you know, but if in doubt the specials are good to promote. If all else fails the crab sandwich is popular and will make you sound like you're letting them in on a secret. Whichever you choose, just say it confidently with a smile and don't sweat it if they ignore you completely and choose something else. There's no right or wrong answer to that one.'

They were interrupted by the little bell chiming as the door opened and a couple in their thirties entered. Marcus nodded to Ledasha to go over.

'Er, hi,' she said. 'Would you like to see the menu?'

'Yes please. We're not too early for lunch?'

'No, it's okay. Take a seat anywhere.' She reached behind her to get two of the menus and handed them over. 'Give me a wave when you're ready to order.'

She turned her back on the couple and grinned at Marcus. So far, so good. She was slightly surprised that she was actually enjoying having a job. The bell tinkled again and she spun back round with a smile.

'Morning!' she said brightly. 'Would you like to –' She froze as she took in the customer who'd entered. Wearing a long coat, and a wide brimmed hat which kept half of his face in shadow, the new arrival looked exactly like the man who'd been on the other car at the cliff railway. The one from the security camera who'd gone off with Logan the day before.

21

The man removed his hat and watched her expectantly. His oily black hair was combed neatly across the top of his head, although even from her position Ledasha could see it was too long and scruffy at the back. His small, ferrety eyes were unnaturally close together, and there was something about the way he eagerly licked his thin lips that made Ledasha unnerved.

She realised he was still waiting for her to finish her sentence. '– Eat?' she managed, reaching for a menu.

The man inclined his head slightly as he accepted the menu, and Ledasha gestured for him to take a seat by the window.

'W-would you like a drink?' she asked.

'A pot of tea, please. And a cheese sandwich,' he added, handing the menu back to her unopened.

Ledasha took it and turned, but saw Marcus watching her with a raised eyebrow. She stared back at him inquisitively, then cringed as he mouthed the word 'bread' at her. Twisting back round, she held the menu close to her chest with both arms. 'Er, sorry, would you like that on white bread or brown? And do you want spread?'

'Brown. With butter please,' replied the man, who picked up the roll of cutlery and meticulously unfolded it, placed the knife and fork to one side, and draped the napkin over his lap.

'Right away.' The other couple gave her a little wave as the door chimed a third time. She glanced at Marcus who nodded to show he'd heard the man's order, reached for two menus and handed them to the new arrivals, asking them to sit anywhere they liked, then took out her notepad and returned to the original couple. She still felt flustered when she returned to the kitchen a couple of minutes later.

'A tomato and pepper omelette, and a jacket potato with tuna,' Ledasha said as she ripped off the page from her notebook and clipped it onto a rail above the counter.

'And the first order?' asked Marcus.

Ledasha looked at him blankly for a second. 'The cheese sandwich? I thought you heard?'

'I did. You still need to write it down, avoids any mistakes. What was that all about anyway? You looked like you'd seen a ghost when he walked in.'

Ledasha took a quick glance over her shoulder then turned back to Marcus. 'It's him,' she whispered. 'The man from the camera. You know,' she added when she received a blank look in return. 'The CCTV footage from yesterday, crossing the road.'

Marcus craned his neck to look past Ledasha into the dining area. 'You sure? That image was pretty fuzzy.'

'It's him, I'm sure of it.'

Marcus shook his head. 'Well, don't go doing anything rash. He's a customer right now, I don't want you accusing him in here.'

Ledasha looked sullen. 'Alright. Can I take a break when he leaves though? See if I can follow him?'

Rolling his eyes, Marcus turned to the chef. 'You hear that Dan? Reckons she's James Bond now. This is the real world Dash. You can't go disappearing off from your job to go chasing customers around town. The detective work will have to be done on your own time.'

Ledasha was torn. She wanted to keep working there but finding Logan was her priority, and this might be her only hope of tracking him down. Reluctantly, she reached behind her back, undid her apron and with a defiant look took it off and held it out to Marcus. 'Fine,' she said. 'I really want this job but I can't risk losing him. If he knows where Logan is and I didn't do something I'd never forgive myself.'

Marcus paused, then nodded and took the apron. 'Well, good luck I guess'

Ledasha turned away. She could feel tears welling up which surprised her, but she was determined not to cry in front of the others. She stormed out through the cafe, unable to resist a quick glimpse at the man sat by the window. He was reading a book and didn't look up. The bell tinkled as she left, and without looking back she strode off down the road.

'Dash, wait,' called Marcus behind her. She stopped to watch him jogging a couple of steps to catch up. 'Here, you did a couple of hours yesterday and more today, take this.' He held out a twenty pound note. 'If things work out with your friend and you still need a job after, come back and see me.'

Ledasha wiped her cheek with her sleeve and gave him a small smile of thanks as she took the money. 'Thanks. And I'm sorry to run out like this. I just, well, I have to.'

'I understand. Go and find your friend. See you around Dash.'

He turned and went back to the shop, leaving Ledasha standing on the pavement. She took a deep breath. Leaving the cafe was the right thing to do, she knew. The reason she was here in Lynton wasn't to serve tourists tea and cake. Logan needed her, that was all that mattered now.

Two cars passed as she planned what to do next. When the man left he only had two choices of where to go. Either down the road towards the car park and bus stop, or in the opposite direction out of town. There wasn't much that way so Ledasha figured the other way was her best bet. She didn't want to go far in case he took one of the side lanes, but it had to be somewhere she could stay hidden and still be able to watch the door for his departure.

Another cafe across the road was perfect. She could get a drink and watch for him to come out. Crossing over, she went in and ordered a coke, then found a seat by the window with an unhindered view across the street. It was hard to guess how long this might take. The man had only ordered a sandwich but he also looked to be in no particular rush as he'd sat there with his book. If he ended up getting a second drink, or maybe a cake, he could easily be another hour. She took a sip of her drink and gazed absent-mindedly out of the window.

After twenty minutes Ledasha had finished her drink and was still staring intently at the cafe across the road. Lots of other people, and several cars and vans, had passed her line of vision, and she'd subconsciously filed them away in the back of her mind, but there was no sign of the man with the hat. One of the cafe staff, a woman in her sixties wearing an old fashioned full length beige pinafore with a matching hat, finished wiping the table next to hers and moved over to Ledasha. 'You finished with that?' she asked, pointing to the empty glass.

'Oh, yeah,' she replied, noticing a badge with the name Mary on her lapel. 'Thanks,' she added, pushing the empty can across to her.

Mary picked up the glass and can and leaned over to wipe the table. Ledasha had to sit back and lift her elbows up to give her room. Feeling exposed suddenly, she realised she might be asked to leave if she continued to sit there with no food or drink. Having no phone must be making her look even more conspicuous but there was nothing she could do about that now. 'Um, would it be possible to have a glass of water?'

'Help yourself. There's some over there.' She pointed to the far end of the counter.

Ledasha looked back across the road but there was no sign of movement, so she quickly went and filled a glass from a big ornate dispenser. Sitting down, she scanned the street in case her quarry had slipped out in the few seconds she'd been away, but all was quiet and she settled back into her surveillance.

Without realising it, she finished the water and sat cradling the empty glass. She was so distracted she didn't notice Mary reappear next to her. 'All done?'

'Huh? Oh, right.' She looked down at her glass. She desperately needed the loo but she couldn't leave her seat in case she missed anything. 'Um, no, I'll just get another one. Sorry, is it alright to sit here? It's just I'm waiting for a date but my phone broke and I'm worried I'll miss him.'

The older woman softened instantly. 'Oh, of course love. Here, you stay there, I'll get you a refill.' She took the glass from Ledasha and went over to the dispenser. 'Don't look so nervous dear,' she said as she returned. 'You want to play hard to get, in't that right Joan?' she called across to her colleague behind the counter.

'Treat 'em mean, keep 'em keen,' she replied loudly as both women laughed. Several customers looked at Ledasha who felt her face prickle with embarrassment. She shrank back into her chair.

'Aw, don't worry dear,' said the waitress. 'If I remember rightly he'll be just as terrified as you.' She pottered off to wipe another table and Ledasha, keen to avoid eye contact with any of the people now watching her, turned back to the window.

She gasped and almost knocked her glass over as she saw the man walking away from the cafe. He was wearing his long, dark coat and hat, and his bag was slung over his shoulder as he marched purposefully along the road. Ledasha grabbed her bag and ran for the door, nearly colliding with Mary. 'I think I saw him,' she said hurriedly as she skidded past.

'Treat 'em mean,' shouted Joan as Ledasha pulled open the door and sprinted through. The sound of cackling laughter followed her out onto the street. Ledasha turned left and ran past the window where she'd kept watch. The pavement ended but there were no cars, and people were ambling along the road. She saw the man disappear round a bend fifty metres ahead and chased after him, slowing as she approached for fear of running into him lurking behind the blind corner.

The road continued past a church but there was a turning to the left, while on the right a pedestrian lane ran down the hill with lots of tourist shops. With a rising sense of panic she couldn't see the man anywhere. She'd have to pick one and hope for the best. The lane to her right was as good as any, and she took a step towards it.

'Dash!'

She spun to face the direction of the voice. Courtney and Tia were running towards her waving, coming up the hill from the direction of the bus stop.

'Wha –?' Confused, Ledasha looked at them. 'What are you doing here?'

Tia shrugged. 'Same as you. We didn't know what else to do so thought we'd come and have another wander round. Where you running off to anyway?'

'There's this man. He's something to do with it, I'm sure. No time to explain, just trust me. Long dark coat, wide grey hat, carrying a bag. Seen him?'

The two girls looked at her uncomprehendingly. 'Um, I dunno, we weren't really looking at anyone. I mean –'

'Never mind,' cut in Ledasha. 'Split up. I'll go down here. One of you check that road, the other go back that way. Don't approach him if you see him, just try and find out where he goes. Meet by the bus stop in ten minutes, alright?'

'Right,' answered both girls together, both with slightly bewildered expressions on their faces. Ledasha was going to have to hope they had enough to go on. She turned and ran off down the lane, pausing to peer into shop doorways as she passed. She'd already lost too much time. The lane opened out onto a cul-de-sac with an estate agent and a chip shop. At the bottom it split further into other roads leading off. There was no sign of the man in any direction. She'd lost him.

She hurried on in case she got lucky, turning left to

head past a library and a primary school towards the car park. The bus stop was at the far end but she lingered to look out over the parking bays for any sign of the man. A car was parking, and a lady was loading her shopping into the boot of another. Off to one side she could see a couple of people getting their ticket from the machine she'd commandeered the day before. But no man in a hat.

Dejected, she gave up and trudged on down to meet the others. Courtney was bouncing up and down on the spot, her fists clenched in excitement and with a wild grin on her face.

'I've done it!' she said breathlessly as Ledasha got nearer. 'I've got him.'

'Got him?' Ledasha exclaimed eagerly. 'How?!'

'Ti went off down that other road right, and I ran back down this way. And I saw 'im, just like that, walking ahead of me. So I waited up there on the slope and watched where he went, right. And get this. He went and got into a convertible.'

'Brilliant,' said Ledasha. 'What type?'

'The type with no roof, that's what type. He sat there and put it down didn't he before he went off.'

'No, I mean what car was it? A BMW or a VW, you know.'

'Oh, dunno. It was blue.'

Ledasha tried not to show her disappointment. A blue convertible was something to go on at least. Even so, she wished Courtney had taken the time to have a closer look before he'd driven off. She realised Courtney was still bouncing up and down manically. 'What?' she asked slowly. 'Do you need a wee or something?'

'I haven't told you the best bit,' she said. 'When he came up to the exit he had to stop to check for other cars, right. So I walked right past him. Funny looking fella. Bad hair, even with his hat on.'

'Yeah, that's him,' Ledasha replied. 'I don't see why you're all hype though.'

'Because I'm tracking him aren't I. When he looked the other way I dropped my phone in the back of his car. When Tia gets her lazy ass back here we'll be able to see right where he's going.'

22

'No. Way!' screamed Tia when she got back a few minutes later and Courtney filled her in. 'That is mental!'

'I shit you not,' replied Courtney, still clearly pleased with herself. 'I mean, it's kinda hackish but I didn't have time to think of anything else. Here, gimme your phone, let's see if it worked.'

Tia fished her mobile out of her bag, unlocked it and handed it over. Courtney sat down in the bus shelter, her fingers buzzing rapidly across the screen. A minute later she beamed and turned the phone round to show the others. A pointer was moving slowly along a map.

'We got 'im,' she grinned.

Ledasha couldn't believe it. For the first time she could remember, Courtney had actually come through. 'We've got him,' she murmured. 'Courts, you're a genius.'

'I know. Come on, let's get a coke and watch where he goes.' She set off back up the hill. Ledasha wasn't sure she could face another drink but as she still needed the loo she was happy to follow them.

'How's your battery?' she asked as they trekked up the slope.

Courtney shrugged. 'Should be good for a few hours. I reckon if he stays in Devon we'll be okay.'

Tia, glued to her phone watching the pointer move jerkily along the A39. 'He's turned off the main road,' she announced. 'Heading south now.'

'This'll do,' Courtney said, going into a corner shop.

'I'm bursting,' Ledasha said to Tia as they waited outside. 'Wait here yeah, I'm just gonna find a toilet.'

'Uh-huh,' Tia replied, not looking up. Ledasha hurried

back up to the main road. She considered going to the place she'd been drinking while watching the cafe but didn't want to get drawn into a cross-examination from Mary and Joan. Or there was Marcus's place itself, but again, it was too soon to go back there. A signpost pointed her further along the high street, where she finally found a toilet in the tourist office building. As she sat down and let out a big sigh of relief, Ledasha made a note not to drink on stakeouts in future. She could have missed him leave and the whole thing would have been a write off.

Hurrying back to the shop she had a momentary panic that the others would have wandered off but thankfully they were both standing near where she'd left them, hunched over the screen.

'Oh, there you are,' Courtney said as she got to them. 'He's just approaching the 361 now. If he turns left that'll take him straight to the M5.'

'If he gets on the motorway he could end up anywhere,' worried Ledasha. 'There's no way we'll be able to follow him.' She followed his progress on the screen for a minute but the feeling of helplessness was too much. 'Come on, let's head back to Barnstaple. There's no point hanging around here.'

'What? We just got here,' complained Courtney.

'There's nothing here,' Ledasha replied. 'I've checked everywhere. We need to come up with a plan on how to get to wherever it is he's going.'

'Fine,' Courtney said grumpily. 'Wait here while I get a magazine or something. There's no way I'm staring out the window for the next hour. I dunno how you stand it without a phone.' She disappeared back in the shop before Ledasha could retort, reappearing a couple of minutes later with Heat and a North Devon Gazette. 'Here,' she said, handing the paper to Ledasha. 'They were giving these away for free, you might as well have it.'

Ledasha took the paper and they strolled back down to the bus stop, Tia providing occasional updates on the progress of the car. The man had crossed straight over the A361 and was continuing south, which was an encouraging sign in terms of staying inside Devon.

They didn't have to wait long and were soon sat upstairs on the double decker on their way back to Barnstaple. Ledasha was grateful for the paper but the more she read it the more cross she got that there was no mention of Logan. All these other reports and nothing about a missing teenager. That was something she'd need to fix. She'd write a report this evening and send it to them. The idea of Logan's face all over the front page gave her a new burst of energy. She'd never contemplated being a reporter before, not until she'd pretended to be one when she'd met Ocean and his friends the previous day. The thought of finding out stories, unveiling the truth, appealed to her.

She started paying closer attention to the other articles, and found herself becoming interested in all aspects of the reports themselves. Yeah, she thought, I could write like this. Better even. Most of the features just didn't grab her as being exciting enough. They covered a few facts, a bit of background, and a couple of quotes from locals, but she felt there was much more that could be said. She could do some proper undercover work, identifying scandals and bringing criminals to justice.

The front page was all about Barnstaple's drug problem. Ledasha had heard there was some sort of new fix going round, like spice but without the full on zombie side effect. A pleasant high, they were saying. There was nothing particularly interesting or groundbreaking in the report, it was just repeating the same rumours. Inside, an outraged customer who'd found an insect in her dinner at a restaurant was so dull she didn't make it past the first paragraph. The rest was adverts for cleaners, a hypnotist to help people give up smoking, and various second hand things for sale. There was definitely scope for improvement. Ledasha got out her notebook to start drafting her report.

'He's stopped,' announced Tia. Courtney scrambled over the back of Tia's seat. Ledasha threw her blank notepad and pen back in her bag and hopped across the aisle, shoving Tia over. Courtney's pointer was still there but wasn't moving anymore. Tia zoomed out slightly. 'He's close to South Molton. A village called Kings Nympton.'

'Never heard of it,' said Courtney.

'Near South Molton?' asked Ledasha. 'That's weird. Take a screenshot. Quick, in case he finds Courts' phone and turns it off.'

Tia held down the buttons and her phone clicked as the screen was saved. 'We've got him.' She looked at Ledasha. 'Now what? Do we tell the police?'

'Tell them what?' Ledasha thought out loud. 'That Courts dropped her phone in some randomer's car? We don't have any proof, they'll just tell us to stop wasting their time.'

'What then?' Tia's eyes widened as she realised what Ledasha was thinking. 'You're not saying we should go there ourselves?'

'That's exactly what I'm saying,' Ledasha replied. 'Look, there's a station not far away, it must be on the line from Barnstaple.'

'What, today?' asked Courtney.

Ledasha raised an eyebrow. 'You got something better to do?'

Courtney shrugged. 'What about Aims?'

Ledasha mulled it over for a moment. 'We should invite her, yeah. But I'd feel more comfortable if someone here knew where we'd gone, in case something goes wrong.'

'What might go wrong?' asked Tia, sounding worried.

'Nothing, I'm sure. But maybe we should tell Reece where we're going. Playing it safe, like.'

'He'll wanna come though,' replied Courtney. 'But if something does go wrong and he gets caught he'll be in real trouble. He's already on a suspended after that knife incident. So are you for that matter.'

'Yeah, well, I'm only sixteen so what's the worst they can do to me? Reece is older, he can't afford to get nicked again, but I can risk it. You both with me?'

'Course,' said Tia, grinning. 'Wouldn't miss this adventure.'

Courtney nodded. 'Well you two won't last five minutes without me there to watch your backs. Of course I'm in.'

'Yeah baby,' beamed Tia. 'Girl power, that's what I'm talking about.'

An hour later they were on the Tarka Line train to Exeter. Aimee had talked her sister into letting her start late at the chippie, and the four of them had bought tickets then taken the first train out. 'What's the plan then?' asked Aimee, looking at Ledasha. There seemed to be an unspoken agreement that she was their ringleader now.

'We watch,' Ledasha replied. 'Find somewhere hidden, see if there's anything suspicious. If he leaves then we can move in for a closer look, maybe even break in if we have to. Until then we wait.'

'What? But that might take days,' said Tia. 'We can't do that.'

'No,' Ledasha sighed. 'You're right. We'll have to take turns, do it in shifts. Let's all scope it out now then we'll catch the last train back later.' She looked out of the window at the passing fields of sheep. The English countryside appeared so tranquil and innocent, a world away from the turmoil she felt inside. 'Then from tomorrow we'll start a rota. He's got to leave eventually.' Ledasha nearly told them she was going to stay. It was warm enough to sleep out under the stars and it would save her the return fare which she could ill afford. One of the others could let Ben and Shivani know she was staying at theirs. No need to get everyone worked up yet though, she'd suggest that later.

'Are you sure about breaking in?' asked Aimee nervously. 'I mean, I know you and Courts used to get up to all sorts of trouble when you was in London but me and Ti, we've never, well –.' She petered out, plainly uncomfortable about continuing.

'Don't you worry,' Courtney answered confidently. 'You and Ti can keep watch while me and Dash do the house. It'll be like old times. Except we're not nicking nothing.' She looked at Ledasha. 'Or can we?' she added hopefully.

'No,' said Ledasha firmly. 'We've been clean for over a year now. I'm not getting back into that. We're here to find Logan, nothing more. If we get banged up we'll be no use to him, will we?'

It took less than twenty minutes for the train to reach Kings Nympton station. The girls followed two other passengers off the train and out into the small car park. Within a couple of minutes the train had departed and the other travellers had scattered, either being picked up or heading off in their own cars. They were left in silence.

23

'What a weird place,' commented Tia looking around the empty car park. A broken basketball net hung limply behind a wire fence, the paint peeling from its backboard. 'This gives me the heebie jeebies.'

'It's just your imagination,' said Ledasha, although she knew what Tia meant. The very air felt heavy with tension as they made their way up the small road leading away from the isolated station.

'What'd they go and build it all out here for?' asked Tia as they set off down the country lane in the direction of Courtney's mobile phone.

'Don't complain,' Courtney replied. 'It's close to where we need to go.'

'Yeah, but still. We're in the middle of nowhere. I don't like it.' Tia's edginess was affecting all of them and an uncomfortable hush fell as they walked. Courtney eased the tension temporarily when she snuck up behind Tia and shouted 'Boo!' as she jabbed her in the sides. Tia screamed then spun and smacked Courtney on the arm, but after a brief laughter from the others they soon lapsed back into an uneasy quiet.

Aimee had been following their progress on her phone. They'd had to cross an empty main street and were now on an even quieter side road. 'We're getting close,' she announced ten minutes later. 'Bit further up here on the right.'

Instinctively the girls slowed down and moved to the side of the road, closer to the protection of the trees. On the opposite side open fields stretched away but the dense foliage next to them now gave them a marginally greater sense of protection.

'Wait here,' Ledasha told them. The last thing she wanted was for them to all burst into view, particularly Aimee who stood out absurdly with her lurid pink jacket on. Part of her wished she'd come alone, although deep down she knew she was glad her friends were there even if they were more conspicuous than she would have liked.

The others stopped behind her, Courtney in the lead with the others peering out over her shoulders. Ledasha glanced back at them then crept forward. She stepped across a small ditch and moved deeper into the trees, carefully picking her way through the undergrowth. A bramble snagged on her tracksuit and she bent to pull it free, receiving a stab from the thorn for her efforts. Sucking the droplet of blood from her thumb, she stepped over more of the weeds. She was watching her feet so closely that the sudden appearance of a farm house up ahead took her by surprise. She froze, then feeling exposed quickly crept behind the nearest tree keeping as low as possible. It was hard to see anything from where she was hidden so after a minute's wait, with no sign of movement or any sound ahead, she moved as quietly as she could to the next tree.

From this vantage point she could see the bonnet of a blue car, and by leaning out further she saw its black, fabric roof.

'That's it,' said a voice behind her. Ledasha jumped and whirled round. She'd been so focussed on the house she hadn't heard Courtney sneak up behind her. The others weren't far behind.

'You sure?' asked Ledasha, trying to calm herself down.

'That's it,' confirmed Tia, still checking her phone. She turned it round to show Ledasha the image on the screen. The pointer was positioned on the courtyard exactly where the car was parked. 'Looks like Courts' phone is still in it.'

Courtney gazed at the car in dismay. 'With the roof up how am I supposed to get it back?'

DEADMAN'S HANDLE

'We'll think of something,' said Ledasha. 'Maybe it's not locked. I bet this is the sort of place people don't need to lock their doors.'

'Yeah, right,' Courtney replied. 'Cars like that lock themselves when you leave them. We need to break into the house to get the keys.' She shrugged matter-of-factly. 'We wanted a closer look anyways.

'We can't go in yet,' Aimee told her as she popped a fresh piece of gum in her mouth. 'He's in there.'

'Well I'm not waiting until he drives off,' complained Courtney, standing up and taking a step forward.

'Wait,' Ledasha said, pulling her back down. 'Let's split up. You two stop here. Me and Aimee can watch the back. Ti, you'll have to text Aims if you see anything. And make sure your phone's on silent.' She already had doubts about whether Courtney and Tia could remain quiet without a ringtone giving them away.

The two girls kept a safe distance from the house, skirting their way around via the woods and the edge of a field. When they were halfway there a high wall appeared next to them, the private garden for a nearby property, and the girls instinctively gave it a wide berth, creeping a couple of metres deeper into the woods. Feeling like she was walking with a beacon, Ledasha gave Aimee a scarf from her bag to cover her hair, and made her take off her bright jacket. The white t-shirt underneath wasn't much better but she figured anything had to be an improvement on the pink. She still needed to persuade her to stop blowing out bubbles.

Fifteen minutes later they snuck up behind a shed at the far end of the garden which gave them a clear view of the back of the house. 'There he is,' whispered Aimee. She pointed to one side of the garden where a man was on his knees, bent over with his hands in the flowerbed. 'What's he doing?' she asked, leaning further out. The man sat up unexpectedly, arching his back and causing the girls to leap back into the safety of the shadows.

'I dunno,' whispered Ledasha. 'I'm not a fricking gardener. He's not in the house, that's all that matters. Let the others know.'

Aimee blew out a large bubble and was about to let it pop when Ledasha glared at her. She slowly let it deflate and pushed it guiltily back into her mouth. Taking out her phone, she typed a quick message. A few seconds later the screen flashed up and she held the phone up to show Ledasha the reply "K. Goin in".

'What if he's got a wife or boyfriend or something inside?' asked Aimee.

'We'll just have to hope he's single.' Ledasha crouched down and moved to the other side of the shed, then crawled through a large bush and lay under a bench looking out across the garden. Aimee wriggled in beside her and they settled down to watch, eyes flicking between the house and the man who was still bent with his back to them. At one point he sat up and shuffled to one side before leaning over again. He'd changed into an older set of gardening clothes and was wearing a pair of thick, green gloves, but Ledasha could tell it was definitely the same man she'd seen in Marcus' cafe. The lank greasy hair was unmistakable.

'Look,' murmured Aimee urgently. Tia was peering out from behind the curtains of one of the upstairs windows. She spotted Ledasha and Aimee under the bench and waved.

'What is she doing?' asked Ledasha, gesturing vigorously towards the man on his knees at the edge of the garden. Tia saw him and, realising he wasn't watching, put her hands to her head and flapped them about, poking her tongue out at the same time.

'She's not so nervous anymore is she?' commented Aimee drily.

Ledasha tried to shoo Tia away, cross that she was messing about. Tia, evidently enjoying winding Ledasha up, lifted the front of her t-shirt to flash her bra at the others then, laughing, waved goodbye and disappeared back inside the house.

'Prat,' muttered Ledasha, but couldn't help smiling to herself all the same.

'Oh crap,' said Aimee. 'He's moving.' Ledasha looked across to the other side of the garden and saw she was right. The man had stood up and was now carrying a tray of something across the garden. She stole a glance at the upstairs window but Tia was thankfully nowhere to be seen. The man reached a compost heap close to where the two girls were hiding and brushed the contents of his tray onto the top, then to Ledasha's horror he started walking directly towards them. They shrank back, listening to the sound of his approaching feet. Even Aimee was frozen in time, her mouthful of gum motionless for the first time Ledasha could remember.

In seconds he was upon them, then just as speedily he'd passed, pulling open the shed door and vanishing inside. They heard the tray being placed on something, then more sounds as unknown things were moved around inside. Ledasha indicated for them to shuffle further back from under the bench so they were more concealed by the large bush behind them. Aimee nodded and backed up carefully. Ledasha followed, reversing on her elbows and knees towards the relative safety of the bush. She was almost there when she heard the door of the shed swing open and a pair of feet appeared next to her.

'Hello, hello. What are you up to then?' said a man's voice as Ledasha's heart sank.

24

Slowly, Ledasha raised her head to look at the man looming above her. His face was sweating, the damp, black hair sticking to the top of his head.

'I – um,' faltered Ledasha. 'I was out walking on my own and got nervous. Thought I'd hide until there was no one around.' She wasn't even convincing herself with that lame excuse.

'By yourself? So what's the girl lying behind you doing? You just happened to bump into her hiding under the bush at the same time did you? Come on, out you come.'

Ledasha twisted round to see Aimee's face just visible below the bush. She gave Ledasha a resigned look and pulled herself out. The two girls both stood, brushing leaves and dirt from their clothes.

'You two need to start telling the truth pretty damn quickly,' said the man, 'or I'm going to call the police and let them deal with you.'

The police, thought Ledasha. Yes, bringing them out would be a good thing. Right now, alone with this creepy man, she felt weirdly anxious. But then, if he was happy for the police to come out, maybe he was nothing to do with Logan's disappearance after all? And there were four of them against just him so they ought to be able to take care of themselves. On second thoughts, she decided, the police might not be such a good idea.

'I – er,' started Ledasha uncertainly.

'Our parents are thinking of moving near here,' said Aimee, cutting in. 'They're off wandering around the village and we thought we'd go off exploring. We saw you but didn't want to disturb whatever it was you were doing so just sort of, hid out, watching.' She looked apologetically at him. 'Sorry. I'm not sure why really. It felt like a bit of an adventure.'

The man stared at them curiously, then seemed to accept Aimee's excuse. 'Hmph. Not heard of any houses on the market. Lost though are you? You'd better come in and call your parents.'

'Oh, no, don't worry. I think I know which way to go now,' said Ledasha hurriedly. She hoped Courtney and Tia weren't still messing about inside the man's house, but the longer she could keep him talking out here the longer they'd have to leave. 'Your garden's nice by the way. Must take a lot of work.'

The man seemed pleased at this. 'It is a bit, yeah. Keeping the weeds out of the veg patch is a constant battle.' He looked at Ledasha strangely for a moment. 'Don't I know you from somewhere?'

Shit, thought Ledasha. They should have left when they had the chance. 'Me? Um, no, don't think so.'

'Yes, yes, I've seen you before.' He looked her up and down, confusion on his face while he tried to place her. 'The coffee shop. That's it. You served me this morning, then ran out. What's going on? You're not with your parents at all are you?'

Ledasha looked at Aimee helplessly, then glanced at the upstairs window for any sign of the others. The man saw her and turned to the house himself. He looked back at Ledasha, suspicions visibly growing in his mind. 'Oh, I see. Come with me.' Before she could react his hand had grabbed Ledasha's arm and he was forcing her up the path towards his back door.

'Ow! You're hurting me. Let go!' shouted Ledasha. She was taken aback by his strength. Aimee ran after them and pushed the man in the back but if he noticed he didn't react. Wrenching the door open, he threw Ledasha into the kitchen, then spun round and pulled Aimee inside as well. He closed the door behind him and locked it, removing the key, then marched past the two girls and into the hallway.

'Come out,' called the man from the hallway. 'I've got your friends, there's no point hiding.'

Aimee looked at Ledasha, a frightened expression on her face. They could hear the man in the next room.

'Do you think they got out?' whispered Aimee.

Ledasha, starting to get over the initial shock, rubbed her forearm and leaned back against the counter. The old stone floor was clean but she could see grime and dust had built up on the windows and the worktop itself was covered in all sorts of random paraphernalia, from oily bits of machinery to unwashed crockery. She was surprised to see a timetable for the cliff railway pinned to a notice board on the wall, alongside flyers for the Paignton to Dartmouth steam railway and, beneath that she could see snatches of other trains in the area.

'I dunno,' she said, trying the locked door. 'Let's hope so. We need to get out before he comes back.' She moved to the right and leaned over the sink to open a window. It was an old frame with a stiff latch but swung open just far enough for a person to get through.

'You go first,' she said urgently. Aimee nodded and climbed up onto the worktop. It was awkward with the taps but she managed to twist herself round and put one leg outside.

She froze, half in, half out, as the man reappeared pushing a scowling Courtney ahead of him into the kitchen. He saw Aimee and sighed. 'Get down,' he said in a weary voice. Aimee paused, but realised she wouldn't make it out before he caught her and reluctantly pulled her legs back in. 'Are there any more of you?' asked the man as Aimee hopped back down onto the floor.

The three girls all looked at each other questioningly, trying to work out silently between them what they should say. 'Alright,' he said, watching them. 'Clearly the answer to that is yes. You,' he said, pointing at Aimee. 'Go and get them. And don't even think about running, I've still got your friends here.'

The three of them waited in silence while Aimee disappeared into the house. They heard her calling Tia's name.

'Keeping a lookout were you?' the man asked Ledasha. 'While your mates broke in and robbed me?'

'No!' said Ledasha indignantly. 'It wasn't like that, honest.'

He grunted and glanced out into the hallway to see Aimee returning with a very nervous looking Tia. They passed the man, who stood with his arms crossed in the doorway, still grubby from the gardening, and went to stand with the others.

'Right. What am I supposed to do with you lot then? You're all under age I presume? Breaking and entering is still a crime you know.'

'I know –' Ledasha started.

'We weren't –' said Tia.

'It's not our fault –' Courtney spluttered.

'Alright, alright. One at a time,' interrupted the man. 'You,' he said, gesturing to Ledasha. 'Something tells me you're the ringleader, am I right?' Ledasha looked at the others who all shrank back, then gave a shrug. 'I'll take that as a yes. So you saw me at the cafe earlier and decided to follow me. Why?'

She looked apprehensively at the others. Courtney gave her a small nod. Ledasha could tell what she was thinking. They'd made a mistake. This man didn't have anything to do with Logan's disappearance.

'It's a long story,' said Ledasha. She took a deep breath then launched into a full account of Logan's disappearance, how she'd seen someone that looked like him on the other train just before Logan went missing. She left out the bit about the CCTV footage in case that got Marcus into trouble, but admitted that when he'd come into the cafe she'd been convinced he was the person that had taken Logan. The man snorted and shook his head in disbelief as Ledasha was talking. When she got to the part about Courtney dropping her phone into his car he raised his eyebrows at her in wonder.

'I recognise you now,' he said, comprehension dawning on his face. Ledasha ended by describing their walk from the station and their surveillance of the house.

'So yeah, I guess you're right,' she finished. 'We were keeping a lookout while the others broke in. But they weren't going to steal nothing, I promise, they was just trying to find Logan.'

The man regarded them all in turn, then shook his head and murmured 'mad' to himself. 'Your phone's still in my car is it?' he asked Courtney. She nodded. 'Clever,' he added, reaching into his pocket. He took out his keys and held them out to her. 'Go and get it.' Courtney looked at him as if suspecting a trap, then stepped forward before he changed his mind, took the keys and left the room.

'Kidnapped a teenager,' muttered the man, shaking his head as he leaned back against the worktop and folded his arms again. He looked at each of the girls in turn. 'What am I meant to do with a ruddy teenager for Christ's sake?' he asked. 'Get them to play crap music all day? Or listen to them slamming doors while moaning about how life's so unfair? No bloody thanks.

Ledasha shrugged. 'Well, I dunno. We just know he's missing. Had to do something didn't we.'

'Kids wander off all the time,' replied the man. 'He probably met some other girl and has been having a lovely couple of days shacked up with her. Did you consider that?'

Ledasha stared at her feet. 'No,' she mumbled sheepishly. Could that be what happened, she wondered. It did make more sense than having been kidnapped mysteriously halfway down the cliff railway. If he'd seen someone he knew at the top, or even hit it off with a girl he'd just met, that might explain it. The driver's confusion about him getting on the train was still weird but when Ledasha thought about it, if she had to drive that train up and down the cliff hundreds of times, day after day, she probably wouldn't remember who'd got on and off either.

She was snapped out of her thoughts by Courtney reappearing in the doorway, holding up her phone and giving it a wiggle to show the others she'd recovered it. She handed the car keys back and muttered a quiet 'fanks' to the man.

'So, like, what happens now?' asked Ledasha. 'Are you gonna call the cops?'

He looked penetratingly back at her. She wanted to look away but held his gaze. Eventually he gave a small shake of his head. 'No. You haven't stolen anything. You didn't even have to break in I suppose, seeing as how my door wasn't even locked. I don't imagine they'll be overly bothered by a mere trespassing, probably means a ton of paperwork they could do without and no doubt you'd be let off with a warning anyway. And I can do that. Let this be a warning. Don't. Go. Breaking. Into. People's. Houses.' He stressed each word as he spoke. 'Your friend will turn up, probably looking exhausted with a big smile on his face, and if not then leave it to the police. That's their job.'

No one said anything as he looked at them again. 'How did you get here? Car?'

'Train,' answered Ledasha.

'Good. Then you'll know where the station is then, won't you. Go on, off you go.' He held his arm out towards the hallway. The four girls didn't wait to be told twice and quickly filed past.

'Kidnapped a teenager,' Ledasha heard him mutter again behind her. 'Bloody hell, can't think of anything worse than having one of them moping about the place.'

Courtney opened the front door and led the way out. Ledasha followed, then the others. She turned back once they were all outside.

'Sorry about messing you around and everything.'

He nodded in acknowledgement. 'Don't try it again, I won't be so lenient next time,' he warned. Then before Ledasha could say anything else he closed the door.

'I swear to God,' said Courtney behind her. 'If Logan's spent the last two days shacked up with some girl he met in Lynton I'll kill him myself.' And with that she turned and stormed off towards the station.

25

Ledasha walked over to the other three girls in the corner of the park and dropped her bag on the grass. Courtney, lying on her stomach and wearing a green bikini top and a tiny miniskirt which showed off her long, tanned legs, glanced up briefly then returned to her phone. Aimee, barefoot with bright pink toenails on display, was wearing her baggy floral trousers and a white t-shirt, and was leaning back against a tree as she sketched the landscape. A bubble popped from her mouth as she drew.

'That's really good,' commented Ledasha as she sat down beside her, as ever in awe of how Aimee was able to catch every detail. The different species of tree all had their own characteristics that Aimee had captured flawlessly, and the play area in the foreground was in perfect proportion. Even the children and parents running around from one activity to another were seamlessly incorporated into the scene.

Aimee shrugged. 'It's a good spot,' she replied. 'Loads of stuff happening, plenty of contrast to make it interesting. Like, you see that old couple over there?' She gestured towards a bench off to one side of the playground. 'Their faces have such amazing character. Children are hard to draw, they're too smooth, but those guys, there's so much going on. I could draw them all day.'

Ledasha smiled. She knew Aimee was able to draw young children as effortlessly as she could the older couple but she saw what she meant about them having interesting faces. 'Do you have to be looking at someone to draw them?' she asked. 'Or can you do it just as well from memory?'

'Dunno,' answered Aimee. 'Probably the same, if I can remember them well enough. Why, you got someone in mind?'

Ledasha sighed. 'Not really. I would have asked you to draw that man from yesterday but we know it's not him now. I've been thinking though. Who was the last person to see Logan?'

Aimee looked confused as she tried to think. 'The driver,' said Tia, who was laying on her back next to Courtney and had apparently been listening.

'Exactly,' said Ledasha. 'The driver. And I bet nine times out of ten the main suspect is the person who saw the victim last.'

'You think it's the driver?' asked Aimee with a doubtful expression on her face.

'I don't know,' said Ledasha. 'I mean, like, he was still there an' all afterwards so I guess he's got an alibi. But there's something funny about the way he was behaving. One minute he thinks Loges is on the train, the next he's not. Kept changing his story didn't he. I think we need to have a closer look at him.'

'Oh, give it a rest,' said Courtney. 'You heard what that guy said yesterday. Logan's banging away on some skank he met after we ditched his sorry ass.'

'For three days?' asked Ledasha. 'Don't feel right to me. How'd his bandana end up on the track? And why's his phone off? Even if he's pissed at us he would've still told his foster parents, surely? I know they can be a ball ache sometimes but you'd let them know after this long. Besides, you saw him, he wasn't pissed with us. No, there's still something very wrong about all this. The police aren't gonna do anything, we need to solve it. Our plan was good yesterday, we just got the wrong guy.'

Courtney made a dismissive noise and turned back to her phone.

'What are you suggesting then?' asked Tia. 'We follow the train driver home?'

'Yeah,' said Ledasha. 'I think we – oh crap.'

Courtney and Tia looked round at her, then twisted their necks further to see what was bothering Ledasha. A middle aged woman in a fawn skirt suit was walking in their direction. She came right up to them and stood looking down at Ledasha.

'Um. Good morning Mrs Huxtable,' she said, looking up at her uncomfortably. The sun was in her eyes so she had to squint to hold the older lady's gaze.

'Miss Hadley,' she replied formally. 'I've been waiting to hear from you, young lady.'

'Yeah, I, um. Sorry, it's all been a bit mental the last couple of days, I meant to call.'

'It's not good enough, Ledasha,' said Huxtable. 'You missed your appointment two days ago. I spoke to Shivani so I know she told you to call me yesterday. These meetings aren't optional you know, you can't just skip them if you're not in the mood. Do you want to end up back in a youth custody centre?'

'No, of course not. It's just –'

'– No, Ledasha. No excuses. I shouldn't have to come down here to find you. I'm very disappointed. Now come on, up you get. We'll walk to my office together so you don't get lost on the way again.' She looked at Courtney. 'And don't forget you're due to see me tomorrow either Miss Bramley. I'm not in the mood for having to come down here twice looking for you girls.'

Ledasha pushed herself to her feet. 'See you later, yeah?' she said to the others. They watched her turn and accompany Iris Huxtable towards the exit. Neither of them spoke until they were out of the park.

'I don't know what's got into you,' Huxtable said eventually. 'I thought you were past all the misbehaving. You haven't missed an appointment for over six months.'

'Sorry,' Ledasha mumbled. She almost left it there but Iris had always been kind to her before and, weirdly for one so old, was someone she felt comfortable talking to.

'Logan's gone missing you see.'

'Logan Reeves?' asked Huxtable, stopping in her tracks and looking at Ledasha. 'I only saw him last Friday. What's happened?'

'Well, that's just it, we don't know,' Ledasha answered. 'He, like, disappeared when we was in Lynton.'

'When we *were* in Lynton, Ledasha.' Iris Huxtable had a habit of correcting her grammar that Ledasha had learned to tolerate.

'Yeah,' she continued. 'We've been really worried, looking for him everywhere. That's why I didn't get back in time on Wednesday. Forgot all about it, I was so stressed. Then Ti and me went to the police, and –'

'The police?' cut in Huxtable, not even bothering to correct Ledasha's use of the word me. 'What did they do?'

'Nothing,' muttered Ledasha. 'They reckon he'll turn up, said it's too soon to class him as missing anyways. So I went back to Lynton myself to look around. Even got a job there in a cafe, then –'

'A job?' asked Huxtable, unable to hide the surprise in her voice. 'Why, Ledasha, that's excellent. Well done. Well, if that's why you didn't call me to rearrange then I think we can justify it, don't you? I'll be able to smooth things over in the paperwork and no harm done.'

The sudden transformation in Huxtable's attitude towards her was such a relief Ledasha decided not to admit the job had only lasted an hour. Best to take advantage of her good mood, clear her slate for the missed appointment and get today's session over with as quickly as possible.

'I need to leave by eleven if that's okay,' she said. 'So I can get the bus in time for my shift.'

'Yes, of course dear.' She started walking briskly again and Ledasha had to run a couple of steps to catch up. 'I could run you over if you like. Perhaps I should see this place where you're working?'

'Oh, no, you don't need to do that,' answered Ledasha hastily. 'Drive me there I mean. It's a long way, and besides, this is something I need to do on my own. If that makes sense?'

Huxtable looked at her for what felt like a long time. 'Yes, yes, I see that. This is your thing. I don't want to interfere. I'm still very pleased though Ledasha. You've shown real maturity and responsibility, both with the job and with worrying about Logan.' They reached a doorway between a charity shop and an off-licence on the high street. Huxtable unlocked it then led the way up the stairs and into a small sparsely furnished office. She gestured for Ledasha to sit on one of the two hard backed chairs facing an empty desk, then moved behind it and sat down herself. 'Now, tell me what happened with Logan.'

Ledasha sat on her hands and gazed helplessly at the antique clock on the wall. The second hand seemed to be ticking at a tenth of its normal speed. Half an hour until she'd be able to escape. Might as well spend that time talking about Logan rather than put herself under the usual spotlight when receiving life advice from Huxtable.

'We went to Lynton on the bus. Wanted a change from hanging around here all day, that's all,' she added when Huxtable raised an eyebrow. 'Logan went off to buy a present for his mum and we wandered over to the cliff railway.'

'And you waited for him there?'

'Yes. Well, no, not exactly. It started to rain see, and there wasn't nowhere to hide –'

'There wasn't anywhere to hide, Ledasha,' chided Huxtable.

'Right, so we jumped on the train to get under cover. We figured we'd find more shelter at the bottom and could wait for him to find us there.'

'But he didn't find you? You haven't seen him since?'

'No. Well, he came to the top station just as we were setting off but it was too late for him to get on. He took a photo of us waving at him and said he'd get the next one. But after that it's like you said – he didn't come and find us. We looked everywhere but there was no sign of him.'

'I see. Well, you're right to be worried, it does seem very out of character. He's a nice boy, Logan. I'm sure it's all a misunderstanding though, he'll turn up with a perfectly good explanation.'

'Yeah, maybe,' Ledasha answered, looking unconvinced herself now. 'Courtney thinks he might have met a girl.'

A disapproving expression crossed Huxtable's face. 'Well, I can't say I endorse that but whatever the reason I've no doubt you'll find out soon. Now, we've only a few more minutes before you need to get going. Can't have you being late for work can we? Tell me, what days are you working so we can schedule your next session?'

Ledasha looked up at the ceiling then back to Huxtable. 'Um, well, we haven't discussed that yet. I'm on trial at the minute. I guess if I do alright they'll talk about it. It's just a summer job anyways, they need the extra staff for tourist season.'

'Of course. That suits you though doesn't it? I mean, you'll be wanting to go to college in September won't you.' Ledasha realised it was a statement rather than a question. Normally, listening to Mrs Huxtable preach to her about how young ladies had a responsibility to educate themselves to the highest level would have provoked her, but today Ledasha just wanted to get out as quickly and painlessly as possible.

'Yes, of course,' she replied with what she worried was too much enthusiasm. 'I haven't decided what course yet, I want to see how my results go, but yeah, I'll definitely stay on to do something. Although I might still be able to work weekends. I'm enjoying it.'

'That's excellent Ledasha. I'm so pleased. You're really starting to show signs of maturing into a very sensible young lady. And crucially you're learning to keep your anger under control. Now, I should let you go. Why don't you give me a call when you know more about your rota so we can have another little catch up?' She stood and walked around the desk, smiling happily at Ledasha as she led her to the door.

'Oh, my phone broke,' admitted Ledasha. For once not having a phone was a handy excuse for not being able to book her next appointment. 'I haven't been able to sort a new one yet, but I'll find some way of getting a message to you. Shivani will help I'm sure.'

Mrs Huxtable nodded appreciatively. 'Yes, I'm sure she will. Although wait a moment.' She bustled back over to her desk and opened and closed a couple of drawers. 'Here we are. It's a bit older but should still work. I think it might even have a bit of credit still on it.' She held out a phone and charger to Ledasha who looked at it sceptically then accepted it with a small smile. She hoped it was a smile anyway, and not as pained a grimace as it felt. The phone was a relic and must have been older than she was. It even looked older than Mrs Huxtable.

'Oh wow. Thanks,' she managed.

'Oh, I know, it's not as flashy as those new gizmos you all have these days with your big screens but it will let you make calls so you'll be able to keep in touch with your friends, which really is all you need isn't it.'

Ledasha let slip an involuntary snort of laughter. The thought of phoning any of her friends and actually speaking to them would freak most of them out.

'I'm glad you're pleased,' said Mrs Huxtable, beaming at her. 'You can keep that until you sort out a new one.'

Ledasha couldn't help but be amused by Huxtable's innocence. How anyone survived with one of these she couldn't imagine.

'Just in case that phone doesn't work anymore, let's pencil in next Tuesday,' said Huxtable as she reached for the door. 'Early. Say, 9am, so you can get off to work afterwards.'

Ledasha's felt suddenly deflated, any happiness instantly erased. 'Okay,' she mumbled.

'Very good,' Huxtable beamed, ushering her out of the

office. 'Have a good day at work dear.'

Ledasha trudged down the stairs, dropping the phone and charger into her bag, her mood becoming more foul with each step. It was so unfair, she thought as she reached the outside door. The thought of a nine o'clock meeting with Iris bloody Huxtable was more depressing than she could cope with right now. She'd have to think of a reason to postpone. Maybe tell her she had training or something. Yeah, that could work. She opened the door and stepped back out into the sunshine. As her eyes adjusted she reached for her sunglasses, but before she could put them on she was suddenly aware of people approaching. Courtney, Tia and Aimee were upon her in seconds, all talking at the same time.

'Woah, slow down,' Ledasha begged. 'What's the matter?'

'It's Logan,' said Tia first. 'They've found a body.'

26

'You what? Where?' He couldn't be dead, thought Ledasha. Not Logan.

'Out on Exmoor,' replied Aimee. 'It came on the radio in the chip shop. I went in early to prep and it was on. An unidentified male found in a field. That's all they've said so far, don't know how he died or nothing.'

'Might not be Logan then,' Ledasha replied hopefully. 'Could be anyone. A farm accident, hit and run, a fight that got out of hand.'

'On Exmoor?' asked Courtney. 'Yeah, renowned fight scene there. Bet it's mental on a Friday night, all them sheep getting lary. Maybe a goat didn't like the way he was looking at him.'

'Alright, no need to get all arsey about it,' Ledasha said defensively. 'I'm just saying, it might not be Loges.'

'Who else is it gonna be?' asked Tia. 'No one else has gone missing.'

Ledasha looked at her. She half wondered if it might be Chelsea's friend Connor, then felt a stab of shame as she realised she was actually hoping for it to be. Still, she had to keep hoping it wasn't Logan. 'Let's find out then. That policeman we went to see the other day. He might be able to tell us. Come on, the police station's only round the corner.'

She strode off, the others quickly falling in behind. They were at the police station within a few minutes. Ledasha opened the door and walked straight up to the counter. 'Sergeant Wilson,' she ordered the officer behind the counter. 'It's urgent.'

He looked her up and down sceptically, then picked up

a phone. 'Sorry to bother you, sir. Four girls to see you.' He listened for a few seconds then turned back to Ledasha. 'What's so urgent madam?'

'It's about the body on Exmoor,' she replied, satisfied at the way it made the officer sit up. He relayed the message down the phone.

'He'll be right out. Wait here.'

Ledasha looked anxiously towards the door she'd been through with Tia when they'd reported Logan's disappearance. It opened less than a minute later. Sergeant Wilson was momentarily taken aback to see her there. He glanced at the others then back to Ledasha, a frown appearing on his face as he spoke.

'What's all this about then Miss, er –'

'Hadley,' Ledasha reminded him.

'Hadley, yes. Dash wasn't it.' He looked behind her and nodded in recognition. 'And Tia Maria, right? What's this about the person they've found on Exmoor then?'

'Is it Logan?' asked Ledasha. 'Our friend who's missing. Is it him that you've found?'

Wilson relaxed and let out a deep sigh in understanding at why the girls had come by. 'The body hasn't been identified yet, and I'm not at liberty to discuss the case.'

'Yeah, but is it?' Ledasha pressed. 'Could it be?'

'I'm afraid I don't know much about it at this stage. The detective inspector and the pathologist are still out there. I've only heard very limited details but more will be released soon.'

'But, couldn't you just tell us what you do know?' Aimee's voice betrayed her exasperation. Wilson eyed her sympathetically, then at the others who were all watching him eagerly.

'Come and sit down,' he said, ushering the four girls over to a row of seats in the waiting area. 'Look, I really don't know any more than the information that's already been released. But even if I did I couldn't tell you. It might have a bearing on the case, and it will be up to the inspector to decide what information is made public, and when. I'm sorry, I know you're worried about Logan, but we have to follow procedure.' He gave a small apologetic shrug. 'I will make sure to keep you updated with anything which might connect this case with Logan though, I promise.'

Ledasha felt her cheeks flushing with anger but at the back of her mind was aware Wilson had used Logan's name twice, which reassured her a little that he was at least treating him as a real person and not some figment of the girls' imaginations.

'I need to get back now, but you have my number,' said Wilson. 'Call me if you hear anything, or if you need something from me. I'll keep you updated best I can.' He stood and acknowledged the other girls, then went back through the security door. The four of them wandered back out into the sunshine, Ledasha bringing up the rear. She felt deflated after the visit to the drab police station, made worse by feeling guilty that she'd wanted some news that it could be Logan to put an end to the uncertainty that had been gnawing away at her for the last few days.

'That's good then, right?' said Aimee. 'It still might not be Loges.'

'Yeah, could be anyone,' replied Courtney, putting her arm around Ledasha and giving her a squeeze. 'Dash is right, it'll be a farm accident or something. It's probably nuffing to do with Loges, he's still shacked up with some bird he met in Lynton, am I right?'

'Right,' Tia and Aimee said together. Ledasha knew they were only trying to put on a brave face but a small part of their positivity rubbed off on her.

'Yeah,' she said defiantly. 'Yeah, he's fine. But we still need to find him so I can punch him for putting us through all this, agreed?'

Courtney held her hand out, palm down. 'We'll find him,' she said. 'Ain't no one messing with him while we're on the case. All for one, right?'

Tia put her hand out on top of Courtney's, followed by Aimee. They looked at Ledasha who thrust out her own arm determinedly and placed it on the top. 'And one for all,' they all said in unison.

27

'You still reckon that guard's a bit fishy then?' asked Tia as they got off the bus in Lynton and walked up towards the town.

Ledasha nodded. 'There's something he's not telling us, yeah. The whole disappearing act is odd, we know that, but he was acting cagey when we saw him after, then he went off sick. No one was about because it was raining. What if he somehow knocked Loges out and hid him, then came back and got him later?'

'Seems a bit farfetched to me,' said Aimee. 'He wouldn't have had long before the train had to set off again.'

'Yeah, but wasn't there some kind of delay?' asked Courtney. 'When we was waiting at the bottom. It didn't go up straight away did it? What if that was because of what was happening to Logan?'

'You're right,' said Tia. 'I forgot all about that. It was only a minute though wasn't it?'

Ledasha shrugged. 'That might be all it needed, on top of the normal turnaround time. There's that funny little ticket office next to the track. And maybe it wasn't even Loges who sent the message. The driver could have done it then ditched the phone. And don't forget his bandana was on the track. Maybe Logan was trying to send us a message.'

They'd reached the lane leading to the station on the cliff top. Ledasha could see Marcus' cafe further along the road, while behind her was the restaurant where she'd sat waiting the previous day.

'What now then?' asked Courtney. 'If he's back at work

do we go and talk to him?'

Ledasha pondered that for a moment. 'No. I don't want to draw attention to us. Logan went missing three days ago. No one's been to ask him any questions since we spoke to him. No police, nothing. If he does have something to do with it he's going to be thinking he's got away with it by now.'

'What then?' asked Courtney again.

'Same as yesterday,' replied Ledasha. 'That worked brilliantly.'

'Yeah, right up to the part where he caught us and I nearly shat myself,' muttered Tia.

'Well, apart from that bit,' admitted Ledasha. 'But we'll be more careful this time. And we've got more time to plan it out.'

'You can piss right off if you think I'm losing my phone again,' Courtney told them grumpily. 'Don't know what I was thinking doing that. Could have lost it on that wild goose chase, mental.'

'You don't need to,' said Ledasha. 'We can spread out, coordinate our movements. We'll switch around, keep our distance so he doesn't clock on that we're following him, then next time we'll make sure no one's at home before we go in.'

Courtney looked reassured. 'Sick. Alright, us three can do that, but you're no use. You need to get a phone man.'

Ledasha rolled her eyes and reached into her bag. 'I've got one,' she said, holding it up.

Courtney's mouth dropped as she stared at it. 'What on earth is that?'

'Don't. Huxtabitch gave it to me. So I can book my next appointment with her. I need to charge it somewhere but it should work, I can text you at least. It's better than nothing I guess.'

'Jesus, I know she's old but that thing's from the stone age,' Courtney said, shaking her head. 'Fine, let us know your number and we'll make do.'

'I don't know it,' realised Ledasha. 'Tell you what, you and Tia go and hide out somewhere. You need to be able to watch this lane, it's the only way for him to come.'

'What if he leaves at the bottom station?' asked Tia.

'Crap. Okay, one of you take the top, one wait at the bottom. But stay out of sight. Me and Aims can go to the cafe I was working for a drink. Marcus'll let me charge the phone I'm sure. Then I'll text my number. If anything happens let Aims know.' She hesitated then held out her hand again in the middle of the group. They all looked at it briefly then put their own hands on top, lifting them in the air with a silent acknowledgement before they separated. Ledasha watched Tia head off towards the pathway leading down to the bottom of the cliff, while Courtney took up her vigil on a bench nearby.

Doubts started to creep in the closer Ledasha and Aimee got to the cafe. There was no guarantee Marcus would be at all as welcoming as she'd made out, especially after she'd abandoned him in the middle of her shift. She didn't know where else she'd be able to charge the phone though so, steeling herself, pushed open the door. It was busy with the lunch rush but there was a table at the back of the room closest to the kitchen. Marcus looked up from serving a customer and raised an eyebrow curiously when he saw her. Ledasha pointed to the empty table and he nodded then turned back to the table he was serving.

They sat down and Aimee picked up the menu. 'What do you recommend then?'

'The special,' Ledasha replied instantly. 'Or the crab sandwich,' she added, smiling to herself.

Aimee looked at her suspiciously. 'What are you smirking at?'

'Nothing. It's all good, from what I saw. Wasn't exactly here long enough to find out.'

Marcus bustled past them to the kitchen to deliver the order he'd just taken, reappearing with a lasagne and baked potato for the customers seated behind Ledasha. 'Be with you in a moment Dash,' he said as he passed. 'Bit rushed at the minute.'

She watched him deftly serve the bowls, and saw a lady at another table trying to get his attention. Marcus returned to Ledasha without noticing her. 'What can I do for you?'

'We were going to get some lunch, and,' she replied sheepishly, 'I was going to ask if I could plug my phone in. But you're pretty stacked here. Want me to help out for half an hour? You don't have to pay me, it's my way of saying sorry for running out on you.'

Marcus looked down at her, then at Aimee. Before he could open his mouth the lady behind called out 'Excuse me!' and he turned to deal with her query. 'Alright,' he said a minute later when he came back. 'Thanks. Run and wash your hands and grab your apron. You can charge your phone in the office. Can I get you a drink?' he asked Aimee as Ledasha jumped up. 'On the house, Dash will earn it for you.'

Aimee grinned. 'Nice one, ta. Coke please.'

'Coming right up,' replied Marcus, spinning round to take another order. Ledasha ducked behind him and into the office, where she plugged the ancient phone in and found her apron on the back of a chair. It still had the same notebook and pen in she'd used previously. Moving hastily into the kitchen, she smiled at Dan who was somehow shaking two frying pans while simultaneously peering into one of the ovens. 'Dash, my main girl, welcome back!' he beamed as he starting laying out salad on two plates.

'Don't get used to it,' she replied as she washed her hands. 'I'm just helping out.'

'So you say, girl, so you say.'

Marcus stuck his head in the doorway. 'All set? Coke for your friend, jug of tap water for table four, then take the order for table one. Dan, how are those omelettes doing?'

'One minute boss.'

'Okay, then serve those omelettes to table eight before you see to table one. Got all that?'

'Coke, water, omelettes, table one, I'm on it,' Ledasha replied, who placed three glasses on a tray then went to the fridge. She really hadn't expected to be back here, certainly not so soon, and had surprised herself when she'd offered to help. Truth be told, she now felt slight rush of pleasure being back here.

'Keep me posted if you hear from the others,' she whispered to Aimee as she delivered her drink. It was no great surprise to see she'd taken out her sketch book and was casually drawing a perfect depiction of the condiments and napkins on the table. 'Your omelettes will be out in one minute,' she said politely to the couple in the corner as she passed on her way to deliver the water. Marcus was standing nearby taking a card payment for another table, but he nodded approvingly at Ledasha.

The next forty minutes were non-stop as she took over the running of the room, even telling Marcus at one point to go and take a break. 'Yes, ma'am,' he replied lightheartedly, but he took her up on the offer and retired to the kitchen for five minutes.

'Any news?' she asked Aimee in a quiet spell.

'We're all good. He gets off at three apparently so you can keep working 'til then.'

'What? How do you know that?'

Aimee shrugged. 'Courtney,' was all she said.

Ledasha shook her head, wondering what had been going on outside while she'd been working. She didn't stop to think about it for long as another table needed her attention.

By two thirty the place was beginning to empty out. Ledasha came into the kitchen and leaned back against a big chest freezer. 'Um, sorry,' she said to Marcus. 'I'm gonna have to leave soon.'

'That's fine,' he replied. 'You've already done an hour more than you said you would. I'm grateful Dash, it was pretty manic today and you helped me out big time. The job's still yours if you want it.'

'Um, I dunno,' said Ledasha. She hadn't really had time to consider that he might want her back. 'I mean, I want to, of course. It's just I don't want to let you down again, and we haven't found my friend yet.'

'I thought you might say that. But you're by far the best waitress I've had working here so I'm prepared to cut you a bit of slack. Do you think you can be here for the lunch rush at least? Twelve until two every day? If you need to shoot off after that then fine, I can manage on my own then.'

Ledasha weighed it up. All the way to Lynton for two hours work every day was a lot of effort, although most days she figured she'd probably be able to do more than that.

'Twelve to two? And more if I can make it?'

'The whole day if you can make it, yes. But I'll take lunchtimes if that's all you can spare. Just until you find him, you understand? Good,' he said when Ledasha smiled and nodded acceptance. 'Now, go before I change my mind. Here, take this. It's sandwiches for you and your friend seeing as how you missed your lunch. And don't forget to take that brick you left in my office.'

28

'What's all this about three o'clock then?' Ledasha asked Courtney a few minutes later. They were standing by the entrance to a care home just off the main road.

'Look, don't get mad,' Courtney said defensively. 'I was sat here right, at half twelve, and there's a sign over there saying the last train is at seven pm. And I'm sorry but I'm not sitting here for another seven hours.'

'But he might not be working until the end,' started Ledasha.

'Exactly. That's what I thought. But we didn't know that did we? So I thought, like, bugger this, I'll try and find out. And now we know. You're not the only detective here you know.'

Courtney leaned back, satisfaction on her face. 'Go on then,' said Ledasha. 'How'd you find out?'

'Took a ride, didn't I. Pretty sure he didn't recognise me from the other day. I got different clothes on, and I put a beanie on to hide all me hair. And I just chatted to him, all casual like. I even put on a posh accent, old Huxtable would've been swooning all over me. Said it must be a long day working here all summer. Well, he didn't shut up then, told me all about the different drivers and what shifts they do. He gets in early to run all the daily safety checks. Brakes, cables, I can't remember all of it, I haven't got your brain. Whatever, don't matter. He then says he nips home for a few hours before he comes back at the end of the day to do some final checks before they lock up.'

Aimee looked impressed. 'So we just need to work out the best way of following him now then. Don't suppose you slipped your phone in his pocket?'

'Don' be daft, I'm not risking that again. Don't need to anyway. Get this. I asked him what happens if he gets stuck in traffic and he laughed, saying he only lives a ten minute walk away. So we're sorted for following him.' She paused to look at them. 'This is the bit where you say wow, great work Courts.'

Ledasha shook her head, smiling. 'Not bad, I'll give you that. You'd better keep out the way though, if he sees you again he'll get suspicious. Aims and I can follow him if he comes this way. Does Ti know the timings?'

'She knows,' said Courtney huffily. 'What am I supposed to do now then?'

'Just stay well back. You can follow us at a distance if you have to but make sure you keep well back, at least until we find out where he lives. Grab a drink in here or something,' she added, pointing at the cafe she'd sat at for her stake out the previous day.

'Fine,' Courtney said, standing up and putting her sunglasses on. 'Don't forget about me though, it's me that found out the end of his shift, remember.'

'You did good Courts,' Ledasha said as she walked off. 'Wait!' she called suddenly. 'Let me give you my new number.' She took out the phone and, once Courtney had typed in her own number used it to phone her.

'Got it,' said Courtney as her phone lit up. 'Save yourself the effort, I'll let the others know it.'

'Ta. Text me though, this thing doesn't have any data. We'll keep you posted.'

Courtney wandered into the takeaway leaving Aimee and Ledasha standing on the pavement. Ledasha looked at the road. 'There's only two options really. I'll go down there, you take that way.' She nodded up the road towards Marcus' cafe. 'If he starts walking towards you keep out of sight. Let him pass then when it's safe try and follow him. Carefully.'

'I know, relax. I've seen the Bourne films, I know how

to tail someone,' replied Aimee, heading off towards the cafe.

'Come and find me if you hear from Tia that he's left her way.'

Aimee spun round and gave her two thumbs up. Ledasha set off in the other direction but couldn't go far. The road curved away, hiding her view of the lane, so she loitered by a shop window looking at leather bags and hats. It was five to three. Not long until they were expecting him to leave, but there was no pavement on this narrow stretch of road and every second she felt more and more conspicuous. She hoped he'd still be wearing his railway overalls or he'd be hard to recognise among the tourists.

Her phone gave several loud beeps, three short, two long, then three more short ones, which made Ledasha jump. It was Courtney sending her Aimee's number. A moment later it repeated the eight beeps as Tia's number came through. 'Jesus,' Ledasha muttered to herself, frantically looking for the settings to turn the phone to vibrate. Each key press caused another beep. Mrs Huxtable had obviously never worked out how to turn the sounds off. Satisfied it had been silenced for now, she put the phone back in her pocket and went back to watching the lane.

A few minutes later Ledasha was relieved to see the driver appear at the end of the lane. He was with another man, and they stopped to talk right where she'd been with Courtney and Aimee only fifteen minutes before. The other man had his back to her but she could easily see the driver, still wearing his work overalls, the sun shining off his balding forehead. From here it looked like the bushy hair wrapped around the side of his head was about two weeks overdue a cut.

Ledasha stayed where she was, waiting to see which way the men would go. But then with a mounting feeling of horror, she watched them shake hands and leave. The driver set off towards Aimee, but the other man's face was now perfectly clear. He wasn't wearing his hat today but Ledasha instantly recognised the man whose house they'd broken into the previous day walking straight towards her.

29

Ledasha hastily turned her back on him. She didn't think he'd seen her but he was only thirty metres behind and approaching fast. She hurried off, picturing him closing in, expecting a hand on her shoulder any moment. A lane appeared on her right leading to some more shops. She ducked down, then stepped inside the first place on her right. Pretending to look at some postcards, she watched and waited for the man to materialize in front of her.

'Can I help you?' asked a lady behind the counter.

She looked at him, then back out of the window. She couldn't see the man anywhere. Ignoring the shopkeeper's concerned look she stepped back out onto the pavement and tentatively made her way back up to the main road. There he was, past the lane and walking away from her now towards the car park. What should she do, she wondered. It seemed likely he was heading to his car, and they knew where he lived, so there wasn't a lot of point in following him. Still, seeing him so soon after breaking into his house was unnerving. What was he doing here? And why was he talking to the train driver?

She decided those questions would have to wait. The focus today had to be on the driver. She watched him until he disappeared round the bend in the road, then after waiting for another minute to make sure he wasn't coming back, turned and went back towards Aimee. When she reached the takeaway Courtney stepped out in front of her.

'Did you see him?' she asked excitedly. 'The man. From yesterday I mean.'

'Yeah, he walked right towards me, freaked me out,'

said Ledasha. 'I hid in a shop, don't think he saw me. Did Aims manage to get after the other one?'

'She's on him,' confirmed Courtney. 'Come on, they went this way.' Ledasha glanced in the cafe as they passed and saw Marcus wiping a table. 'I've let Ti know, she's on her way up,' said Courtney. Ledasha nodded absent-mindedly. She was still preoccupied by the unexpected appearance of the man with the convertible. 'There she is,' pointed Courtney, bringing Ledasha back to the present. Aimee was a couple of hundred metres further up the road, peering around a corner with her back to them. She suddenly took off running down the side road.

Ledasha and Courtney automatically picked up their own pace to reach the junction before they lost her. The left side of the street was taken up by a row of terraced houses, a low fence bordering the gardens and separating them from the pavement they were walking along. The entire length of the street opposite was taken up by a long row of white garages behind an old stone wall. Several vehicles were parked alongside the wall and Ledasha wondered briefly what might be in the garages if they weren't being used for cars. In her house Ben always left his van outside. She'd never bothered to look but suspected theirs had become a dumping ground for tools, old bikes and anything else they didn't want to keep in the house. In the past she would have seen it as a target, but those days were behind her.

Reaching the end of the road they could see no sign of Aimee. Panicking, they set off running themselves. At the end of the road they paused to get their bearings. An elderly lady was leaving her house nearby, shopping bag in hand, but otherwise there was no one around.

'Now what?' asked Courtney.

'Split up I guess,' Ledasha replied, looking uncertainly up and down the road.

'Psst!'

Aimee's head popped up from behind a car about

twenty metres away. She waved them to keep low, then disappeared from view. Ledasha ducked down and, followed closely by Courtney, scampered towards her.

'He went in there,' Aimee whispered, pointing to a house opposite. Ledasha risked a quick look through the car's windows. It was a pretty, if unremarkable, mid-terrace home, with a small patch of grass out the front and a path leading to a white front door. As with the buildings on either side, the middle upstairs window had been blocked. Ledasha remembered being taught about a tax in olden times on how many windows you had. Maybe it was to do with that.

'You reckon that's where he lives?' asked Courtney.

'Well, he used his own key to get in,' replied Aimee. They crouched and watched for a couple of minutes.

'Let's fall back,' suggested Ledasha. 'If anyone sees us hiding here like this they'll get suspicious.'

They took one last look at the house for any sign of movement, then stepped back onto the pavement and crept back to the corner of the road. 'What's the plan then?' asked Courtney as they walked.

'We need to get in and search the place,' Ledasha replied. 'Later, when he's back at work.'

'Oh no, Dash, I can't do that again,' Aimee moaned.

'What d'ya mean, again?' asked Courtney. 'You didn't do it last time!'

'We still got busted and dragged inside. I'm not like you two, I've never done anything like that before. I was terrified.'

'It's alright,' Ledasha reassured her. 'You can keep well away. Maybe do some sketches on the cliff top. I did that the other day, no one will find you suspicious. But you'll also be keeping an eye out in case he leaves, so you can let us know, okay?'

Aimee nodded. 'I could do that, yeah. Thanks.'

'Me and you then eh?' grinned Courtney. 'Just like the old days.'

'No. Not like the old days Courts. We're not gonna get caught this time.'

'What if he's got a wife or something?' asked Aimee. 'The house might not be empty.'

'We ring the bell,' explained Courtney. 'Ask for Mandi.'

'Who's Mandi?'

'Don't matter. You make up a name, then when they tell you you've got the wrong house you walk away. It only works once mind, we'll have to watch the place and wait for them to leave if that happens.'

'Let's just hope it's empty then,' said Ledasha.

30

They waited on a bench outside the town hall. There'd been a disagreement on where to hang out, but there was a risk that staying on any of the streets closer to Jim's house might mean they'd miss him if he took a different route back to work. As far as they could tell, whichever way he walked would bring him past their current spot, but they were far enough back from the road not to draw much attention to themselves. If everything went to plan he'd walk straight past.

Just to be safe, at six o'clock Courtney and Ledasha had walked up a lane next to the hall to wait around the corner. Aimee and Tia had been given strict instructions not to stare open mouthed at the driver as he walked past. Ledasha had even made them rehearse looking at their phones as soon as they saw him. At quarter to seven they got their opportunity to act it out for real as Jim appeared right on cue, and passed in front of them on his way back to the railway.

'That was rubbish,' muttered Aimee. 'You didn't take your eyes off him.'

'He didn't see us,' Tia replied defensively. 'But don't tell the others. I'll let them know they're good to go.' She tapped on her phone for a few seconds and a minute later the other two emerged from the lane.

'All set?' asked Ledasha. 'Aims, you go and get yourself set up on the cliff top. Ti, you stay there. Follow him when he comes past, and if we're not out yet find some way of slowing him down.'

'I know,' Tia replied. 'I'm lost, can he give me directions. Go, before he comes back.'

They left immediately and a few minutes later were back at the house. A narrow lane led to the back garden, but first Ledasha waited at the bottom of the path while Courtney rang the bell. She waited thirty seconds then rang it again.

'All clear,' she said, coming back down. Ledasha had broken into dozens of houses before, but not for over a year, and never in Devon. She'd forgotten what the rush was like. It came back to her easily enough. They didn't wait to be seen, but proceeded calmly down the lane by the side of the house.

'Sweet,' said Courtney quietly when they reached the end. No houses overlooked the terraced row from behind. A steep wooded bank rose up, leaving them completely sheltered. She risked a quick peek around the corner to see if any neighbours were outside, but the gardens were silent. 'Let's go.'

Ledasha was impressed at how swiftly Courtney moved. With no hesitation, she was at the back door in a few confident steps and was inspecting the handle before Ledasha had even left the lane. 'Oh, you are kidding me,' she said, looking back at Ledasha.

'What?'

Courtney gave the door a push. 'It's unlocked,' she said in disbelief.

Before any doubts could creep in Ledasha followed Courtney into the house, closing the door quietly behind her. 'Right, ten minutes. No messing about. And no nicking anything. Let's see if there's anything suspicious then get out.'

'On it,' said Courtney, disappearing into the hallway. Ledasha spun slowly in a circle taking it all in. For the second time in two days she found herself in someone else's kitchen, someone who might have something to do with Logan's disappearance. She wasn't sure what she was hoping to find but she was sure this guy had something to do with it. He had been acting very strangely on the day

Logan went missing, and had been off work afterwards. It felt too fishy to be a coincidence, and Ledasha had learned to trust her instincts over the years.

He'd had a snack before heading back to work, thought Ledasha, spotting a mug and plate in the sink. She opened the fridge for a quick look but short of finding a body part she knew it was unlikely to present her with any evidence of wrongdoing. Although the open bowl of liver was a crime in her book.

Moving to the oak worktop by the door, she sifted through a handful of post. A couple of unexciting bills and an invoice from a hypnotist for a thirty minute session to quit smoking. Sixty pounds for half an hour's work. Ledasha figured it would save Jim a fortune on cigarettes if it worked, but still, that was a lot of money. Maybe she should look into doing that for a career. Half an hour of talking sleepily to someone beat a day's slogging away in any other job she could hope to get.

Nothing else jumped out at her in the kitchen so she moved on to the lounge. She could hear Courtney moving around upstairs and hoped she wasn't disturbing anything that would give away their presence, then chided herself as she remembered Courtney's breaking and entering talents. She'd burgled more homes than Ledasha could count. Some of her victims probably still hadn't noticed they'd been burgled, given her skill at only taking selected items of jewellery which many people probably assumed they'd mislaid. She'd only been caught finally when another girl who'd gone with her on one job had foolishly tried to pawn the stolen goods off on an undercover policeman, and had then shopped Courtney as part of her plea bargain.

The lounge was tidy, with a Daily Mirror on a small table beside a single comfy chair facing an old television. Several low bookshelves filled one wall. Ledasha glanced along the spines to see everything from eighteenth century engineering reference books to science fiction novels. She wrinkled her nose. None were to her taste, and none looked remotely connected to kidnapping.

'Aims just texted,' said Courtney from the doorway. 'He's on his way back, time to go. There's bog all upstairs. Find anything down here?'

Ledasha shook her head. 'Nothing,' she said, picking up the Mirror to look at the half completed crossword. She realised she knew the answer to six across, and had to fight an urge to fill it in for him.

'Come on Dash, stop dicking about, we need to go,' urged Courtney.

'Okay, let's go,' agreed Ledasha, dropping the paper back on the table. As it landed she did a double take and lifted it again. A thin folder had been sat beneath it. She gave a start as she turned her head to read the title, and looked at Courtney before reading it out.

'Body found in Lynton Railway water tank.'

31

Ledasha lay on her bed that evening searching for any information she could find about the body in the water tank, but there was nothing at all about it on the internet. She hadn't had time to read the report and wished she'd hung on another few minutes. Courtney could have run interference out the front if Jim had come back too soon. As it was, she was left with nothing to go on.

Still, the report existed, it happened once so it could happen again. Why anyone would want to do that to Logan she couldn't imagine. Could he have had any enemies she didn't know about? Was there something from his past he'd never spoken about? Either way, despite the rain surely someone would have noticed if he was being forced away from the railway and into the water tank.

The only problem was she couldn't work out exactly where the water tanks were. Presumably they were quite near the top station. Whether they were close enough she'd have to find out on her next visit.

She was disturbed by the sound of the doorbell. Opening her door a crack, she heard men's voices, followed by footsteps into the hallway.

'Dash!' called Ben. 'Can you come down a minute?'

Checking her face in the mirror, she closed the door behind her and went tentatively down the stairs. Ben was waiting at the bottom and pointed towards the kitchen. 'Jeff Tozer's popped by. You know him, right? Shivvers said you two already spoke the other day.'

Ledasha nodded and walked past Ben into the kitchen. Mr Tozer was standing talking to Shivani, his back to the door. He turned to face Ledasha, just as Ben came in behind her; in the narrow kitchen she suddenly felt very hemmed in and instinctively searched around anxiously for an escape route.

'Sit down, Dash,' Ben said behind her before she had a chance to get any further than look longingly at the back door. She did as she was told, watching the three grownups apprehensively.

'What is it?' she asked, unable to keep the worry out of her voice. 'Is it that body they found? Is it –?' Ledasha couldn't bring herself to say Logan's name as she regarded them fearfully.

'No,' replied Tozer. 'They haven't confirmed the identity yet, but they are now saying it's a white male, so that's one thing at least.'

Ledasha slumped in her chair in relief. Thank God. It wasn't Logan, there was still hope. 'What's happened then?' she asked.

'Nothing's bloody happened, that's what,' replied Tozer. 'Sorry,' he added, looking at Shivani. 'I've been banging my head against a brick wall with the authorities. I can't tell if they're treating Logan as just another runaway, or whether it's worse than that and they think I've got something to do with it.'

'Oh, no Jeff, they wouldn't think that I'm sure,' said Shivani consolingly.

'Course they would,' Tozer replied. 'How often do you see a story about a missing person, then later it turns out to be someone they knew. Nine times out of ten it's a close friend or relative. They're bound to have us on the list of suspects at the very least. And look at the lad, he doesn't know that many people, it'll be a very short list. So that's why I'm here Dash,' he said, turning to face Ledasha. 'Talk me through it again would you? The day he disappeared. And have a think about whether you've seen him talking to anyone recently. Anyone at all. He's a quiet lad from what we've seen. He's friends with you girls but doesn't hang around with the other boys so much. Since moving to Devon he hasn't been any bother, he's kept his nose clean and not got mixed up with the troublemakers. But we don't see everything obviously. Was he having any problems that you know about?'

Ledasha shook her head. 'No, nothing like that. He'd had issues, I knew that, same as the rest of us. Well, more than most kids round here I guess but, you know. But that was before, when he was in a bad crowd. He hasn't had that here, it's quiet. He hasn't had anything to do with any adults I know of. Other than school obvs.'

'So tell us again about what happened on Wednesday,' Mr Tozer prompted.

Ledasha looked in his eyes, then lowered her own to the table and recited it all again, exactly as it happened. Logan had gone in a shop and they'd continued to the railway. How the rain had got heavier and they'd jumped on the train to escape it. How they'd seen Logan running towards them just as the carriage was beginning its descent. Then she finished up by telling them how they'd waited at the bottom, only realising something was up when Logan failed to appear after the next carriage had come and gone.

'And you saw no one else? No one in Lynton before you split up? Or talking to Logan on the cliff top while you were descending?' asked Tozer.

'We couldn't see a lot through the rain,' replied Ledasha. 'And the train drops pretty quickly, but no, I'm pretty sure there was no one anywhere near him. The place was deserted as we were leaving, and he was on his own when he ran up. He texted us five minutes later to let us know he'd got on the next car. That's what I don't get. He was there. He got on. He told us he was on. The driver told us he got on. But he wasn't there at the bottom. It don't make no sense.'

Tozer drummed his fingers on the table a few times, then shook his own head and looked exasperatedly at Ben.

'I dunno mate. None of this makes sense to me either. Where can he have got to?'

'Are you being totally honest Ledasha,' asked Ben. 'This isn't all some silly game you kids are playing is it?'

'Of course not,' said Ledasha, getting angry now. 'Why would I make it up? I know, I can prove it. He took a photo of us. When he ran up to the station and we was going down, he took a great picture of all of us on the train, with a rainbow and everything.'

'Can we see it?' asked Tozer.

'Well, no, not right now. My phone's broke so I didn't get it, but the others did, they can show you. And there's his bandana,' she added suddenly. 'His purple one. We found it while we was looking for him.'

'Found it? Where?' asked Ben.

Ledasha hesitated. She couldn't admit they were climbing on the tracks. 'It was in a bush, near the top station. I've got it upstairs. So you see, he was definitely there. I'm not lying,' she added desperately.

'It's okay, Dash, we believe you,' Shivani said comfortingly. Ledasha looked down, but not before she saw Shivani frown at Ben.

'Yeah, sorry Dash. I know. I had to ask. Sometimes kids play pranks, that's all.'

'It's not a prank,' she said firmly. 'We're going crazy worrying about him. We're trying everything we can think of. At first we thought it might be something to do with this man what was on the other carriage. While we was going down, he was coming up, so he would have got to the top around the time Logan went missing. But we checked him out and it's not him.'

'Checked him out?' asked Ben.

'It don't matter, just trust me. It's not him.' Ledasha didn't want to get into that story if she could help it. 'Then we thought maybe the driver was in on it. He was the last person to see Logan.' She contemplated telling them her theory about the water tanks, but they'd just tell her not to be silly. Or tell her to keep any from them. Until she knew more there was no need to say anything. 'But we don't think it's him either. He was still there working when we came up looking for Loges, so I can't see how he could have kidnapped him and got back in time.' She was getting tired of having to explain herself to these people. None of them believed her, this was a waste of her time. She pushed her chair back and stood up and strode off towards the door, turning back to make one last comment. 'But I'm not giving up, you hear me? Someone took Logan, and whatever it takes I'm going to find him.'

32

Ledasha woke at eight o'clock the next morning. There was no more news about the body, so after a quick bowl of cereal she decided she might as well head to Lynton. There wouldn't be any way of looking at the water tank during the day so she may as well repay Marcus' generosity by going into work early. By ten thirty she was in the cafe, writing the daily specials on the blackboard while Marcus described some of the ingredients and flavourings.

'You might want to make some notes,' he suggested. 'There's a lot to remember.'

'It's okay,' said Ledasha as she concentrated on making her handwriting as neat as possible. 'I've got it.'

'Really? You got a photographic memory or something?'

Ledasha shrugged. 'I don't think so, but I can remember stuff better than my friends. And I notice things like, say, car number plates. If a car drives past, then I see it again a few days later, I'll know I've seen it before. I just notice things I guess.'

Marcus looked at her curiously. 'That first day you came in here. What was the third item on the blackboard?'

The image of the board popped into Ledasha's head, perfectly clearly. 'Creamy langoustine pasta,' she answered. 'For eleven ninety-five. Although we ran out of the baked goats cheese salad at the top so I guess the pasta moved up to second on the list.'

'And there was an old couple sat in the corner. What colour was his tie?'

'Maroon,' she said instantly. 'With little gold crowns on it.'

Marcus nodded, impressed. 'Sounds pretty photographic to me. Don't know how useful it is in the real world but when you're considering your options for sixth form it's something to bear in mind, having a skill like that.'

Ledasha snorted. 'Maybe. It makes exams easier I guess. Not seen an A-level or BTEC in remembering shit at any of the colleges yet though.'

Marcus smiled. 'Yeah, well, I don't know what I want to do when I grow up yet, and I'm thirty six. If you want my advice pick something you enjoy.' He wandered off to the kitchen and left Ledasha to finish off the blackboard. She hadn't given it much thought since, but the other day when she'd pretended to be a reporter the concept hadn't felt totally ridiculous. She'd have to look up what courses were recommended for that as a career, although the academic side of it didn't excite her as much as the image of investigating crimes, solving problems that no one else could crack.

'Who am I kidding?' she muttered to herself, writing the final item on the board. She was no closer to finding out what had happened than when they'd first realised Logan was missing, and so far her investigative skills had entailed two break-ins, sort of, one of which ended with getting caught. If she was going to solve this one she definitely needed to improve.

33

The shift passed as quickly as the previous day, the Sunday trade making the place even busier. Ledasha had no reason to run off so worked until gone 4pm, when the cafe closed. All the tables were cleaned, the floor swept and everything prepared for the following day when she waved bye, Marcus locking the door behind her.

She checked her phone for the first time since she'd arrived that morning. Courtney had sent a couple of texts asking where she was but apart from that there was nothing.

She walked along the road, looking around her. It dawned on her that a week ago she'd have been scrolling through Instagram or searching for some music. Today she was actually watching people, the road, the buildings. It was all clearer somehow, more vibrant. She shook her head. It wasn't just the lack of a phone, the whole sensation of stepping out into the fresh air after a hard shift at work, that was what was different. The last time she'd sat down was six hours ago on the bus to Lynton, and she figured this must be the longest she'd spent on her feet since, well, ever. But it was a satisfied tiredness, a peculiar feeling that was totally alien but not unpleasant. She smiled to herself. Maybe being a grown-up wouldn't be so bad after all.

She turned the corner and started to walk down the lane to the cliff top. Some market stalls were set up along both sides, most with large gazebos to protect their owners from the sun. She scanned ahead, looking to see if any were selling anything interesting, and stopped dead. The man with the hat, the one whose house they'd broken into, was walking towards her. And yet again he was deep in conversation with Jim, the train driver.

They hadn't noticed her yet, so she hurriedly turned away and stepped up to the closest stall. A trestle table was laid out with random bit of old machinery, repurposed as lampshades and other items. She could feel her face becoming flushed as she intently studied a piece of copper pipe that was curled around to give it a stable base, before rising up to hold a candle stick. Keeping her back turned, she sensed the two men approaching. Within a few seconds they were right behind her, their voices unmistakable as Jim said something about a classic motorbike exhibition coming up.

And then they were past. She breathed a deep sigh and risked a glance in their direction. Too late, she realised the man with the hat had paused and looked back, directly at her.

'I don't believe this,' he said, stopping. 'Are you following me again?'

Jim had taken a couple of steps further on but returned and stood beside his companion, looking at Ledasha curiously. 'Wait a minute,' he said. 'I know you don't I? You're the one who lost her friend.'

Ledasha had nowhere to hide. The two men were standing between her and the road, and behind her led only to the cliff top and the top station. She stepped forwards nervously.

'Yeah, um, hi.' She ignored Jim and addressed herself to the first man. 'No, I wasn't following you or nothing. I was just here looking for clues about Logan. I come here every day,' she added, trying to make the tone of her voice sound as sad and helpless as possible. Before either could reply, she made a snap decision that attack was the best form of defence. 'Why are you here?'

'I work here love,' replied Jim, laughing. 'And William here is one of our engineers. He has to come and sort out the odd issue sometimes.'

'Ah,' said Ledasha. 'So that's why you were here the other day? And on Wednesday when Logan went missing.'

'I was here two days back, yeah. That's the only time this month. Last visit before that was for the lifting and loads equipment checks in June.'

Ledasha looked at him. 'But I saw you. On the train. The car. We was going down while you was coming up.'

'Not me,' said William. 'Spent the whole of Wednesday in the garden. Needed to plant out my brussels and get on top of the weeding.'

This didn't make any sense, thought Ledasha. Why was he lying, unless he had something to hide? She closed her eyes and thought back to the day Logan had disappeared. The four of them were on the train going down, and she'd definitely seen William, his back turned, talking to Jim. Was it definitely him though? He'd had a long dark raincoat and a wide brimmed hat on that day, but it had been raining heavily so that wasn't unusual. When he'd come into the cafe he'd been wearing the same outfit.

Or had he? Comparing the two images in her mind, she sensed something wasn't quite right. The hat. The one in the cafe had a dark grey band around it. The same colour as the hat itself, barely noticeable, but she now realised it was different to the one on the train. Still, that was no proof. Anyone could change their hat, especially if it had got wet.

She opened her eyes and scrutinised them again. They seemed slightly perturbed by her odd behaviour but she ignored them. Something still wasn't right.

'Height,' she said quietly to herself. She closed her eyes again, picturing the scene on the railway car as it flashed by, then reopened them and looked back at the two men. 'I'm an idiot,' she muttered.

'You what love?' asked Jim. 'Are you okay?'

'I'm good,' Ledasha replied. Seeing the two men standing together had highlighted the difference to the image she had in her head. 'It wasn't you on the train that day was it? The day Logan went missing.'

'I already told you that,' William replied, sounding irritated.

'It was someone shorter,' Ledasha went on, looking at Jim now. 'The man talking to you, wearing the raincoat and hat. He was she same height as you, wasn't he? Who was it?'

Jim shook his head. 'You can't expect me to remember some random punter from, what, four days ago?' asked Jim. 'I mean, yeah, if they were standing right in front of me maybe, but I must go up and down that cliff a hundred times a day. We've thousands of passengers during the week at this time of year, more at the weekend. Nah, I'm sorry, I'm usually fairly good at remembering who's been on before but I really have no recollection your friend, or this other mysterious passenger you keep talking about.'

Ledasha was getting more and more frustrated. The man had blatantly been talking to Jim all the way up, he must remember him. And then Logan had been the only person to get on, and with his purple bandana he must have been pretty memorable. Even if he'd lost that before he got on, his tufty dreadlocks were pretty hard to forget. How could Jim be so clueless?

She could see she wasn't going to get anywhere right now. Mumbling thanks, she turned and walked off towards the cliff edge. She avoided the temptation to look back, though she was in no doubt the two men would have watched her and shaken their heads at her peculiarity. They wouldn't follow her though, she was pretty sure of that. It was a hot July weekend, and there was a steady throng of tourists milling around by the cafe, and a long queue for the train. So different to when she'd first visited only a few days earlier.

She took out the old phone Mrs Huxtable had given her and texted Courtney. At Lynton. Meet here l8r to chk water tank? She hit send, then added a second message. Train closes at 7. She held the phone, waiting for a response, but after a minute none had come. Ledasha turned her back to the sea and contemplated joining the queue to go on the railway down to Lynmouth but it had grown even longer while she'd been standing there. As tired as she was from being on her feet all day, she resolved to walk it instead. Wandering back to the main road, she was relieved to see no sign of Jim or William as she made her way around the bend to the top of the cliff path. After a few minutes she began to regret her decision, her thighs aching with the steep descent.

Ledasha paused on the first bridge crossing the railway to watch the cars pass beneath her. She shook her head at the thought that she'd climbed down that track. What had she been thinking? Yeah, she'd found Logan's bandana but what use was that? Certainly not something worth risking her neck for.

She looked back up the slope, trying to picture how it had ended up in the bushes alongside the railway. It could have been thrown from the window while the car was moving. Or dropped from the top perhaps. The breeze could have easily carried it that far. It would have to have been after the car had left the station otherwise the carriage would have been in the way. She tried to visualise what might have happened. It must have been Logan, surely? Was he trying to send them a message? He was being forced to go with someone but in a last, desperate attempt to leave a trail he'd discarded his bandana. Could there be other clues? They'd only been looking for him before, not any of his things. Ledasha was suddenly cross with herself. That had been four days ago. Any other clues he might have dropped would likely have been swept away long ago. She'd left it too late.

The market stalls at the top would make it hard to search right now anyway. She filed it away for something to do after everything had closed down for the night, then continued winding her way down the slope until eventually the bottom station appeared before her. The path brought her out onto the beach road adjacent to the railway. Crossing the road to the wall facing the station, she sat with her back to the sea just as she'd done with the others while they were waiting for Logan to join them. She watched the carriages come and go a couple of times, replaying that day over and over again in her mind.

'Ledasha, hello dear,' said a voice next to her.

Startled, Ledasha looked down. 'Mrs Huxtable. Er, hello. What are you doing here?'

'Well, I have you to thank,' replied the older lady. 'When you said in my office about your trip here, I rather got a fancy to visit. It's been years since I came to Lynmouth, used to do it all the time with my daughter.'

Ledasha nodded, unsure what to say. She'd never thought of Mrs Huxtable as a mother before. She was more of a granny if anything. It still didn't sound a convincing reason to come. Had Iris been checking up on her? It was lucky Marcus had given her the job again if she had. She'd have to ask him if any busybody old ladies had been in to ask about her. God, she hoped Huxtable wouldn't actually come back tomorrow as a customer. She'd cringe if she had to serve the old bat.

'I expect you're worried about Logan aren't you?' asked Huxtable. The unexpected turn of conversation threw Ledasha.

'Um, yeah, I am,' she replied.

'I am too,' replied the older lady. 'He seemed to be doing so well recently, it does seem very out of character to go off like that.' She looked back at the railway. 'And this is where you say it all happened?'

'Yeah,' Ledasha replied, feeling guilty at her uncharitable thoughts towards Huxtable. She only had their best interests at heart, even if Ledasha didn't always appreciate the lectures on bettering herself. Presumably Logan had received identical lectures on how he could be doing so much more with his life. 'Mr Tozer said he was going to see the police again, see if he couldn't get more interest in Logan's case.'

'That's good,' Huxtable agreed. 'Perhaps I should speak to them as well. I'm surprised they haven't been to see me already come to think of it. They'll be wanting details of his history. I think you're right dear, I should go and see them.'

Ledasha wasn't entirely sure it had been her idea but was pleased someone else was showing an interest at least. And, she couldn't help thinking selfishly, any time Huxtable spent with the police talking about Logan was time where she wasn't bothering Ledasha.

'Well, don't make yourself ill looking for Logan, dear. Regardless of the police I'm sure he'll turn up sooner or later. Probably hungry and ready to eat poor Mr and Mrs Tozer out of their home. He can't live off that box of fudge for ever now, can he?' She gave a small laugh at the thought, then seemed to realise joking about Logan might upset Ledasha so became serious again. 'I'm driving back to Barnstaple shortly if you'd like a lift?'

The thought of half an hour stuck in a car with her anger management counsellor filled Ledasha with horror, but she hoped she was able to mask her dread. 'Oh, no, I'll be okay thanks Mrs Huxtable,' she replied as sweetly as she could. 'I'm quite enjoying the sea air, I think I'll hang out here a little longer.'

For a moment she thought Huxtable was going to try to persuade her otherwise, but thankfully she gave a small nod. 'How lovely. Well, in that case I'll bid you farewell. I'll see you for your appointment next week then. Byesy bye.'

Ledasha watched her walking away. Dappy old bint, she thought. Good luck to Sergeant Wilson if he had to endure a visit from Iris Huxtable. He might even decide to go out and look for Logan just to get away from her. Ledasha gave a small snort, cheered by the image of her hounding him into taking the case more seriously. Maybe if they solved it the kidnapper would somehow end up assigned to Huxtable for counselling. She grinned at the thought of it. Now that really would be a punishment.

34

'O.M.G.' exclaimed Courtney an hour later, her mouth wide open in wonder. Ledasha had just described how she'd bumped into William, the man with the convertible, walking along with Jim. 'And he recognised you?'

'Course he recognised me. He's hardly likely to forget cross-examining us in his own kitchen is he? It was weird though. Said he wasn't in Lynton on the day Loges went missing. He's some sort of part-time fixer on the railway, and he claims he was nowhere near the place then.'

'Well don't ask me,' Courtney pointed out. 'I didn't even see him. You're the one with the photographic memory. Was it him?'

'I dunno,' Ledasha replied hesitantly. 'I was sure it was, but now.' She shrugged. 'Could be, could not. It was only a quick glimpse as the other carriage went past, but seeing him today he looked taller than whoever that was.'

They were sitting in the bus shelter at the bottom of Lynton, next to the car park where Courtney had dropped her phone into William's car. Ledasha had been waiting there when Courtney's bus arrived and they were waiting there until the railway closed.

'Did you tell Aimee and Tia about this?'

'Yeah,' replied Courtney. 'Aims is working at the chippy tonight. Ti's got some family thing going on. These Devon girls just can't be relied on. It's up to you and me again.'

Ledasha gave a small grunt. She'd have preferred the others to be there in case something went wrong but maybe it was better keeping it between the two of them. Her and Courtney could take care of themselves. Tia and

Aimee weren't like them, they had more to lose.

'Remember that time we broke into that warehouse in Eltham,' Courtney said, the traces of a smirk on her face. 'The one we thought had all them new iphones in?'

Ledasha couldn't help grinning. 'I still can't believe you were stupid enough to trust Wayne with that tip off. He was always a liability, the prick.'

'He was,' nodded Courtney, smiling. 'Fricking out of date cabbages, that was in the first crate I checked. Carrots in the next. All the out of date veg from the market. Should've known it wasn't right, you could smell it a mile off.'

'Should've taken the most rank stuff to chuck at him. Useless tosser.'

'Yeah,' Courtney replied, a wistful look on her face. 'They were good days. I'm not saying I wanna go back to that but we had fun, didn't we?'

'We did,' agreed Ledasha. 'But we're not going back to that life. Jim's house yesterday, these tanks tonight, it's all for Logan. We're doing the right thing, looking for him.' She checked her watch. The railway had closed an hour ago and everywhere felt quiet. 'Ready?'

'Ready,' confirmed Courtney, standing up and putting her phone in her pocket. They strolled back up the hill and cautiously walked round to the top station. A middle-aged couple were standing on the cliff top gazing out to sea. The girls moved further down the wall and stood facing the same view. After ten minutes the others moved on, leaving Ledasha and Courtney alone.

'Time to go,' said Courtney, wasting no time in heading towards the top of the track. Ledasha was glad it was her who had come. Getting into tight spots didn't faze Courtney, and once she put her mind to something she knew she could rely on her to see it through. 'You say the water comes from a tank?'

'That's what I read, yeah,' confirmed Ledasha. She examined the pipe used by the drivers to fill the carriages at the top station. 'Looks like it comes from over there,' she said, pointing towards the retaining wall behind them.

'Right. Let's find out then shall we?' said Courtney, striding to the wall. 'Here, give me a boost will ya?'

Ledasha bent down, her hands locked together. In seconds Courtney was up and over the wall. 'Yeah, this is it,' she called down. 'There's a big metal door in the floor here, must open up into the water tank.'

'Is it locked?' asked Ledasha.

'Yeah, padlock. Won't take long to get through that.'

'Okay, well, help me –'. Ledasha stopped talking. She'd been facing back up the lane and had seen someone appear at the far end. Stepping behind the hut, she hoped fervently she hadn't been spotted. 'Someone's coming,' she called up quietly to Courtney. 'Keep your head down.'

Time seemed to slow down as she crouched, hidden behind the hut. She heard whistling and footsteps approaching, then someone unlocked the door of the hut and went inside. She realised she'd been holding her breath and let it out slowly. At least whoever it was hadn't seen her. Peering up at the retaining wall she saw Courtney's head pop up. Ledasha thumbed towards the hut to let her know whoever it was had gone in. Courtney waved her to come and climb up but Ledasha shook her head. Their gatecrasher could come out at any moment and stumble right into them. Safer to wait it out.

Courtney rolled her eyes and disappeared again. Ledasha kept as still as she could, terrified she'd step on a twig or knock something over that would alert the person to her presence. She could hear them rummaging about inside, oblivious to anyone else being nearby. After a minute or two it went quiet. She wondered if they'd come back out, but glancing around the edge of the hut she could see the door still open. As she considered her options a chair creaked inside. Whoever it was had apparently settled in and was in no rush to leave. That decided her. Scampering over to the wall, she put her foot against it and jumped, managing to get her hand on top. Pulling herself up, she dropped down into the undergrowth behind. A startled Courtney opened her mouth to say something but Ledasha put her finger to her lips.

She didn't dare peek back over the parapet in case the person in the hut had heard something and looked outside out of curiosity. Lying still, she raised an eyebrow quizzically at Courtney. In response, she was handed the padlock, now removed from the metal door. Courtney grinned back her. 'Still got it,' she whispered smugly.

Ledasha crawled over for a closer look. Putting her hand on the tank she could almost feel the power of the water beneath. She knew it was diverted from a nearby river and held here ready to fill the railway cars so the weight could take them down the cliff. There must be an overflow to divert the rest of the water elsewhere, she figured. The river would provide a constant supply after all.

She glanced in the direction of the wall, then back at Courtney. 'Shall we lift it?' she asked.

Courtney shrugged. 'May as well try, although it's a pretty big door. Might be heavy.'

'Might creak too,' pointed out Ledasha. 'Go slowly.'

Courtney nodded and reached for the handle. It moved barely a centimetre before she had to lower it again. 'It's heavy,' she confirmed. Shifting onto her knees to get more leverage, she grasped hold again with both hands.

'Wait,' said Ledasha. Looking around, she saw a fallen branch and dragged it towards her. 'Okay, try again.' As Courtney pulled upwards, Ledasha pushed the branch under the corner to wedge the door open. Courtney relaxed and tentatively let go, rubbing her palms.

'At least it's well oiled,' she said, pointing at the hinges. 'Not a squeak.'

'Let's hope that continues,' agreed Ledasha, twisting the branch beneath the door to push it open further. She moved to the open edge. 'Ready to give it another shot? I'll push from this side.'

Courtney brushed her hands together a couple of times then placed them firmly on the handle again. She brought her feet forwards and lifted her knees so that she could lean her weight back. 'Ready,' she said. As Courtney heaved, Ledasha leaned forwards and used the branch to help widen the gap until she could get her own hands beneath it. Giving it a big shove, the door suddenly lifted more quickly than they'd expected. Courtney, her full weight pulling backwards almost stumbled and fell back into the scrub behind her. Ledasha was not so lucky. As the door picked up speed, she found herself unable to keep up with it. Thrown off balance, she had just enough time to shout 'Shit!' before momentum carried her over the gaping hole. Her palms slapped the underside of the door as she found herself spread-eagled above the chasm. Looking down she could see the cold, dark water churning beneath her.

Ledasha's shout caused Courtney to jump and release the door. The abrupt drop as it fell to the floor tipped Ledasha beyond the point where she could hold herself up. Her head banged the edge of the opening and everything went black as she crumpled into the darkness.

35

The shock of plummeting into the icy water instantly knocked the wind out of Ledasha. Having never learned to swim, panic overwhelmed her as she desperately thrashed about searching for something to hold onto. She was vaguely aware of the bright sky above her, now blurry from the splashing of the water, but otherwise all around was total darkness. The effect was utter disorientation, coupled with a numbing pain from the cold.

She couldn't breathe, and as her head went under again, plunging her into the freezing water once more, Ledasha thought this was it, this was how she would die. The next time she went under there'd be no coming back. Her hands swung wildly, her legs bicycling violently below. She became vaguely aware of the light dimming above her. This was it then. The oppressive darkness closed in and an eerie calm fell over her. In a moment of peaceful clarity she idly wondered if she should stop struggling and accept her fate.

'No,' she shouted to herself. This was not how she was going to die. She gave a powerful kick and reached up for the opening. Her hand flailed about, desperately searching for something to hold onto but finding nothing but air. She started to descend again, then suddenly another hand gripped hers. The unexpected lifeline made her jump, and she started to slip, her wet fingers making her difficult to hold, but then another hand snatched at her sleeve, roughly tugging her back up. It's Courtney, thought Ledasha, kicking hard to make it easier for her. She must have managed to lean in far enough to reach her.

Her slippery hand gave way but Courtney's hold on her

arm held strong and Ledasha felt the back of her collar being grabbed. With a lurch she was hauled higher and then somehow Courtney was holding her under the armpits. An almighty yank brought her through the opening. Her lower back banged painfully into the hinged doorway, nearly sending her tumbling back into the murky water. Instinctively, Ledasha snatched at the edge of the hole to prevent herself falling, then another pair of hands appeared and held on tightly. Ledasha looked round in confusion, her legs still dangling inside the tank, to see a terrified Courtney staring back at her.

Puzzled, Ledasha wiped her eyes with her free hand and twisted further to see who was holding her.

'Keep still,' grunted a strained voice. She caught a fleeting glimpse of Jim, the driver from the railway, before he gave one final heave to drag her from the watery tomb. She landed, shattered, on her back, with an equally exhausted Jim trapped beneath her.

Rolling off, she got to her knees before a coughing fit hit her. Water poured from her mouth, whether from her stomach or lungs she wasn't sure. Her eyes watering, her throat burning, she trembled uncontrollably while the retching gradually subsided. Courtney put her arms around her, hugging her tightly, as tears streamed down her face. They were both startled by the crash of the tank door closing behind them.

'Wait here,' said Jim, stepping past and disappearing around the corner. He returned a couple of minutes later with a blanket. 'Come on, let's get this on you. The kettle's on in the hut and I've turned on the portable heater. We need to get you warmed up.'

'I'm sorry,' managed Ledasha.

'Yeah, well, let's worry about that later. We need to get you fixed first. I'll call for an ambulance, get you checked out properly.'

'Oh, no, she'll be okay,' said Courtney quickly. 'Won't you Dash?' Jim grunted and helped Ledasha to her feet.

He walked her round to a path which led down to the top station. Ushering her into the small hut, he turned Ledasha around to face him. Her teeth had begun to chatter and her hands were shaking.

'You need to get out of those wet clothes,' said Jim. 'Here, take these.' He reached behind him and passed her a set of oil-splattered overalls hanging on the back of the door, then removed his own jacket and draped it over the back of a chair. 'Your friend can get you changed, I'll wait outside.'

'Is she alright?' asked Courtney, looking dubiously at Ledasha whose shaking was becoming more pronounced.'

'Yeah, should be. Shivering's a good sign. The initial shock from the cold water will have brought all the blood and warmth to her core. Now it's happening in reverse, sending the heat back to her extremities. Should pass in ten or fifteen minutes. Now, hurry up and get her changed. I'll be out here.' He stepped out and closed the door behind him.

'Bloody hell Dash,' Courtney said, turning to face her. 'I thought you were a gonner then.'

'W-w-what h-h-h-happened?' Ledasha asked, struggling to fight the tremors.

'You bloody fell in the water didn't you. Holy shitballs Dash, you scared the life out of me. That was like, well mental.' She paced up and down the small room as she spoke. 'I screamed and tried to reach you, but you was too far down. Then he appeared out of nowhere. Shoved me out the way and somehow managed to grab you and haul you back up. Jesus Christ Dash. He saved your life.'

Ledasha stood there shivering, wrapped in the blanket, while the enormity of it all sank in. She could see Courtney was suffering from shock, or adrenaline, or something. Ledasha wasn't sure what, but even Courtney didn't normally swear quite that much, and she was finding it almost as hard to keep still as Ledasha was.

'Come on, help me get changed,' she said. It proved

tricky, peeling her sopping t-shirt over her head while still shaking violently. As Courtney tugged down her tights she vaguely wondered if she should be embarrassed but was past caring. Still shivering, she clumsily let Courtney manhandle her feet into the legs of the overalls and pull the outfit up. It was way too big for her, the ends of the trousers flapping on the floor with her bare feet inside. Courtney saw a plastic bag on the table and dumped all of Ledasha's wet clothes and shoes into it while Ledasha struggled into Jim's jacket. Courtney didn't say anything, but dropped the bag on the floor and leaned in, giving Ledasha a huge hug to try to warm her up.

'How d-do I l-look?' asked Ledasha, stepping back and wrapping her arms around herself. Courtney regarded her critically. A small snort of laughter escaped her, and within seconds both girls were giggling hysterically. They were interrupted by a knock on the door.

'You decent?' called Jim. Ledasha nodded at Courtney, who opened the door uncertainly and stood to one side to let him in. He took one look at Ledasha, seemed satisfied with what he saw, and moved to the far corner and rummaged in a drawer. Fetching out a woolly hat he handed it to her then turned back to a kettle and some mugs sitting on top of a small cabinet. Putting in a tea bag, he poured in the hot water and added two spoonfuls of sugar without asking. 'No milk I'm afraid but this will help. Here,' he said, passing her the mug. Ledasha took it, her still trembling hand slopping it over the sides. 'You?' he asked, holding up an empty mug for Courtney, who shook her head.

Jim bent and delved into the bottom of the cabinet, pulling out a small hot water bottle. 'Gets cold in here out of season,' he explained as he filled it and handed it to Ledasha, before making himself a hot drink. He leaned back against a table strewn with papers and oily rags and eyed Ledasha shrewdly; she looked away, ashamed at what had happened, and focussed instead on her tea. The cup was only shaking sporadically now, although she found it was worse as she moved it to her lips so kept it locked against her chest with both hands while she waited for the trembling to subside.

'Looks like you'll live,' commented Jim. 'I'd still feel more comfortable if you were checked out properly.'

'I'm fine,' replied Ledasha sullenly, then realised how ungrateful she sounded. 'Thanks to you. You saved my life.'

'No need to get all dramatic about it. Your friend here was about to get you. You might've even made it out yourself.'

Ledasha shook her head. 'I can't swim, and Courtney couldn't reach me. If you hadn't turned up when you did I'd be gone.' As she said it an overwhelming sense of hopelessness hit her, and it took all her willpower to fight the urge to cry.

'Well, you ought to learn to swim, living by the coast and all. But I'm not sure it would have been of much use to you today. Cold water shock can cause even seasoned swimmers to panic so don't beat yourself up over that. And I can't force you to go to hospital, but I'm afraid I do need to fill out a report, and file a crime reference, given that you deliberately broke into the storage tank. What on earth were you thinking?'

'It's going to sound stupid now,' admitted Ledasha. 'We're still looking for our f-friend Logan, and I read that someone once drowned in the water supply tank for the railway. I got worried and thought m-maybe that's what had happened to Logan.'

'That's the stupidest thing I ever heard,' Jim said, shaking his head. 'That tank is securely locked. He couldn't have fallen in by accident, and there'd have been witnesses around if someone else had tried to push him in. It's not easy accessing it either, you girls must have gone out of your way to get in.'

'But it happened before, didn't it?'

'That was a hundred years ago!' exclaimed Jim. 'How did you hear about that anyway?'

A hundred years, thought Ledasha. Bugger. She hadn't noticed a date when she'd looked at the article in Jim's living room. She could hardly tell him where she'd seen it either. 'I er, –.' Ledasha was momentarily lost for words as she wondered desperately what to say. Courtney came to her rescue.

'I read it on the internet somewhere. Can't remember where, I was just searching for anything to do with missing people and the railway.'

Jim grunted. 'Hmm, well, it's still a stupid idea. Christ, you could have drowned for God's sake. You're lucky I –' He was interrupted by the door opening and a large, cross looking man stepping into the hut.

36

'Jim,' the man nodded. 'What's all this about then?' He looked at the girls warily, his face ruddy behind his black bushy beard, whether from rushing to get there or his natural appearance Ledasha wasn't sure. The man was huge, almost filling the doorway and making the whole room feel uncomfortably crammed. He left the door open but she had a sense of all the air in the room having been sucked out.

'Evening chief,' Jim replied amiably. 'It's all under control now, not as bad as I feared when I rang. Girls, this is Mark Scanlon, one of our directors. My boss,' he added, although Ledasha had already worked that bit out. The shock from the cold water had passed now, and although she felt bedraggled standing in dirty overalls with her hair all tangled, she was starting to feel stronger again and more alert. She even felt a curious warm glow as her body sent heat back to her extremities. The sweet tea was definitely helping.

'Right then,' said Scanlon, perching on the edge of the desk and folding his arms as he addressed the girls. Ledasha found herself transfixed by his brown checked shirt straining to contain his stomach, half expecting the buttons to ping off at any moment.

'Jim called and filled me in on the essentials. We need to go through some formal procedures, alright? Although this is all pretty unprecedented.' He looked directly at Ledasha. 'I'm guessing you're the one who went for a swim. First things first, do you feel well? Do you need further medical attention?'

'I'm fine,' Ledasha replied defensively. 'Look, I'm sorry,

it was all a big mistake.'

'Yes, it was,' cut in Scanlon. 'And I'm here to make sure we learn from it and prevent it ever happening again. So why don't you tell me in your own words what happened?'

'Is she in any trouble?' asked Courtney before Ledasha could reply.

'That depends,' replied Scanlon. 'We take the safety of our customers and staff extremely seriously. And, if I understand it correctly, not only did you risk your own life but you also endangered Jim's. So yes, if you two don't give me a very good explanation of what's gone on here then I'll have no choice but to take this further, and that could well mean the police getting involved and whatever consequences for you that might bring.'

'But –,' started Courtney.

'No,' Scanlon interrupted her. 'No buts. You don't seem to appreciate the seriousness of your actions. Now, I'll ask again. What happened?'

'Don't say anything Dash,' Courtney urged.

Ledasha's eyes flicked between Courtney, Jim and Scanlon. 'It's okay,' she decided. 'Best to clear things up now. I want to help,' she said to Scanlon. 'I was stupid, and Jim saved my life.' She went on to explain why they were there and how they'd picked the lock for the tank and forced it open, slipped and fell in the water and subsequently been rescued. Ledasha gave a small shrug after finishing her tale. 'That's all there was to it really.'

Scanlon looked at her for a moment then nodded. 'Very well. Jim, this'll need to go down as a near miss report. We'll need your names and addresses first.' He leaned across to a shelf and lifted down a thin red ring binder, opening it and flicking through to the right section. Picking up a pen from the desk he clicked it on then looked at Ledasha expectantly. She briefly considered giving a false name but knew they'd already drawn enough attention to themselves at the railway looking for Logan and if Scanlon went to the police it wouldn't take them long to find their way back to her. She sighed, and went through the usual rigmarole of explaining the spelling of her name, then added Ben and Shivani's address.

'And you are?' Scanlon asked, looking past Ledasha.

Courtney folder her arms defensively and looked down at the floor. 'Courtney Bramley,' she replied sullenly. 'Um, Dash,' she added. 'The last bus leaves in about ten minutes.'

Scanlon looked at his watch then back at the girls, then finally down at his form. 'I guess I can fill the rest of this in. Look, the important thing is you're okay, but I'm afraid I am going to have to report this. Relax,' he added, when he saw the girls about to protest. 'I'm not going to press any charges so you won't get into any trouble, as you call it. I doubt the police will even need to speak to you, but all the same, we can't brush this under the carpet either. Everything needs to be done properly. Now you two had better run along if you're to catch your bus.'

Ledasha wasn't overly happy with the way things had gone but the small hut felt oppressive, an effect of both the heater and a lot of people in the confined space. She was ready to agree to anything just to get out of there. She removed the woolly hat and hot water bottle and gave them to Jim, then shrugged off the jacket. 'You all warmed up again, love?' he asked.

'Yeah,' Ledasha replied. 'I, well, I mean, um.' She stepped forward and put her arms around him, hugging him tightly. She surprised herself by the action. 'Thanks for saving my life,' she managed to get out.

Jim patted her on the back awkwardly. 'Just glad to see you're alright. Now run along, you can bring the overalls back another time, no rush.'

Ledasha nodded and stepped back. 'Fanks,' muttered Courtney as well, then they sheepishly stepped out of the hut and walked quickly away without looking back.

'You okay?' asked Courtney once they were alone.

'Yeah,' Ledasha replied, as she pulled her shoes out of the plastic bag and hoisted up the baggy overalls to slip them on.

'Lucky your phone wasn't in your pocket,' pointed out Courtney. 'Remember when I dropped mine in the bog that time and it stopped working completely for two days? It must've dried out 'cause it suddenly woke up next morning and was completely fine.'

Ledasha glanced at her then screwed the bag up in frustration. 'Shit man, this is all turning into a nightmare. What are we going to do now?'

Courtney glanced at her watch again. 'Run I guess. We've got four minutes or it's a long walk home.'

37

Ledasha was quiet for most of the fifty minute journey back to Barnstaple. The bus had been empty and she'd hung her clothes on the back of some of the seats, but they were still too damp to wear when they pulled into the station. It was getting dark by the time she said bye to Courtney, and she trudged home in the dirty overalls feeling very sorry for herself. The security light came on as she walked up the path, and she paused to rummage around in the plastic bag for her key. The door opened before she could find it and she saw Ben looking down at her.

'You made it then,' he said. 'Come on, in you come, there's someone here to see you.' He stood to one side and gestured for Ledasha to go through. Hesitantly, she stepped past and walked into the lounge. Her heart sank as she saw Sergeant Wilson sat on the sofa, opposite a disappointed looking Shivani.

'Well, well. Miss Hadley,' said Wilson. 'Here at last. I understand you've had an eventful evening.'

Ledasha's eyes widened in surprise. 'You know?'

'I know,' Wilson nodded. 'The cliff railway reported the incident, and seeing as I was already investigating Logan Reeves' disappearance in Lynton the file came through to me.'

'You remember his name at least,' answered Ledasha defiantly.

'Ledasha,' snapped Ben, anger in his voice. 'You do not speak to Sergeant Wilson like that.'

'This may come as a surprise to you Miss Hadley,' said Wilson testily, 'but we do sometimes know what we're doing. A missing teenager isn't something I'm likely to forget.'

'Yeah? It seemed that way the other day,' pointed out Ledasha, ignoring the look she was getting from Ben. 'What have you found then?'

The sergeant shook his head. 'That's not how this works. We're not here to talk about Logan Reeves right now. I'm here because you've been caught trespassing on railway land and causing criminal damage. Do you deny it?'

'But it is all to do with Logan,' protested Ledasha.

'Do you deny it?' asked Wilson again more forcibly.

Ledasha glanced at Ben, who looked furious. 'No,' replied Ledasha reluctantly.

'Good, we're getting somewhere.' He turned to Ben and Shivani. 'Would you mind giving me a minute alone with Ledasha?'

When her foster parents had stepped out, Wilson got up and closed the door behind them and turned back to Ledasha. 'What's going on then?' he asked, his tone fractionally more genial. 'What does all this have to do with Logan?'

Ledasha stared at him, thrown off guard by his change of tone. Was this some kind of trap, she wondered, but couldn't see how. She walked over to a comfy chair but realised just in time she was still wearing the grease-splattered boiler suit, so paced up and down in front of the gas fire instead.

'It's going to sound crazy,' she began. She stopped to look at Wilson, who stood patiently watching her. She began pacing again, then finally started talking, tentatively at first but soon the words were tumbling out. She left out the bit about how she'd discovered the report on the previous drowning, and when it had happened, vaguely alluding to it being a while back. 'We was desperate, see? No one else is doing nothing so we had to.'

'That's not your job though is it?' Wilson replied. 'It's mine. If you'd had concerns about the water tank you should have reported it. You don't go breaking in and risking your own neck with that damned fool dive you took.'

Ledasha looked up angrily. 'Report it? What good would that do? You think we're making this whole thing up. You wouldn't have done nothing. No one's doing nothing! You'd have nodded politely, made a few notes in your stupid book, then ushered us out and forgotten all about it. We'd be wasting our time. And Logan's still out there, missing or, or...' She tailed off, realising that she'd been shouting but not wanting to finish what she'd been about to say.

Wilson waited in silence. 'Finished? Right, let me speak plainly. We are taking this seriously. Very seriously. Particularly in light of the person discovered on Exmoor yesterday.'

Ledasha looked up sharply. 'Do you know who that is yet? It's okay, I know it isn't Logan. Mr Tozer told me last night.'

'We do know the identity,' confirmed Wilson. 'And the family are being informed as we speak. There will be an announcement later so you'll hear the details then. I can't say any more for the moment.'

'Is it Connor? Connor Derrington?' Ledasha could tell immediately from Wilson's reaction that she was right. 'It is, isn't it? I found details of his disappearance on the internet,' she explained. 'I was searching for cases like Logan's where people had vanished, and he came up.' She gave a small shrug. Now wasn't the time to admit she'd been to South Molton to look for Connor's friends, she was in enough trouble as it was. 'Seemed similar to me anyway, the way it was reported.'

Wilson considered her for a few seconds then made a point of taking out his pad and scribbling a note. He glanced up at her briefly, jotted down another couple of words, then flicked back a couple of pages. 'As I was saying, we are taking Logan seriously. I spent most of yesterday morning interviewing Logan's foster parents, Jeff and Becky Tozer, then had a very frustrating afternoon trying to track down his biological parents.' He paused as Ledasha snorted derisively. 'I take it you're aware of his mother's situation, and the lack of any father. Today I went through everything again with your friends Tia and Aimee. If I'd been able to get hold of you then we'd have had another chat as well. As it was, your foster parents were next on my list of interviewees.'

'Ben and Shivani? They didn't have anything to do with it?' Ledasha replied, confused.

'I know, it's for background on Logan's case. He's in foster care, like yourself. Been moved round a lot like you too. Been in trouble a few times as well. Like you.'

Ledasha glared at him. 'You been checking up on me?'

'Had to. When someone goes missing, you'd be surprised how often the person reporting it had something to do with the disappearance. It would have been negligent of me not to do a background check. Your concern seems genuine, don't get me wrong, but then again, there are a lot of convincing wrong uns out there who can turn on the charm when they want to.'

Ledasha was furious. 'You think I had something to do with it! With Logan disappearing? That's why you've been going round talking to people all day? To find out more about me? When you should be out there looking for who's really done it. I don't believe it, you've been after me the whole time.'

'Woah woah, slow down. Keep talking like that and you will start actually sounding guilty.'

'Why are you telling me this if I'm a suspect?' asked Ledasha.

'Because despite all the nonsense you've pulled in the past you're not a suspect.'

Until a minute ago it hadn't crossed Ledasha's mind that she might be, but the unexpected accusation then immediate clearing of her name made her feel disorientated. 'I'm not?'

'You're not. For one thing, you've a pretty solid alibi, unless all your friends are in on it as well. And to be blunt, it's rare to find a group of teenagers who can get their stories straight on the simplest thing. You four have been consistent enough that I'm happy with your version of events. Plus, if you were involved, drowning yourself is a pretty extreme way of trying to throw us off the scent.' He shook his head. 'Nah, your heart's in the right place, I'm not such a bad judge of character. But now I want to find out more about the fostering side of things, and your carers here seemed like a good place to start.'

'But they didn't really know Logan,' said Ledasha, still reeling. 'He's never been put with them.' It occurred to her she didn't know that for sure. Logan had been moved around different foster parents when they'd first come to Devon, she knew that much, but he'd never mentioned that he'd stayed with her current family. 'Has he?' she asked uncertainly.

'No, he hasn't,' Wilson confirmed. 'But they know more about him than you realise. They know the Tozers who're caring for him at the moment, and they may have known some of his previous families too. I'd hoped they might have been able to give me a better idea of Logan's past. Turns out there wasn't much to add unfortunately. But I have notified other forces in the area and distributed Logan's photo to them and the media. In short, I do believe you, and I believe there is cause for concern regarding Mr Reeves' disappearance. So I can promise you I am doing all I can to find him.'

'But you made out this happens all the time,' said Ledasha. 'We thought you weren't going to do anything.'

'I was trying to put your mind at rest, stop you worrying. And it's true, teenagers abscond with alarming regularity. But like I also said before, most turn up after a day or two. We're past that now, so rest assured we are treating this with the importance it deserves. However, I must stress the 'we' in that sentence. We, the police. Not you. Now, I appreciate any information and support you're able to give but that does not include active investigation on your part, am I clear?'

Ledasha nodded. She'd made a fool of herself falling into the water tank, and the likelihood that Connor was really dead had knocked the wind out of her. Poor Chelsea, she ought to give her a call.

'Now,' said Wilson, 'about your activities this evening. The railway have confirmed they don't wish to press charges. Personally I think you should offer to pay for the damage you caused but they haven't asked for that. As it is, I don't think this needs to go any further.'

'Really? You mean that? I'll pay Mr Fuller back for the lock, I promise.'

'Then I think we're all done. Let's go and give the good news to your carers shall we?'

Ledasha loitered behind Wilson in the hallway while he explained to Ben and Shivani that Ledasha wasn't in any trouble, and that she'd agreed to make amends for the damage she'd caused. She could tell Ben was still angry with her but he thanked Wilson for his help and showed him out. Closing the door he turned to face Ledasha and looked at her for a few moments before shaking his head. 'Go to bed,' he said, then walked past her to the kitchen leaving her standing there with Shivani.

'Ledasha –'

'Don't,' Ledasha replied. 'Just, don't.' She ran up the stairs and locked herself in the bathroom, then turned the shower on as hot as it would go.

38

Ledasha arrived at the Cliff Railway in Lynton at half past nine the next morning, well before she was due to start her shift at the cafe. Jim was kneeling by the railway polishing the brasswork on the car with one of his colleagues.

'Er, morning,' she called. She held up a plastic bag containing the overalls she'd borrowed.

Jim stood and came over. 'Morning. You're looking better, all fully recovered from your adventures yesterday?'

'I am. Thanks to you. I've got your clothes here. And this. It's not much but I wanted to say thanks again.' She handed him a small box of chocolates. It hadn't been planned, but when she'd walked up the hill from the bus stop she'd passed a gift shop and decided on an impulse to pop in.

'Ah, you didn't need to do that, love. Just glad you're okay. Got time for a cuppa?'

'Um. Yeah, thanks, if I'm not disturbing you?'

'You're alright, we don't open for another twenty minutes and have completed the daily checks. How do you take it?'

She told him one sugar as he went into the hut and flicked on the kettle. Unsure whether to follow him, Ledasha waited outside. A couple of minutes later he returned with three mugs, handing her one and taking the other over to his colleague before returning.

'I haven't been paid from my job yet,' Ledasha told him, 'but I'll call by as soon as I am, if that's okay? And don't say no, I need to pay you.'

Jim nodded. 'Fair enough. Any news on your friend's

case'

Ledasha shook her head. 'Still a mystery. I thought I saw him with your friend, the engineer guy with that hat, but apparently I was wrong.'

'Well, I can't see how William can be involved but there is something peculiar about the whole thing. Whenever I try and think about that afternoon I come over all funny. It's a weird feeling, very confusing. Can't explain it.'

'Yeah, it all seems unreal to me too,' said Ledasha.

Jim's colleague appeared beside her, taking a packet of cigarettes from his pocket and tapping one out into his hand. He lit it and stood next to them, ready to join in their conversation.

'Come on Malcolm. You know I can't stand those things.'

Malcolm rolled his eyes. 'Yeah, yeah, I know. Wasn't long ago you smoked like a chimney, can't get used to you not having one.' He wandered to the top of the railway and leaned on the railings, looking down at the track heading to Lynmouth.

'He's right, I used to get through forty a day. Tried giving up a few times of course but never could. Went to see a hypnotist in the end.'

'Yeah, I saw –.' Ledasha froze. She'd been about to admit she'd seen the invoice in Jim's kitchen.

'Eh? Saw what?' asked Jim.

For a moment Ledasha stood there unable to speak. Then a brainwave hit her.

'What? Oh, the hypnotist. Yeah, I saw an advert in the paper the other day. It worked for you then did it?' She tried to keep a calm face. That was close, how can she have been so careless? She needed to make her excuses and get out of there before she said anything else that might incriminate her.

'First time,' answered Jim, seemingly oblivious to Ledasha's panic. 'Remarkable really. I came out of there after just one session and didn't want anything to do with cigarettes after that. No idea what was said to me while I was under. Some kind of magic whatever it was.'

'Really?' asked Ledasha. 'Just like that?'

'Just like that. Some minds are easier to persuade than others apparently. Guess I should probably be insulted at that, but I don't care. Got me off the fags and if it's because I'm easy to manipulate then that's fine by me.' He chuckled as he said it.

'Maybe we should get this hypnotist to put you under again,' Ledasha said idly. 'See if they can help you remember exactly what happened when Logan was on your train.'

Jim looked thoughtful. 'Aye, maybe. Not sure I want to be going under too often mind, probably not good to mess around in there too much.'

'Oh, I was only joking,' Ledasha said quickly. Which was true, although now it was out there she wondered whether there might be anything in it. Probably not, she decided. Jim saw so many customers going up and down the cliff every day that even a hypnotist would struggle to get him to pinpoint that exact journey in his memory.

She drank the last of her tea and handed the mug back. 'That's just what I needed. Again,' she smiled.

'Solves all the world's problems, a good cup of tea,' agreed Jim, peering past Ledasha at the railway. A few people were starting to gather by the gate leading to the top car. 'Looks like it's nearly opening time,' he said, checking his watch. 'All set Malc?' he called over. His colleague gave him a wave and opened the gate, letting the first customers on. 'You take care of yourself now,' he said, turning back to Ledasha. 'No more nonsense putting yourself in danger, agreed?'

Ledasha had no desire to fall in a dark tank of icy water again, or to go climbing around on a steep cliff railway track in the middle of the night, but she somehow suspected this wasn't the end of her perilous activities. She would do whatever it took to get Logan back, but knew enough not to say that now. 'Agreed,' she said, her fingers crossed behind her back.

39

Ledasha still had a couple of hours to kill until her shift at the cafe, and wandered aimlessly to the cliff top where she could gaze out to sea. She needed to think. There was something bugging her, something at the back of her mind that she couldn't quite connect with. What was she missing? Was it something to do with Connor maybe? She wasn't sure why his face had popped into her head all of a sudden. She still hadn't heard any more since his body had been identified. She still felt guilty at the relief she felt when Mr Tozer had told her it wasn't Logan, but now felt awful that Chelsea must have heard the news by now. She'd told Ledasha to call her if she needed someone to talk to, but right now maybe it was Chelsea who needed her. Rummaging through her bag she found her notebook and flicked through until she got to Chelsea's number.

It rang six times, and Ledasha was convinced it was about to go to voicemail, when Chelsea's voice came on.

'Hello?'

'Hi, um, Chelsea. It's Dash. From Barnstaple. I came to see you the other morning?'

'Dash? Yeah, yeah, how's it going?'

'I'm good. I, uh, well, I heard about Connor. I just wanted to say sorry.'

Chelsea took a while to reply. 'Thanks.'

An awkward silence followed, Ledasha not sure what else to say.

'You okay?'

'Not really,' replied Chelsea. 'I'm angry. This is all so messed up. I guess I should have expected it, you know? But while he was still missing I always hoped that meant he was still out there, having fun or something. You know what I mean?'

'I know.' Ledasha knew exactly what she meant.

'Aw, shit man, I'm sorry. I've been so hung up on Connor, I wasn't thinking. There's no news then?'

'Nah, feels like I'm getting nowhere. That's partly why I called. Hope you don't mind. I just needed someone to talk to.'

'Yeah, sure man. Where are you?'

'Back in Lynton. Still digging around. Keep wondering about Connor too, can't help feeling there's some sort of connection between the two of them.'

'Connor and your mate? Because of the train thing?'

'Disappearing from them, yeah. It's really weird, right? Shame that fairground where Connor went missing isn't there anymore. I wouldn't have minded asking them some questions, see if anyone there has anything to do with the Cliff Railway.'

'Wouldn't have thought so, but no harm in asking. It's only a small company from what I remember, they pretty much just travel around Devon. They won't be far away.'

'No way, really? I thought they'd be miles away by now. Can you remember what they were called?'

'Yeah, hang on, I'll see if I can find them.' Ledasha tried not to get excited while the line went quiet. If they were still nearby then maybe there was some kind of link to Logan. She kept the phone to her ear as she leaned against the wall, looking out at the view. A seagull was perched a few metres away, eyeing Ledasha disdainfully. She leaned on one elbow, facing the bird who lifted its wings once, then again, before settling back down to its resting position. Ledasha was about to make a sudden movement to shoo it away when Chelsea came back on the line.

'Dash? Still there? Got it. Finley's Fairground. Devon's finest apparently. They're in Ilfracombe, there until next week.'

'Holy shit, that's awesome, thanks Chels.'

'Want me to come with you? I need to get out of here, do something useful. I can pick you up if you like.'

'You've got a car?' asked Ledasha, surprised.

'Nah man. Got a moped though. It's only 50cc but it'll get us there.'

'Well, yeah, great. I mean, if you're sure. I need to get to work now, I got a job at a cafe here in Lynton, but I should be free by about two if that's any good for you?'

'Yeah, two's good. I'll head on over, drop me a text when you're out.'

*

Ledasha stepped outside and happily flicked through the envelope of cash Marcus had just given her. Her first pay packet. It wasn't much, but was the first time she'd been paid for doing something legal. She couldn't deny it, it felt good.

Taking out her phone to text Chelsea, she saw a string of messages waiting for her. Aimee and Tia had already got to Ilfracombe and were chilling out in the harbour until she got there. Courtney couldn't come as she had her weekly appointment with 'bloody Huxtable'. Ledasha grinned as she read it, until she saw her next message was from Mrs Huxtable herself wanting to confirm their next meeting. And there was one from Chelsea, letting her know she'd arrived in Lynton and had pulled in by the town hall.

She looked up. The town hall was where she'd popped to the toilet a couple of days before, just a short distance along the road. Sure enough, Ledasha could see Chelsea leaning against the low stone wall separating the car park from the pavement. She was holding a bike helmet and had another perched on the wall next to her. Ledasha waved and walked over.

'Thanks so much for this,' she said as she approached.

There was an awkward moment as she half leaned in to hug Chelsea, then they laughed as they pulled apart.

'Here,' Chelsea said, handing her the second helmet. 'Ridden pillion before?'

Now seemed the wrong time for Ledasha to admit she'd spent a large part of her early teenage years stealing mopeds with her friends and racing around the streets of south London.

'Once or twice,' she replied.

'Sweet. All set to go then?'

Ledasha nodded, donned her helmet and slung her bag onto her back. Chelsea had parked the moped behind a Land Rover, so she got on first and backed it out of the space. Pointing it towards the road she waited for Ledasha to climb on behind her. 'Hold on,' she called, then eased out and set off towards Ilfracombe.

It had been a while since Ledasha had been on the back of a bike, and the sense of freedom brought a smile to her face. It dawned on her that she hardly knew Chelsea, and they were heading off into the unknown, but that added to the thrill of the adventure. Holding on tightly to Chelsea's waist, she thought about how good it felt, despite the noise coming from the engine as it struggled out of the town.

Several times on the journey to Ilfracombe, they encountered hills which slowed them to a crawl. The roads were mostly quiet and cars overtook them easily, although once or twice oncoming traffic forced vehicles to hold off and sit perilously close behind them. Ledasha found it terrifying and exhilarating at the same time, and she clung on until Chelsea laughed and had to call back to tell her to relax.

She turned off to the right at one point and took the quieter road past the beach at Combe Martin, although by the time they reached the top of the hill out of the town there was a big queue of angry looking traffic behind them. Chelsea stopped briefly in a lay-by to let them pass, then set off again, finally arriving in Ilfracombe just after three o'clock.

'Can you get to the harbour?' Ledasha said, shouting to be heard over the engine. 'Some friends are meeting us there.'

'No problemo,' Chelsea called back, winding her way around the town until they reached the port. She pulled up alongside two cars with a small gap between them and let Ledasha off before she backed the moped into it. Ledasha took off her helmet and watched Chelsea admiringly. Maybe she should use her cafe earnings to save up for her own moped, she thought. There'd been no need for one in Barnstaple, or London, but in the last week she'd spent more time travelling than she ever had in her life. The idea of being able to go anywhere, whenever she wanted, was very tempting, and the promise of the freedom it would bring was intoxicating.

'What are you grinning at?' smiled Chelsea as she removed her own helmet.

'Nothing, just thinking how much I enjoyed that,' said Ledasha, checking her phone. 'Come on, let's find the others. They're in an arcade by the lifeboat station apparently.'

40

Tia and Aimee were sitting outside the lifeboat station when they got there. Ledasha introduced Chelsea, and explained how she was a friend of Connor, the boy whose body had been discovered.

'Sorry man,' said Tia.

Chelsea gave a small nod. 'Thanks.'

'Do they know how he, well, what happened to him?' Tia asked.

'They announced it just before I left the house,' Chelsea answered. 'Overdose apparently, that new drug everyone keeps talking about. It's bollocks, Con wasn't a user. Someone's made it look that way to put the cops off.'

'And you reckon he's connected to Logan somehow?' asked Tia.

Ledasha shrugged. 'That's what we're here to find out. The fairground where Connor was last seen is here this week. I want to talk to the guy running the ride he was supposed to have been on.'

'Yeah, we saw a sign for the fair, it's on the other side of town,' Tia replied. They chatted as they walked, Aimee popping bubble gum the whole time while Ledasha described what had happened the previous night at the railway with Courtney.

'Shit dude, you were lucky,' said Chelsea as Ledasha relayed the experience in the water tank.

'Yeah, if that guy hadn't, like, been there you could have been in real trouble,' agreed Tia.

'I'm trying not to think about that,' said Ledasha. 'Such a stupid thing to do, it all happened so quickly. He's been really nice about it though. Even Sergeant Wilson wasn't a total dick when he turned up. Told me how much work he's been doing looking for Logan. Feel a bit bad that I didn't trust him before.'

'Yeah, well, they never found Connor until he turned up dead so forgive me if I don't get too excited at that,' Chelsea muttered, then realised what she'd said. 'Oh, but I'm sure they're taking your case more seriously. I didn't mean, you know. Sorry.'

'It's okay,' Ledasha answered. 'That's why haven't given up yet, can't rely on anyone else to find him.'

'There it is,' pointed Aimee. A handful of stalls from the fairground were just visible on a lawn ahead. A carousel dominated the middle. Around the edges a helter skelter, stalls and other rides made up the rest of the fair. Including the ghost train.

'Let's do this,' Ledasha said, walking purposefully towards it as the others hurried to catch up. 'I'll do the talking,' Ledasha continued, 'but jump in if something's bugging you.' She'd never been the nervous type, and had been in enough fights in her past not to be fazed by talking to a stranger, but she felt a few butterflies in her stomach as she approached the ride. Five cars were queued up ready to go, and the edges of the ride were adorned with scary images of monsters and vampires. Ghost Train was written in large writing above it all, and Only For The Brave was above the entrance. A lone man was in a booth by the first car.

'Hi,' said Ledasha, walking up to him.

He looked at the group of girls. 'Four?'

'Um, no, we're not here for the ride. Do you have a minute?'

'What for?' he asked, suspicion in his voice.

'It's a bit awkward. I was hoping you could tell me a bit about that missing person case last year. The one in South Molton?'

He raised both eyebrows in surprise. 'The missing kid? What do you want to talk about that for?'

'I'm just interested, that's all. Is it right you were the last person to see him?'

The man gave a big sigh before responding. 'What do you want to go dragging all that up again for? The kid ran off. No one's heard from him since because he doesn't want to be found. That's all there is to it.'

It seemed the man hadn't heard about Connor being found, or at least, if he'd heard about the body he hadn't connected it to the boy who'd gone missing from his ride the previous year. That suited Ledasha, and she wasn't about to enlighten him now in case he thought she was implicating him and scared him off. Still, it was obvious he wasn't going to talk without a good reason.

'There is more to it now,' Ledasha replied. 'Someone else has gone missing. Disappeared from a train ride. I know it might sound crazy but there are loads of similarities to what happened to you last year. Can I tell you about it and then you can decide if you want to talk?'

The man looked at the other girls, then to the fairground beyond. 'Go on then, it's quiet, I could do with a fag break anyway. Hang on.' He got up and opened the door of the booth behind him, coming round to talk to Ledasha. He lit a cigarette, breathed it in deeply and blew the smoke out through his nose. 'What's this about another kid then?'

'It's our friend,' Ledasha began. 'Logan. We was in Lynton the other day. Do you know they've got this railway there? Goes up and down the cliff?' The man nodded as Ledasha continued. 'Well, Loges got on the train at the top, but when it got to the bottom he'd gone. Vanished into thin air. It doesn't make any sense. Then I was online looking for missing people and found the article about Connor Derrington, how he went missing the same way. Got on your train, but when it got to the end of the ride he'd disappeared. That's right isn't it?'

He took another drag on his cigarette before replying. 'Yeah, that's about the size of it. It was all a bit weird, but I figure he must have been messing about. Got on the car and started the ride, then jumped off partway round and hid in there somewhere. Or climbed out when I was dealing with another customer or something. There's plenty of ways he could have done it. Only, I didn't see him leave. And he definitely wasn't inside when I went to look for him.'

'When did you do that?' asked Ledasha.

'Look for him? Straight away when the empty car came back. I wasn't feeling great from what I remember, bit woozy for some reason, but when the car appeared with no one in it I knew that wasn't right. I could remember him paying his money and getting in, clear as day. But what happened next is a mystery. I went round the back but there was no sign of him, so I went in and followed the track all the way to the end, checking in any dark corners he might have hid. Even called my mate Terry over to keep an eye on the front and he didn't come out that way, so like I said, mystery.'

'And did the police turn up the same day looking for him?'

'No, didn't see them for a couple of days. I was at home, off sick and had the telly on. Saw the lad's face on the news, recognised him from the ride so gave them a call.'

'You were ill?' Ledasha asked. 'Does that happen often?'

'No, never. Haven't had a day off in ten years apart from then. Lucky timing I guess or I might not have seen the news.'

'Yeah, lucky, I guess. Were you properly sick then?'

'No, no, nothing like that. Just felt groggy, must've picked up a bug somewhere. I was fine a day or so later, can't keep me down for long.' He flicked the stub of his cigarette away. 'I need to get back to work. I've told you all I know about that day. Now, I hope your friend turns up but I can't see how it's anything to do with that lad that took off last year. You're looking for something that's not there.'

Ledasha nodded in agreement, but her mind was racing. She'd never been more sure that she was onto something. Jim, the train driver in Lynton, had said he felt dizzy the day Logan had gone missing, and then had to take the next day off sick from work. And now this guy was saying exactly the same. There had to be a connection. But what? The man had already turned and gone back to his booth, and the four girls moved further away so they could talk without being overheard.

'Did you get that?' asked Ledasha.

'They were both off sick,' said Aimee. 'The day after Logan and Connor went missing.'

'Exactly,' agreed Ledasha. 'Why would that be?'

'Because they're involved in some way? In the kidnapping?' suggested Tia. 'They were busy doing something, and faked their illnesses?'

'Maybe,' mused Ledasha. 'We should let Sergeant Wilson know at least, he'll want to check if this guy has an alibi for the day Logan went missing. Doesn't feel right though. They seem more confused than deliberately trying to hide something, don't you think? I can't explain it any other way, it's more a sense that they're telling the truth, they just can't remember.'

As she said it, a sudden thought hit her. It all fell into place in her head in a split second.

'That's it,' she said, more to herself than the others.

'What's it?' asked Tia. 'You alright Dash? You look like you've seen a ghost.'

Ledasha stared at the spot where the cigarette stub had landed. That was the only flaw in the scenario that had come to her. The cigarette was wrong, it didn't fit with how this must have panned out. 'Wait here,' she said to the others. She strode back to the ticket booth.

The guy rolled his eyes when she appeared in front of him. 'Now what? I've told you everything.'

'Have you ever tried to quit smoking?' asked Ledasha without any kind of preamble.

'Quit? Nah, sommat to do, sat here all day. Thought about it once or twice maybe but a man's gotta have one vice.'

'Oh,' said Ledasha, disappointed. She'd been sure that was the connection, but she must have got carried away putting it all together. 'Okay, thanks,' she added, taking a step away to head back to the others. She stopped, another thought occurring to her. 'That's your only vice is it?'

'Well, no,' laughed the man. 'Can't say it is. I wouldn't say no to a beer or two of an evening. And don't tell anyone but the fags are usually more of the herbal variety, if you know what I mean. But I'm doing better than I used to. I quit the gambling at least.'

Ledasha was sure he could hear her heart thumping as she took a step back towards him again. 'You quit gambling,' she asked, as casually as she could. 'You stopped one day, just like that? Or did you get some help?'

'Funny you should ask actually. Yeah, always had a problem with it. The debts were piling up, and I was spiralling down fast. One big win would clear it, you know? Except it never did. You'll never guess how I kicked the habit in the end though.'

Ledasha knew with absolute certainty how he'd managed to stop, but wanted to hear him say it. 'No idea. How?'

He laughed again. 'This will sound mad, but in the end what cracked it was going to see a hypnotist.'

41

'Huxtable?' exclaimed Tia and Aimee together when Ledasha came back to them a few minutes later. 'No way, that's mental!'

'It has to be,' said Ledasha. 'I never really paid attention before, but the sign on her door lists all the therapy she covers. Counselling, addiction support, hypnotherapy. Shit, why did I never realise before.'

'Who's Huxtable?' asked Chelsea, looking bewildered at the whole conversation.

'My therapist,' Ledasha snorted. 'Don't ask. I got into some trouble with the police, long story. Ended up getting moved down here to Devon, under the condition I visit a therapist every week for anger bleeding management.'

'Yeah? How's that working out for you?' Chelsea grinned.

'Bollocks, waste of effing time.' Ledasha shook her head.

She suddenly froze as a thought struck her. 'The fudge,' she murmured. 'I never told her about the fudge.'

'You what?' asked Tia, evidently concerned that Ledasha was cracking up.

'I told Huxtable Logan had stopped to buy a present for his mother. Then when she saw me by the beach in Lynmouth she said some rubbish about him coming home to get food. He can't live off that fudge forever, that's what she said.'

'So?' asked Courtney.

'Well how did she know about it? I can't believe I didn't spot it sooner. She's been extra nice this last week and all, giving me a phone an –.' She stopped and looked wide-eyed at the others. Reaching slowing into her pocket, she took out the phone Huxtable had given her, peering at it suspiciously.

She unlocked the screen then turned it off. 'She's been tracking us the whole time,' Ledasha said quietly.

'On that thing?' asked Tia, wrinkling her nose. 'Not bloody likely.'

'Why not,' replied Ledasha. 'It's old, but you can probably still fit some sort of tracker on it somewhere.'

'You sure you're not being paranoid?' asked Tia. 'I mean, like, I don't know her, only seen her when she came to see you in the park, but she came across as a feeble old biddy to me. She couldn't have taken Logan, surely?'

'Can you remember what she looked like Aims?' asked Ledasha.

'I guess so,' Aimee replied. 'Ti's right, she's pretty old.'

'No, I mean, could you draw her? Now? I wanna show it to the guy on the ghost train over there, see if he recognises her.'

Aimee sat down on the grass and took out her sketchpad. While she drew, Ledasha toyed with the phone Huxtable had given her. 'Any of you know about this sort of thing? Could she have done something to it?'

'I've seen it in TV shows,' offered Chelsea. 'You need to bin it, now. Ditch the sim and battery separately.' They all looked at her. 'What? It was on Fast and Furious. Or was it Killing Eve? I dunno, something I saw anyways. Pull it all apart and chuck it Dash.'

Ledasha nodded and did as Chelsea suggested, walking to a bin next to a candyfloss stall to drop the pieces in.

'How's this?' asked Aimee when she got back. She held up her pencil drawing of Huxtable's head and shoulders.

'Perfect,' said Ledasha taking it from her. 'Never ceases to amaze me what you can do. Wait here.' She went straight to the ticket office for the ghost train. A minute later she was back.

'That's her,' she told the others. 'He recognised her

straight away, no doubts.'

'Holy shit,' Chelsea replied. 'This is big.'

'Now what?' asked Tia. 'We need to go to the police, tell them everything.'

'I agree,' said Ledasha. 'We've enough to go to Wilson. I need to show him I'm being helpful anyway after I ballsed up at the railway yesterday. Um, can I borrow one of your phones?'

Tia rolled her eyes and handed hers over. Ledasha dialled Sergeant Wilson's number.

'You remember it?' asked Chelsea as it rang.

'She's a freak,' explained Tia as Ledasha gave her a withering look. She held up her finger to make them be quiet.

'No answer,' she told them, cancelling the call. 'I'm sure we're right about this, aren't we? The guy on the ghost train ID'd her, but what does that prove? He went to her to quit gambling. Doesn't explain how she kidnapped Connor. Same on the railway. We can go and check if that's who Jim saw for his smoking. The invoice in his kitchen didn't say her name otherwise I'd have made the connection sooner. Dammit,' she swore. 'She's been ahead of us the whole time. Bitch.'

'Yeah, but even if this Jim guy did see her,' pointed out Chelsea. 'You've got the same problem. How did she get your friend off the train?'

'I don't know. But if she has been listening through the phone somehow then she already knows we're onto her. We need to follow her, now, before she does a runner or worse. She's already killed Connor, Logan could be next.

'What are you saying?' asked Aimee.

'I'm saying I don't know where Sergeant Wilson is,' said Ledasha. 'And I don't know how long it'll take him to get my message. We can't wait. Courtney has her appointment with Huxtable right now, so we know where she is. We need to get to her before that meeting ends and follow her. She'll lead us to Logan.'

42

Chelsea was keen to stay with the others, telling them that if this woman really had something to do with Connor then of course she was going to help. She could only fit Ledasha on the back of her moped so they left the others to catch the bus back to Barnstaple while they went ahead. The bike couldn't go quickly enough for Ledasha now, and she swore to herself that if she ever did save up to get one she'd go for the fastest she could afford.

It was almost five o'clock by the time they got back to Barnstaple. Chelsea parked the bike in a side road near Huxtable's office and they cautiously peered round the corner for any sign of her. It was quiet, but Ledasha was still conscious she could be watching out for them from her upstairs window.

'Put your helmet back on,' suggested Chelsea. 'She won't be able to tell it's you then.'

Ledasha couldn't think of a better plan. She took a couple of pins from her bag and fastened her hair back to disguise herself further, then squeezed her head back inside the helmet. 'I'm going to watch from over there,' she told Chelsea. 'Wait by the bike. She doesn't know you, it should be safe. If she comes out I'll give you a wave and we'll try to follow her.'

She walked away, crossing the road and trying to look as normal as possible. Every movement felt unnatural to Ledasha, as if Huxtable's eyes were scrutinising her from behind, already knowing who was walking conspicuously past in a bike helmet on such a hot summer's day.

When she reached a small grassy area opposite Huxtable's window she ducked behind a bush and dropped to the ground, removing her helmet so she could see where she was going. The undergrowth was thick but there was a gap allowing her to shuffle underneath and crawl through. She stopped well short of the front to ensure she wasn't visible, but still have a good view of both Chelsea and the entrance to Huxtable's office.

She wished she had a phone on her. Hiding here all alone, Ledasha felt vulnerable despite the cover. If someone came up from behind she'd have no warning until they were on top of her, and she was sure her loud breathing would draw the attention of anyone within a hundred metres. She realised she should have checked to see if the office was already shut. If it was this was going to be a long and boring wait for nothing. If not, it was getting close to five o'clock and Ledasha suspected Mrs Huxtable was someone who would leave promptly. She'd find out soon if that was true.

Glancing across to the side road, she saw Chelsea give her a subtle thumbs up. Ledasha returned the signal, feeling much calmer now. She wasn't alone in this, and her new friend was keeping a close watch on her, and Ledasha wriggled into a more comfortable position for her stakeout. It struck her as odd that this was the second time in a few days that she found herself laying hidden on the ground while staking out a building. Last time she'd had Aimee right next to her, but Chelsea's presence across the road was reassuring enough.

She was startled by Huxtable and Courtney appearing at her office door. Courtney walked off towards the town centre, while Huxtable locked the door and walked towards some nearby cars. Ledasha gave a wave and pointed in Huxtable's direction. Chelsea peered around the corner and got a good look at her as she got into a blue Fiesta, then ran back to get her bike. As Huxtable drove off Chelsea stopped at the curb in front of Ledasha. 'Jump on!' she called.

Ledasha scrambled backwards out of the bush and ran

to the pavement, pulling her helmet on as she went. She swung her leg over the seat and held on tightly to Chelsea's waist. 'Go!' shouted Ledasha over the noise of the engine.

43

'Don't get too close', Ledasha called out as they set off after the Fiesta. It was a narrow one-way road and they could see Huxtable's car disappearing from sight around a bend ahead. Chelsea got the moped up to speed but eased off when they could see the car again. At the end of the road Huxtable indicated left then merged onto a small roundabout before turning onto a faster road out of the town.

Chelsea tucked in behind a red Audi and accelerated as best she could. 'She'll be quicker than us on the main road,' Chelsea shouted back. 'I'll do my best to keep up but we might lose her. Do you know where she lives?'

'No idea,' Ledasha shouted. The high pitched whine from the moped's tiny engine was deafening as Chelsea pushed it as hard as she could. Ledasha was relieved to see traffic building up ahead causing Huxtable to slow down. As Chelsea eased to a stop behind the Audi Ledasha leaned forward to speak to her. 'Rush hour, that'll help.'

'Let's hope so,' Chelsea replied as the traffic started moving again. They slowly made their way out of Barnstaple, Huxtable's car remaining comfortably in sight. After ten minutes the road began to clear and the cars ahead started pulling away. As soon as there was a gap in the oncoming direction the red Audi accelerated and overtook Huxtable, leaving the girls directly behind her. She was plainly a slow driver and Chelsea backed off slightly as she comfortably kept pace.

'Lucky the old bat can't drive,' called Ledasha. A couple of cars overtook them in quick succession, then swiftly caught and passed Huxtable. Ledasha turned and glanced behind her to see a long queue of cars. 'She must piss people off driving like this every day!'

'Don't complain. I'm going flat out. If she was any quicker I'd have lost her ages ago.' Three more cars sped past, leaving a wide gap but still causing Chelsea to wobble slightly. Ledasha held on more tightly to her waist. The road undulated regularly, and they sped up as much as possible on the downhill stretches to gain momentum for when the slope changed to uphill. That meant closing the gap with Huxtable, ending up a lot closer than Ledasha would have liked on several occasions, but she knew they had little choice if they weren't to lose her.

The road flattened out and Huxtable pulled ahead, but then when she was almost out of sight she indicated left and slowed to turn into a side road.

Chelsea slowed too, and carefully followed into the turning, not wanting to find herself right on top of Huxtable. She needn't have worried; there was no sign of her on the empty road ahead.

'Shit,' Chelsea swore. 'Where's she gone?' She accelerated, but Ledasha tapped her on the shoulder.

'Don't rush. We must be close, doesn't look like there's much else down here and we might miss a turning. Let's take it easy and keep our eyes open.'

Ledasha saw Chelsea's helmet dip in acknowledgement as she eased off the throttle. They went slowly down the winding country lane, slowing for a brief check whenever they passed a gate or farmhouse. The few buildings they passed were very isolated, but there was no sign of Huxtable's Fiesta parked outside any of them.

'We've lost her,' said Ledasha when they got to a crossroads.

'There's still a chance,' replied Chelsea, turning off the engine and looking at the options. 'Which way do you reckon?'

The turning to the right went down a steep slope, the trees on either side of the road reaching over the top to create a dark and uninviting tunnel. To the left the slope led uphill. 'Don't fancy either of those on this thing,' pointed out Ledasha. 'No offence, but hills aren't exactly its forte, especially with two people on it. Straight on's best I reckon.'

'None taken, gets my vote too.' Chelsea started the engine again, crossed the road and set off in the same direction. A couple of hundred metres further along they discovered they'd made the right decision. A farmhouse was set back a little way from the road, its wooden gate open and two vehicles parked on the gravel driveway. A white van, and Huxtable's blue Fiesta. Ledasha tapped Chelsea's side and called out to keep going, although she realised the instruction had been unnecessary as Chelsea wasn't foolish enough to pull straight into the drive.

A few hundred metres later they came to a farm gate. Chelsea stopped the bike and cut the engine. 'That was her, wasn't it?' she asked.

Ledasha stepped down onto the ground and unclipped her helmet. 'That was her,' she confirmed as she removed it and shook her hair out. Chelsea kicked down the bike stand and dismounted, taking off her own helmet and resting it on the seat. 'That's a bit weird isn't it?'

Ledasha followed Chelsea's gaze. The roadside was lined by a row of trees, broken only by the gate. Beyond the gate however, the field was shielded by a large hedge. Any vehicle entering would have to turn immediately and drive along parallel to the road, between the trees on one side and the hedge on the other.

'I can't see a lock on the gate,' observed Ledasha. 'If we can open it that hedge will give us plenty of cover to hide your bike.' She walked over for a closer inspection. Lifting the latch, she swung the gate easily.

'Your Mrs Huxtable has no idea about security,' Chelsea observed, as she kicked back the bike stand and rolled it into the field. 'This seems safe,' she added as she parked it.

Ledasha closed the gate behind them. 'Now we just have to find a way in. Let's be extra careful though, okay? A quick look at what's going on, and we'll call the others if we see anything strange.'

Chelsea nodded. 'That way I guess.' She pointed back in the direction of the house, and they set off along the grassy passageway. Ledasha tried to peer through the hedge to see the field beyond but it was too dense.

'We're very exposed here. Reckon we can get on to the other side of this thing?'

Chelsea looked the hedge up and down. 'Might be able to squeeze underneath. Could get dirty.'

'I don't care about that if it means finding Logan. Do you want to wait here?'

'No I bloody don't,' Chelsea replied, getting down on her hands and knees and examining the base of the hedge more closely. 'It is pretty dense but I think we can do it. Come on, I don't like being out here anymore than you do.' She flattened herself to the ground and pushed her way beneath the foliage. 'Ow, bugger,' she muttered at one point, but kept going. Ledasha surveilled the channel apprehensively, half expecting Huxtable to jump out on them any moment, but Chelsea's legs scrambled through and disappeared leaving Ledasha on her own.

'It's clear,' hissed Chelsea. 'Mind the twigs, some of them are sharp.' Ledasha was slightly slimmer than Chelsea, who had already widened the gap, so Ledasha was able to clamber after her more easily. She pulled herself to her feet on the other side and gazed at the scene ahead.

'What is all this stuff?'

'Some sort of greenhouses,' replied Chelsea, looking at row after row of plastic tunnels, each at least three metres high. 'I've seen them around. Guess it's tomatoes or something that grows better indoors. Let's have a gander.'

She walked up to the nearest one and opened a door in the end. A pleasant aroma hit them from inside. 'Smells good, whatever it is,' Chelsea said as she stepped inside,

Ledasha following right behind. The tunnel was filled with an unusually shaped plant, slightly taller than her and covered in yellow bell-like flowers hanging from the branches.

'Any idea what these are?' asked Chelsea, gently lifting one of the yellow flowers.

'I dunno,' replied Ledasha, 'but they're giving me the creeps.'

'It's called borrachero,' said a voice behind them. The girls spun round to see Huxtable standing inside the doorway they'd just come through, flanked by two teenage boys. Ledasha looked the other way for an escape route but two more boys were walking purposefully down the tunnel from the far end, cutting them off. The two who'd come in the door behind them moved to each of the girls and held them tightly. 'It has other names,' continued Huxtable, casually approaching the tree and stroking it tenderly. 'The get-you-drunk tree is one translation, but it's more commonly known as Devil's Breath. A rather theatrical name I know, but apt. Allow me to demonstrate.' With that she lifted her free hand and blew a yellow powder into Ledasha's face. She felt her eyes glaze over, and could hear Huxtable continuing to speak as if from far away, then everything went blank.

44

The ceiling came slowly into focus, criss crossed by strange lines that shouldn't have been there. Ledasha blinked a few times and tried to sit up, but her head was pounding. Where was she? It was all a blur, hazy memories of a lifeboat and being on the back of a motorbike. Had there been an accident? She put her hand to her throbbing forehead and swore.

'Now now dear, we don't need language like that do we?' came a voice by her side. Ledasha squinted until the blurry outline of the person speaking came into view behind the same crosshatch that was on the ceiling. Iris Huxtable was sitting on a hard-backed chair. It took Ledasha a moment to register that she was knitting. And that the lines weren't on the ceiling or Huxtable. She was in a cage.

'Mrs? Mrs Huxtable?' she slurred. 'What are you doing here? Where am I?' It was all so confusing, and Ledasha found it exhausting even asking the questions.

'Why, you're my guest Ledasha. Just rest for a minute, your memory will come back shortly. You only received a very small dose.'

'Dose?' asked Ledasha blearily. She closed her eyes and tried to make sense of all the images swimming around in her head. There had been a red sports car. And Chelsea had been there. That was it. She'd met Chelsea and gone to Ilfracombe to meet the Ghost Train operator. Had she bumped her head on the ride somehow? 'There was a red car,' Ledasha said slowly, clinging onto the image.

'That's right dear. It was much easier to keep an eye on you once he overtook me. You know, it's quite a challenge driving so slowly, I was worried I was going to lose you more than once. Your friend really needs to get a faster bike. Not that it matters now of course.'

'We were following you?' Ledasha was puzzled, but then it started to come back to her. 'We were following you,' she repeated more confidently. The single light bulb hanging from the ceiling was coming in and out of focus as she fought the nausea. What was wrong with her?

'Go on, dear,' encouraged Huxtable, looking up from her knitting to give Ledasha a sinister smile.

'You did something to the guy on the Ghost Train didn't you?' A surge of euphoria hit her as she had another thought. 'And Jim at the railway. Hypnotised them so they'd forget you were there.'

'Well, hypnotism is a generous way of putting it,' Huxtable admitted. 'I never did quite master how to do it. Not reliably. Not without a little help.'

It was all coming back to Ledasha now, although the banging in her head was disorientating. She propped herself up on her elbow and rubbed her temple again.

'Yes, you will have a bit of a headache,' said Huxtable matter-of-factly. 'Don't worry, it'll pass.'

'What was it?' asked Ledasha. 'That stuff you blew at me.'

'Devil's Breath? It's a dramatic sounding name I know but I rather like it. Those polytunnels you stumbled into are growing it. Well, the borrachero trees it comes from. It's from Ecuador originally but grows well here given the right conditions. It's very labour intensive to harvest unfortunately, but the good news is I've managed to cultivate my own willing workforce.' She smiled to herself as she said it. 'The drug softens them up, makes them more susceptible, then it's a simple matter of applying suggestion to keep them working.'

'And that's what knocked me out?'

'In a manner of speaking. The drug alone isn't quite that effective, although we're getting better at refining it.

We combine it with another crop from my other site, which makes it more profitable, very profitable I should say, as a hallucinogenic. It's proving to be very popular with the younger crowd. Teenagers really will take anything these days, it's remarkable. But no, it didn't knock you out, just slowed your senses enough that my own instructions became more effective. It's more like a post hypnotic suggestion, but with a bit of chemical assistance to ensure complete surrender. A perfect cocktail of physical and mental stimuli to induce psychosis, if you like. I must confess I do enjoy the challenge of taking that initial control. Everyone's different. If it's any consolation you took longer to crack than your friend.'

'Chelsea? Where is she?'

'Oh, don't worry about her. Or Logan for that matter.'

'So you did take Logan as well.'

'Of course. He's the perfect subject. A history of trouble, running away from home, drugs in the family. No one's going to put much effort into looking for him are they?'

'But how? How did you do it without anyone seeing?'

'Well, I was just having a bit of fun you know. Mr Fuller had been a client of mine. His treatment was over but he'd been particularly easy to put under and I was curious about where I could go with it. I went to Lynmouth to see him at work. There was no one else around so I administered the drug, and before we'd reached the top I'd persuaded him that I wasn't there. As far as he was concerned he was all alone and he couldn't see me standing right in front of him. Otherwise he was functioning completely normally. Remarkable really what you can do with the human brain.'

'And Logan was just in the wrong place at the wrong time?'

'Or the right place at the right time, depending on your point of view. He recognised me immediately of course. Well, I nodded hello and walked quickly away. Couldn't exactly stop for a chat, could I? Mr Fuller would have thought Logan was mad having a conversation with thin air. But then I thought, why not? Like I said, Logan's perfect for me. He'd gone inside by the time I got back. Fuller had already closed the door and was shutting off the water supply. I told him to go up to the front, keep facing forwards and to count to a hundred before departing.'

'And then you used the same drug on Logan to get him to go with you?' said Ledasha, picturing Huxtable leading him away, Logan completely unaware of what he was doing.

'It all seemed too easy really. He resisted of course, fought the effects of the drug as long as he could. Even had the presence of mind to pull the scarf off his head and throw it out of reach, as if leaving some clue about his whereabouts when he was abducted might save him. It wouldn't, obviously. I amended my weekly reports to convince anyone who came asking that he was obsessed with running away. And that should have been the end of it. If you'd listened to me and left it alone you wouldn't be here now. I didn't want to do this you know. You had so much potential. Teenage boys are worthless creatures, easy to manipulate and no one will miss them. I wanted more for you Ledasha. But you spoiled it all by getting involved where you didn't belong. All this trouble over some boy who would have forgotten about you in five minutes. It's very disappointing. Pathetic, really. I misjudged you.'

'Logan wouldn't forget me,' insisted Ledasha. 'He's a good person.'

Huxtable dismissed the comment with a wave of her hand, then went back to her knitting. 'So misguided. Oh well, it's unfortunate but nothing we can't resolve. You've brought me your new friend Chelsea. I don't normally like to use girls but I'm sure she'll be a more than adequate replacement for Logan, so he can be disposed of. And you're going to help me with that Ledasha.'

45

Ledasha didn't like the sound of that. She was going to have to escape. Somehow. If she was left alone for a few minutes she might be able to break out of this cage. Failing that she'd overpower Huxtable once she was let out. She was an old woman after all, no match for Ledasha who'd survived years fighting with people much bigger and stronger.

'What do you mean? Disposed of?'

'So sad, isn't it, how some teenagers lose their way these days? The whole world's against them. It's not fair. Life's not worth living. Don't you think?'

'No! I don't think that at all.' Ledasha could feel her face flushing, fear and anger growing inside her. 'And nor does Logan.'

'So you say. Others will see it differently. They'll look at the two of you, when you're found, and see two troubled kids, always struggling to fit in, always angry at the world. That misspent youth of yours, always causing trouble, it will be easy for them to believe your suicide pact was simply a cry for help.' Huxtable turned to face her. 'Then they'll move on and you'll be forgotten about.'

'And how do you plan to do this, you evil bitch?' Ledasha was still angry, but she could sense her fear being replaced by a cold hatred.

Huxtable paused from her knitting and contemplated Ledasha, amusement on her face. 'Oh, I wouldn't want to spoil the surprise dear. Much less traumatic for you not to know, don't you think? Now, get some sleep. It's going to be an exciting day tomorrow.' She stood up, holding onto her knitting and the needles in one hand and the trailing ball of wool in the other, then opened the door to the hallway. 'You can scream if you like. No one will hear you.'

Huxtable flicked off the light, plunging the room into total darkness, then swept out and closed the door behind her. Ledasha heard a key turn in the lock, which seemed a little overcautious given she was already locked inside the cage. She tried to visualise the room to get a better understanding of her surroundings. Although she hadn't been paying much attention while Huxtable had been in there, her mind relived the conversation, zooming in on different areas of her peripheral vision. The only window was blocked by some kind of padded insulation. It appeared Huxtable's claim about not being heard needed a backup, although it was also a useful way of disorientating most captives. Not me though, Ledasha thought, determination growing inside her.

With the window blocked Ledasha had no idea what time of day or night it was. From the way Huxtable had spoken about getting some sleep it might be late evening, but she could just as easily have been messing with her mind. Ledasha tried to look for a chink in the cover but couldn't even work out where the window was. She closed her eyes again and pictured the cage. It was against a wall, in the corner, and might have been designed for a large dog or something similar. There was room to lay down, and she could perch on her knees, but standing up was out of the question. The mesh itself was pretty small, just big enough for fingers to fit but there was no way she'd get her whole hand through. Not that there was much point in doing so, as nothing was within reach. The door had a single lock. Ledasha pictured it in her mind for a few seconds, nodded to herself, then continued her mental survey of the room.

The only furniture was the chair Huxtable had been using, and a thin, narrow mattress behind her in the cage. Other than that the room was bare. She gripped the door of the cage and shook it gently to test it, but as she expected it remained securely shut. The lock had looked pretty basic though. Sitting down cross-legged in front of it, she ran her finger over it.

'Misspent youth,' Ledasha muttered to herself as she reached her hand to her head and pulled out the two hairpins she'd put in earlier. She carefully bent them against the floor then threaded them into the lock, feeling for the pressure points. A satisfying click announced her success.

She pushed the door a centimetre out to confirm it was fully unlocked, then put the pins back into her hair making sure they were concealed. Ledasha wondered if the hinges were squeaky, but realised it was a risk she was going to have to take. She needed to plan her escape before making a move though. Remove the window padding first to see if that could be a possible way out, but do it slowly and cautiously in case there was some kind of alarm wired up. It seemed far-fetched but Ledasha was starting to suspect Huxtable had been kidnapping teenagers for a while, and it must take a particularly shrewd individual to have done it so successfully for so long.

She decided once she moved she would need to move fast. Chelsea and Logan were here somewhere and both were in danger, but the probability of finding them without being caught herself was low. As desperate as she was to rescue them both and take them with her she knew it was too risky. Unless she happened to stumble into them on her way out they'd have to wait until she was free and could raise the alarm.

Okay, she thought to herself. Window first. If she could open it then no dithering, climb out and run. If not, try to break out through the door. Again, no stopping to look around, just get out as quickly and quietly as she could.

And then what, Ledasha wondered? Escape overland on foot? She knew they were somewhere remote, countryside was all she'd seen on the way in and Huxtable had warned her that calling for help was a wasted effort. There must be other farmhouses in the area, but finding them in the dark might be tricky, especially if Huxtable was on to her by then. She could spend ages trying to cross fields or woods only to end up lost. And she couldn't afford to waste time. The sooner Huxtable discovered she was missing the greater danger the others would be in.

Could she make it to the bike? Presumably Huxtable now had the keys. That wasn't a big problem, Ledasha had boosted plenty of mopeds before, but it would slow her down. Then she'd have to push it back to the gate, open that and only then make her escape. It would all add to the delays but the alternatives didn't seem any better.

Yes, the bike was her best bet. If she could get to it she stood a chance. A good chance. This was it then, now or never. She took off her jumper and held it against the hinges, hoping it would muffle any squeaks. Satisfied she'd done as much as she could, Ledasha held one hand on the top hinge, put the other on the grill of the door and pushed.

46

Over the last couple of years, before being moved to Devon, Ledasha had broken into a lot of garages. She'd occasionally gone into houses and shops as well, but they had alarms and she'd never been comfortable with the thought there could be people inside. Garages were never protected. The rewards weren't as high but there was always something worth taking. Bikes, tools, even a surfboard once. The trick was not to dither. Opening a window or door slowly just prolonged any screeches from rusty joints. Do it quickly and smoothly, and more often than not the window was open before it had a chance to squeal.

The same approach worked on the cage. She sensed a very slight resistance, an almost imperceptible pause in the swing which she was sure would have made a noise if she'd been more tentative. She didn't wait to find out if anyone had heard anything. Grabbing her jumper, she crawled out and stood, tying it around her waist as she moved. Within a couple of seconds she was at the window, reaching to pull away the padded cover. Her hands stopped in mid air as she remembered her plan to check for alarms. Delicately leaning into the alcove she examined the edges of the window frame and sill. Nothing obviously visible. She reached to one side of the padding with both hands and gently peeled it back a few centimetres. It was dark outside, well past sunset, and Ledasha could now see she was on the first floor of the building. Climbing down would be dangerous, but possible, and still preferable to going through the house. She eased the covering back another couple of centimetres, but froze as a wire appeared, attached to the back of the insulation and leading down into a small hole drilled in the windowsill.

'Shit,' Ledasha mouthed silently. She didn't move for a few seconds, then cautiously pushed the padding back into place and listened. There was no sound from elsewhere in the house to suggest she'd triggered an alarm. She stared at the padding for a minute, considering whether there was any way to prise it off the window but keep it attached to the wire, but she knew any movement was risky. She'd have to take her chances in the house. At least she wouldn't have to clamber down the outside in the dark.

Moving over to the door she repeated the exercise, feeling all around the edge for some sign of an alarm. Nothing was noticeable, but it could easily be hidden. She toyed with turning the light on but worried that might draw attention, plus she wanted her eyes to be accustomed to the dark once she was out of the room.

She decided there was no choice but to go for it as she bent to examine the lock. It was stiff and heavy, but after a few attempts she felt the latch thud back into the door. She stood up and bent her head left, then right, shaking her arms out and taking a few deep breaths, steeling herself for her next move. Don't run, but don't dawdle either. Calm, swift movements, making sure to stay absolutely silent throughout. She put her hand on the knob, took one more deep breath, and turned.

Again, she moved quickly, opening the door in a single confident, fluid movement. Ledasha smiled for the first time. 'Shoulda put a bolt on the outside,' she thought. The landing was pitch black, but her eyes were used to it now and she could make out a corridor with doors leading off it. Stairs were at the far end.

She regarded the doors longingly. Was Chelsea behind one of them? There was no way to tell. It could just as easily be Huxtable or some of her gang. She shook her head and faced the stairs instead. It was the only sensible route out. Was it too obvious though? Huxtable had been particularly thorough so far, with the locked cage and locked door, not to mention the hidden alarm on the window. Somehow it still felt too easy to Ledasha. There was no explanation other than a sixth sense telling her heading that way would lead into a trap.

At the opposite end of the corridor was a window. Uncovered this time. She took one more look at the stairs then turned and headed the other way. There was no sign of any alarms or booby traps around the frame. There wasn't even a lock. Outside, Ledasha saw some kind of walled garden at the back of the house, but there was a gate in the wall, and if worse came to worst it wasn't too high to climb. Even better, she could see a small roof directly below her, some kind of porch over the back entrance, as solidly built as the rest of the farmhouse.

She'd spent too long here, she knew. It was time to go. Turning the handle, she pulled open the window as quickly as she dared then climbed through and lowered herself slowly onto the roof of the porch. It sloped away from the building but the shallow angle enabled her to crawl down on her stomach and dangle her legs over the end. Putting her weight on her hands, she swung herself down and landed lightly on the ground. Tia would be proud, thought Ledasha.

She took a moment to decide on her next move. She could see spotlights around the house and garden. They were off right now, but no doubt sensors would pick up any movement. How long would she have before Huxtable and her brainwashed minders responded? A minute, maybe two? Not enough. Unless she could get through that gate in the corner and block it from the other side. It would surely be locked though, and she'd have no time to open it. Over the wall maybe? That was as likely to trigger the spotlights as anything else, but presumably by the time Ledasha got there they'd be on already.

Okay, decision time. Edge slowly around the house and

make her way towards the gate. Try that first and if it opened, get through then barricade it if possible. If not then don't hang about trying to pick the lock. Climb straight up and over the wall using the birdbath next to it to get a head start. If the lights came on at any point the plan stayed the same, but from then on any thoughts of creeping slowly could be forgotten. She'd have to run flat out and not stop until she was far away. Or caught.

She moved, crouching low but staying on two feet, searching constantly for movement sensors. Strange there weren't any. Maybe Huxtable was so confident in her internal security she'd never had to worry about having more outside. Or perhaps wildlife in the countryside caused too many false alarms. Either way, Ledasha was happy to get to the gate without any trouble.

It was locked. She sighed, weighing up the time it would take to pick it. Two stiff looking bolts at the top and bottom, on top of the heavy duty keyhole in the middle of the gate, convinced her she'd be there a while. Just when it had started to feel like things were going her way. Never mind. A short hop over the wall and she'd be clear. Behind her the house remained still, everything dark and peaceful. She crept further around the wall until she reached the birdbath she'd seen earlier, then climbed on top, briefly worried she was about to crash as it wobbled slightly. The top of the wall was just out of reach, but with a small jump she got her fingers on top, her feet planted securely against the side.

The spotlights flooded the garden instantly, illuminating her in their glare. She looked back at the house. The sensors must be set to pick up movement above a certain height. What an idiot! Cross that she'd been so careless, she clambered up. Only then did she notice the wire running along the top. 'Clever bitch,' muttered Ledasha. The bright lights had ruined her night vision and all she could see was blackness beyond.

Adrenaline was pumping through her now. She was

about to lower herself down to the other side, but stopped herself when she figured that might not lead anywhere. Without knowing what she'd be jumping into she was reluctant to head that way. Standing up, she ran along the top of the wall instead, away from the gate since Huxtable would have to go out that way to come after her. She could make out the polytunnels in the next field. If she was lucky they could lead her back to the moped.

Reaching the corner, she lowered herself as far as she could down the outside of the wall and let go. The landing was soft, but a second later she realised her feet were stuck some thick mud, the suction holding her tight. She wavered for a moment then fell backwards, away from the wall, sitting down almost in slow motion. 'Bollocks,' she castigated herself, twisting round onto her knees and dragging her way out. The mud was sucking at her, sapping her energy, but she was strong and forced her way through it towards a grass verge only a metre away. The gate creaked open at the far end of the wall just as she reached the firmer ground. Hauling herself up, she ran towards the field with the tunnels, scrambled over a chest-high gate and stumbled blindly onwards.

She yanked open the door to the first tunnel but left it as a decoy and ran past the next two before she turned and sprinted up the gap between them. There was nowhere to hide or catch her breath, but if she could get to the end without being seen there was a chance she could lose them. Voices and footsteps carried through the still night, and a sense of terror swelled inside her. She forced it down, trying to get control of her fear. This wasn't the first time she'd been chased and had to find her way out of a dangerous situation. Get a grip, she told herself silently as she kept running as lightly as she could over the thick grass.

Risking a quick glance behind her she was relieved to see no one there. They must have fallen for her diversion and gone inside the first tunnel. There might be others though, and they'd see her long before she made it to the end of the row. She saw entrances coming up on either side, halfway along each tunnel. Ledasha spun to her right, away from the direction of the voices, and tugged open the door, closing it silently behind her. The air was damp and much warmer, the humidity cranked up to suit the weird bell-shaped flowers lining the path. Creeping between two of the plants she squatted down and rested for a minute, breathing deeply as she tried to slow her pulse.

This is stupid, she thought. She was foolishly crouched waiting for them to find her. Now wasn't a time to hide, or to try outmanoeuvring her pursuers by cutting back on herself. She needed to put distance between them, it was as simple as that. Standing up, she moved onto the dirt path leading down the middle of the tunnel and made her way stealthily towards the far end. She was almost there when a door crashed behind her and she dove off to the side, ducking between two of the plants.

'You take the next one, I'll check in here,' said a male voice. Whoever it was hadn't seen her, but they weren't leaving. The door rattled shut as the second pursuer moved on, but watching through the foliage she could just make out the first one moving slowly towards her. Ledasha shrank back, keeping low and trying to camouflage herself amongst the leaves. Her tracksuit was all muddy from her fall from the wall but she knew her t-shirt was still glaringly white.

Slipping her dark jumper from her waist she slowly pulled it over her head and slipped her arms through. Not perfect, but she needed all the help she could get. The footsteps were getting closer now.

'Come out, come out, wherever you are,' taunted the boy. She couldn't see his face but he sounded young. She didn't know how many were out looking for her, or whether they were drugged teenagers under Huxtable's control or willing accomplices. Even if she evaded this one she might find herself outnumbered as soon as she turned the next corner. Better to take him out of the equation now while she had surprise on her side. Attack is the best form of defence had always been her motto.

She scanned around for something to use as a weapon but cowering down among the plants all she could see was the fine dirt from the flowerbed. It'll have to do, thought Ledasha as she scooped up a handful. The boy's feet were almost on top of her now as he slowly made his way along the path. Ledasha knew this was her chance. Springing to her feet, she swung her arm up and flung the dusty grains of dirt in his face. She had a split second to register that it wasn't Logan, although whoever it was couldn't have been much older than sixteen, before her other hand was jabbing forward, striking him hard on his Adam's apple while he was blinded.

His hands went to his throat as he gasped for air, but Ledasha, rebounding slightly from her punch was already swinging her foot up hard into his groin. He crumpled with the force of it, unable to cry out because of the trauma to his airways, and she finished him off with a merciless knee to the face which left him sprawled on the floor. She looked at him, curled up and gasping for breath, and was satisfied he wouldn't be going anywhere for a while. She could have followed it up with more kicks but something inside her told her to hold off, that he might not know what he was doing if Huxtable had him entranced.

'Stay down,' she warned, then spun and ran towards the far end of the tunnel. Reaching the door, she paused to listen for anyone outside. Hearing nothing she opened it and peeked out. There was no sign of life, but she saw with surprise the tall hedge they'd crawled under earlier. The bike might still be on the other side, and the gate to the road right next to it. Ledasha sprinted flat out and dove to the ground, crawling through the dirt to get through to safety. The hedge was thick but she could see the open grass beyond as she pushed herself along.

Her arms reached the clearing, followed quickly by her head and shoulders. One more push and she was half out, when from nowhere a huge weight pressed down on her back, forcing her flat onto the ground. She struggled and squirmed, trying to shake it off, but her left arm was pinned to the floor while other hands grabbed her right. She tried to look up, but they were on top of and behind her. All she could see was the moped, parked agonisingly close.

'Well done, Ledasha,' came Huxtable's voice, a little out of breath. 'No one's ever made it this far before. I knew you were special.'

Ledasha's face was being pushed into the earth, a strong hand holding the back of her head, and she spat out a mouthful of dirt. 'Get them off me!' she snarled, struggling against the heavy knees pressing down on her lungs.

'Yes, that'll do boys. We don't want to leave any marks on her now, do we? Pick her up, let me look at her.'

She felt hands reach under her shoulders, dragging her roughly to her feet. Like a wild animal, she windmilled her right arm backwards to shake off her assailant, swinging her fist back up into the other boy's stomach. He groaned and bent double, as the first wrapped his arms around her and held her tight. Ledasha kicked out with her feet, catching the injured boy in the face, then stamped down hard on the foot of the one holding her. He managed to hold on, as Huxtable took a step closer and held out a small tube. Ledasha took a deep breath and screwed her mouth and eyes closed, determined not to breath anything in, but nothing happened. She held it for a few more seconds, waiting for the powder to hit, but before it did her captor squeezed her chest tightly and she involuntarily gasped. As she took another breath she felt the powder hit her face and the inside of her mouth, and heard Huxtable's voice. Then, just as before, her vision went fuzzy and she gave up the struggle.

47

Ledasha woke slowly the next morning, her head thumping. She felt very groggy. Opening her eyes, she realised she was back in the cage, but this time a teenage boy was sitting outside. She closed them again before he recognised she was awake.

Lying still, the events of the night before gradually came back to her. She cursed herself for having wasted precious minutes hiding among the plants when she should have made straight for the moped. Now she was back where she'd started, only worse because this time she had a guard watching over her.

'Psst. Are you awake?' she heard the boy whisper.

Ledasha kept very still. This could be a trap, and she needed to shake off the wooziness before talking to anyone.

'I want to help you,' came the voice again. 'I don't know how, but if I can I will, I promise.'

She opened one eye to look at him. He was thin, his hair long and unkempt and his clothes scruffy, but he had a childlike innocence to his face, his freckles standing out against the pale skin. He smiled when he noticed her watching him and shuffled forward on his seat, checking behind him in case they were being observed.

'She told me to guard you, but I managed to fake my last dose of the drug she uses on us so I'm more with it than normal.'

Ledasha propped herself up on one arm. 'Really?' she asked sceptically. 'You expect me to believe that?'

'It happens sometimes,' he shrugged. 'I dunno how long I've been here, it's all patchy, but I know she gives us a drug that messes with our heads, and sometimes it's not a full hit. Could just be luck, or maybe she's skimping on the dose, I don't know.'

'If this has happened before, why haven't you escaped?'

'It's not that easy. One boy, Connor his name was, local lad, showed me how to fake taking the drug. Well, he nearly got out a few months ago, even made it over the wall like you. But he got stuck in the mud on the other side. She made us bring him back inside, then that's the last I seen of him. Been too scared to make a run for it since then in case she does the same to me.'

'Can't you overpower her? You're stronger than she is.'

He shook his head. 'She's always got a couple of other lads close by, ones that are totally under her control. I ain't had the chance to do nothing. Not yet anyways. Got to pick the right moment, you only get one shot.'

'And I blew mine,' rued Ledasha.

They were both quiet for a minute. 'Can you get a message out?' Ledasha asked him. 'A text, or phone call or summat?'

He shook his head. 'If I could do that I'd have been out of here months ago. None of us have a phone, and there's no way I could get to hers. I don't even know where we are, or what her name is.'

'Iris Huxtable,' Ledasha explained. 'She does counselling and shit like that. I was sent to her for anger management. Don't ask. And we're, well, I don't know exactly. About twenty minutes south west of Barnstaple.'

'Barnstaple?' asked the boy. 'Where's that?'

Ledasha looked at him, surprised. 'North Devon. Where are you from then?'

'Reading. Last thing I remember for sure is going to the cinema with me mates one night. October half term. What month is it now?'

'It's July. Shit man, we gotta get out of here. Can you get me out of this thing? Together we could do it, we can get away.'

He glanced around nervously. 'I dunno. The cage is locked and she has the key. How did you get out before?'

'Oh, it's pretty easy, I ju–' Ledasha stopped herself and regarded him suspiciously. 'Wait a minute. If you were mates with Connor surely he told you where you were? You said he was a local.'

'Well, I, I,' he stuttered.

'You're just trying to find out how I got out before, aren't you?' asked Ledasha angrily. 'She's still controlling you. Can you understand what I'm saying? She's taken over your mind. Fight it! Get her out of your head!'

'I, no, she, I.' The boy looked towards the door, confusion on his face. A moment later it opened, and Huxtable walked in clapping slowly. She'd changed out of her usual frumpy skirt suit and was wearing olive green cord trousers and a yellow blouse, with heavy brown walking boots.

'Well done Ledasha. I said you were smart. Didn't fall for my little trick, did you? Run along you,' she added, looking at the boy. 'Your breakfast is in the dormitory.' She waited until the boy had left, then pulled over the chair and sat in front of Ledasha again. 'Come on then, tell me how you got out.'

'Go to hell,' answered Ledasha.

Huxtable eyed her shrewdly. 'Very well. It won't help you, but may have been useful knowledge for future guests. I do like to learn from my mistakes. No matter.' She stood and moved the chair back against the wall. 'Two of the boys will be in to collect you shortly. You can struggle if you like. They're a bit upset at how you got the better of them last night and will enjoy having an excuse to hurt you.'

She left the room, locking the door behind her. Ledasha waited a minute, scanning the room for cameras. She couldn't see any, but it was uncomfortable crouching in the low cage so she decided it was worth risking it. Besides, it would annoy Huxtable. She picked the lock and crawled out, then moved the chair so it was facing the door. Sitting down, she reclined as best she could and put her hands behind her head. She was determined not to give the guards the satisfaction of seeing her cowed, and knew Huxtable would be irritated to find her sitting here. Ledasha smiled grimly to herself. She wasn't sure how yet, but she resolved that somehow she would find a way out of this. And next time there would be no mistakes.

48

Ledasha didn't have to wait long. Ten minutes later the door opened and two large teenage boys stepped into the room. They looked at each other, slightly taken aback that she wasn't in her cage as expected. Ledasha took the opportunity to throw them further off guard by standing up and stretching.

'Come on then boys, let's do this,' she said, walking up to them. They stood still, confused, so she held one arm out to the open door. 'Lead on then sunshine. Or do you want to follow me?'

He contemplated the key in his hand then put it in his pocket. 'Come with us.' They each took one of Ledasha's arms and forcibly led her to the door, but it wasn't wide enough for them to go through together and they stumbled.

'Here, let me help,' offered Ledasha, then she elbowed the one on her right in the stomach, not hard but it still made him take a step back. She cocked her head towards the door, indicating to the other boy that he should lead. 'After you then,' she added brightly. The boy behind her propelled her roughly through the doorway. .'Really? Is that the best you've got? How did I ever allow myself to be caught by you overgrown lumps of cabbage?'

They led her along the corridor and down the stairs. As they reached the halfway point, the stair creaked loudly, then again on the next one. Ledasha nodded to herself, pleased she'd made the right decision the previous night to head in the other direction.

At the bottom she was led outside onto the forecourt at the front of the house. The white van was still parked on the gravel next to the Fiesta. Huxtable was standing behind the van, its doors open.

'Put her in with her friend,' said Huxtable. 'You both get in the back as well. I'll go and lock up.' Ledasha watched her walk back to the house. She saw a sign naming the place Hollowbrook Farm before she was shoved roughly towards the van.

Ledasha glared at the boy who'd pushed her. 'Do that again you get a kick in the balls.'

'Get in,' he said, grabbing her arm and forcing her to move. Ledasha searched for a way out but she was being held tightly, and for all her bravado she didn't think she'd get far if she tried to break away from them here. Besides, it sounded like Chelsea must already be inside the van, and despite last night's escape attempt, if she was going to try again she'd take Chelsea with her next time. As the boy pulled her round to the back of the van Ledasha looked inside, keen to see her new friend.

'Logan!' she exclaimed. It felt like weeks since she'd seen him, and his sudden appearance in the van startled her. Of course. She remembered Huxtable saying the night before how she'd be getting rid of both of them. With a suicide pact.

'Dash, mate, am I glad to see you,' he replied, relief on his face. 'Huxtable said she had a surprise for me. How did you get here?'

'Long story.' One of Ledasha's guards tried to force her inside. 'Back off,' she snapped at him. 'I'm getting in, keep your paws to yourself.' She stepped onto the footrest then shook off the boy holding her and threw herself at Logan. She hugged him tightly, overcome with relief.

'I'm scared Dash,' Logan said quietly, as the two other boys climbed into the van. 'Huxtable's had me working in her greenhouses but she said we're going on a trip, and I'll be free soon. You think she means it?'

'No,' Ledasha replied. There was no point sugar-coating it. 'She doesn't. She's planning to do us in. We need to find a way out of here.' The van felt very claustrophobic with the boys blocking the exit. Huxtable reappeared outside and closed one of the rear doors.

'Where are you taking us?' asked Ledasha. 'You said we had some sort of suicide pact last night. What is it? An overdose?'

'No, that didn't seem right for you,' Huxtable replied, her hand on the other door. 'Besides, I've already used that this week. Doesn't do to repeat the same methods too often, people get suspicious.'

'So what is it then? I want to know.'

Huxtable considered her thoughtfully. 'Why not. The anticipation of what's to come will make it all the more unbearable. You and Logan are going to take a walk, near Umberleigh. It's not far so don't worry, you won't be back here for long.'

'And what's in Umberleigh that we should be afraid of?' asked Ledasha. 'Some big cliff for us to jump off?'

Huxtable shook her head. 'No, no, quite the opposite. It's very flat. A little village with a pub, a pretty river running through it.' She paused, then added 'And a small train station. There's a level crossing just outside the village, keeps cars and people off the tracks when a train's passing. I thought you two might like a closer look.' She smiled and turned to the two boys guarding them. 'This one can be tricky. If you see her trying to escape, or her friend, you can sit on them for the rest of the journey.' She closed the second door, shutting them inside. The opaque windows let some light through but it had become very gloomy inside.

'What's she talking about?' asked Logan nervously.

The van started up and they were rocked about in the back as it made a tight turn on the gravel driveway. 'She's going to make us walk onto the track when a train's coming,' Ledasha replied, holding onto him as the van turned onto the road and accelerated. She was surprised at how calm she sounded, despite the desperate urgency of their situation. Huxtable was wrong; the uncertainty had been worse, making her angry and stopping her from thinking. Now she knew what Huxtable had planned she felt more composed, and the confines of the van forced her to sit back and weigh up their options.

'She what? Dash, we gotta stop her, this is mental.'

'Shh, let me think,' Ledasha told him. Logan was clearly agitated, and if they were going to get out of this it would be up to her. She tried to picture what Huxtable had in mind. They would be given the mind control drug and given instructions to step onto the track, then presumably to walk towards the train. Or lie down and wait for it to hit them. Either way, the end result would be the same.

Ledasha wasn't sure where they were, other than it was south of Barnstaple somewhere. All she knew about the train line was that it also headed south east out of the town, so Huxtable was probably telling the truth when she'd said it wouldn't take them long.

That left them with two choices. Overpower their guards now, and somehow try to get out while the van was moving, or wait then try to escape once they arrived. Ledasha didn't like the thought of that. It would mean leaving it very late, and if anything went wrong there'd be no more chances. No, the sooner they made it out of here the better. That meant either the double doors at the back, which were blocked by their two guards, or the sliding side door opposite her, which would almost certainly be locked. A cursory glance behind confirmed there was no other door on this side. The front cab was blocked by a partition so there was no way through that way, and the tiny skylight in the ceiling would be no use as an escape route.

She looked at the first teenage boy, seated on the opposite side at the back of the van. He was big, very big, bent over with his thick forearms resting on his knees as the van rocked them all gently about.

The other boy wasn't very different. He was sitting

more upright, his huge arms folded across his large chest, his shorts showing off legs that appeared to be pure muscle. Both were gazing out of the back windows, showing no interest in their captives, totally confident in their superiority. If it wasn't for their spotty faces Ledasha might have thought they were much older, given their bulk. She couldn't help but stare at them in wonder.

'You two like to work out, huh?' she asked. Both boys ignored her. She tried again, more loudly. 'You. With the white t-shirt, you must be pretty strong. Spend a lot of time in the gym do you?' The boy moved his head as if he'd just noticed her for the first time, but otherwise remained as he was with his arms resting comfortably on his knees. After returning her stare for a few seconds he went back to his original position, dismissing her without a word.

'What is it with these two?' she asked Logan quietly. 'Huxtable must have hypnotised them into working out twenty four hours a day. And given them some steroids or something. No way can that be natural.'

Logan looked at them and shrugged miserably. He was tiny in comparison and had a helpless, defeated demeanour. Ledasha turned her attention back to the two muscly boys. Okay, they were very big, and very strong. Possibly not too bright though. Or if they were, whatever trance Huxtable had put them under seemed to be slowing down their senses. They were clearly solid units, but Ledasha wondered if they were quite as tough as they appeared. Lifting dumbbells and doing squats for hours on end was no substitute for street smarts when it came to close quarters fighting. And Ledasha had plenty of experience at that. Even so, she'd only get one shot against two opponents as big as these. Taking them on in this confined space would need some thought, and ten minutes must have already passed since they left the farmhouse. She might not have much longer.

As casually as possible, she scanned the van looking for

something she could use as a weapon. There were some dust sheets on the floor, but nothing solid to hit them with. Right now, she didn't care that they were under Huxtable's control, and were likely to be as innocent as she was. If it came to it, it was them or her, and she knew she couldn't hesitate to put them down if the chance arose. Still, it would take everything she had to even stand a slim hope against them. Launching herself, with her whole bodyweight behind her, might mean she could knock out the one opposite her, then a solid kick to the face of the other may just give them the few seconds they needed to get the door open.

The van stopped, and Ledasha had a fleeting panic that she'd left it too late, but then it turned onto another road. She was thrown across to the other side of the van, then as it accelerated again she fell towards the two large boys, landing on the floor between their feet. They ignored her as she sat on the floor rubbing her hand.

Interesting, thought Ledasha. They hadn't moved at all. What was it Huxtable had said to them? If you see her trying to escape.

Her.

'No way,' Ledasha said to herself. It couldn't be that easy, surely. Would they take every instruction that literally while they were under her control?

She picked herself up, then sat on the opposite side this time, dusting off her legs as she faced Logan. Attacking two bodybuilders felt foolish now. They would have brushed her off then sat on her for the rest of the journey. An idea was forming in her mind. It was risky, but something was telling her this was the right thing to do. She bent down and picked up one of the dust sheets.

'Dash,' Logan whispered, his voice sounding strained. 'What are you doing?'

She held the dust sheet against the side of her head, bunched up in her hands but still covering her face.

'I've got a plan,' she answered quietly. 'If it doesn't

work, promise me you'll dive for that door and try to get out. Don't think twice okay? If they stop me you won't be able to do anything, so don't even attempt it. You run, you hear me? Run and find help. You need to get to that crossing before the train does or I'll be finished.'

'Dash, no way man. I can't leave you.'

'You have to,' she assured him. 'If this works perfectly we may both get out, but if I don't then I'm relying on you to get away and find a way to save me. Promise me Loges.'

He looked at her nervously, then nodded.

The van rocked as it changed gear to go up a hill. Ledasha knew she couldn't waste any more time debating this. There was no point anyway; she already knew it was crazy.

Shaking out the dust sheet, she took hold of two of the corners. Neither captor showed any interest in her, which reassured Ledasha she was doing the right thing. She poked the corner of the sheet into a metal groove along the ceiling, pulling it tight so it snagged and stayed firmly in place. Leaning across to Logan's side, she did the same with the other corner. And now you can't see me, thought Ledasha.

She tried the handle of the sliding door but as she expected it was locked. Removing her hairpin, she bent it into shape and started to work on the lock.

'Dash! Watch out!' Logan's shout behind her made her look up. The second boy's hand was on the dust sheet, tugging it down. His face appeared over the top and he stared at her for a couple of seconds, then realised this fitted with the instructions he'd been given. Ripping the dust sheet away, he advanced towards her.

Ledasha didn't stop to think. Plan B hadn't worked, so she was back to Plan A. Snarling, she flew up from her crouched position, concentrating every bit of her momentum into her fist, now aimed squarely at the boy's nose. He didn't react, the speed of her attack taking him completely off guard. His nose exploded, the sickening crunch reverberating through Ledasha's arm. His eyes widened in surprise, but again Ledasha moved too quickly for him, her left hand swinging round and catching him hard on his ear. He wobbled, dazed, still holding onto the sheet. Grabbing it, she lifted it over his head with both hands and wrenched it roughly down, bringing her knee up to meet the boy's face.

As soon as it connected, she yanked again, sidestepping so he was thrown behind her. The other boy looked up in surprise, his arms still resting on his knees as if he'd only just grasped what was going on around him. Ledasha didn't wait for him to catch up, but reached for the skylight, pulling herself up then lashing out at the second boy's head with both feet. Her heels landed perfectly, catching his stunned expression and slamming his head into the side of the van.

As she dropped back to the floor, Logan jumped past her and landed on top of him. 'Go!' he shouted. 'Get the door.'

Ledasha leapt across, jerking up the handle and pushing open the door. It was hard to tell how fast the van was going, but there was no doubt it was moving pretty rapidly. She gripped the door tightly; for the first time, she felt a flash of fear and looked back at Logan grappling with the second boy. It wasn't a fair contest, and a moment later with an almighty shove Logan was thrown off, crashing into the other boy still stumbling around at the back of the van with the dust sheet still over his head. Logan collided with him and they both fell against the back of the van, tangled together as they were rocked about. The noise must have alerted Huxtable in the front as she hit the brakes. The second boy, who'd been scrambling towards her, was sent tumbling back into the other two, and Ledasha's arm felt like it was about to be pulled off as she clung onto the door. As the van skidded to a stop, she took one glance at the three boys in a heap behind her, then turned to the open doorway and jumped.

49

They were on a narrow country lane. Ledasha didn't know what was behind her, and didn't wait to find out. She ran. Up ahead she could see buildings and a church tower, so she sprinted towards them. A sign told her the village was called Atherington. It was slightly uphill, and she could feel herself tiring, but knew she had to keep going.

'Get her!' came a shout from behind. That was Huxtable, thought Ledasha, as she put on a fresh burst of speed. She could hear footsteps behind her, then the van itself reversing back up the hill. The lane was too narrow for it to turn around and it was emitting a high pitched whine as it attempted to close the gap. She risked a look back. One of the boys who'd been guarding her had jumped out and was halfway between her and the van, closing quickly.

A driveway led off to the left, the first house on the outskirts of the village. Ledasha rejected it instantly. There was no car parked outside and no other obvious sign anyone was home. Next came a wooden gate on her right hand side, but that was closed and again the place felt empty. Where is everyone, she thought desperately. The village itself was now only fifty metres away, and Ledasha guessed the boy was half that distance behind her. If she could reach the high street then surely there'd be someone around who could help.

The hill was really starting to take its toll now and she knew she was slowing. The road narrowed further as she closed in on the buildings, just a single lane for cars travelling in both directions. She reached an old stone wall on her left, with a grassy bank facing it. The sound of the boy's feet behind her felt terrifyingly close. She could stop and fight but he was a big lad, and angry, and she didn't have surprise on her side anymore. Keep running, that was her only option. She was so close, the church and a post office almost within reach, but the village felt deserted.

A thump suddenly hit her in the back and she went sprawling to the floor. A second later the boy was on top of her, pinning her to the ground. A knee pressed hard into her back, and a strong hand gripped her wrist, the other clamped over her mouth to stop her calling out. She twisted and kicked and tried to bite him but couldn't shake him off. He had her.

She saw the van come to a stop not far behind where the road had become narrower. The other boy jumped down, and Ledasha could see the fury in his eyes as he approached, blood all over his face and shirt from his busted nose. He kicked her hard in her side, pain shooting through her. Ledasha let out a muffled cry, cursing him and angry at herself for not being quick enough to get away. She'd got so close, if only she'd run faster she would have been safe.

'Get off her!' came a shout from above. Ledasha recognised Logan's voice, then the weight lifted from her side and the hand left her mouth as the boy holding her down was pulled away.

'Logan! Forget about me, run!' shouted Ledasha. She forced her head round and could see Logan on his back now, tussling with her assailant.

'Get her in the van,' hissed Huxtable from nearby. The boy who'd kicked her lifted her easily and spun her round to face Huxtable. 'Quickly,' continued Huxtable. 'Before anyone sees her. Then help get the other one in.'

Ledasha could see Logan thrashing about on the floor with the other boy, but could tell he was fighting a losing battle. Before she could say anything she was thrust roughly forwards, causing her to stumble and almost fall again. She was about to turn round to have a go at the boy behind her when she realised he wasn't holding onto her anymore. He was so confident he'd won that he was arrogantly pushing her in front of him. This was her chance. Her last chance. Ledasha steeled herself, then jumped forwards and punched Huxtable full in the face.

The boy froze in shock as he watched his leader rock backwards unsteadily. She wobbled for an instant then dropped to her knees. Ledasha didn't wait to savour the moment, but immediately ran down the side of the van. Finally reacting to the situation, the boy started to follow her, but she ran around the front of the van and made to come back up the other side. He moved to his right to block that route, and they each feinted left and right at opposite ends of the van. Ledasha knew the longer she could evade him the better the likelihood of someone else arriving.

Anger finally overcame the boy and he dove down one side, forcing Ledasha back the other way. The boy doubled back but she'd already reached the back of the van again. Huxtable was trying to get back up, but Ledasha pushed her into the boy's path and the collision brought them both down. She kept moving, level with Logan still wrestling on the floor, but the boy he was holding reached out and grabbed her ankle as she passed. She tried to shake him off but he was holding tightly, then Logan threw himself onto the boy's arm and he yelled out in pain, releasing her.

'Go!' shouted Logan. Ledasha wavered, aware she'd shouted the same to him only minutes before. She couldn't leave him here like this. Then she saw the other boy clambering to his feet and knew she couldn't wait.

'I'll get help,' Ledasha called down to Logan. 'Hang on.'

She turned and sprinted up the road, Huxtable shouting 'Leave him, get after her!' as she ran. Ledasha had reached the row of houses now though, and banged on the first door before running on to the next and doing the same. Glancing back she saw one boy close by, and the other not far behind, so left the door and ran up the middle of the road towards the post office. Two customers came out as she was halfway there, at the same time as a car came round the corner towards her.

She spun around and saw the boys stop in their tracks, uncertain what to do now there were witnesses. One of the doors Ledasha had banged on opened and a man stuck his head out. Across the road, another car pulled up at a junction. Ledasha started laughing with relief. It felt as if the whole world had descended upon them.

'Come one step closer and I'll scream,' she said to the two boys. Logan limped up from behind, trapping the two between them. They looked around, startled, as the people in the village closed in to see what the commotion was all about.

She could see Huxtable torn over what to do, but the road was filling up with people now. Ledasha pointed towards the van and shouted. 'They kidnapped us! They're still holding others prisoner, get them!' She wasn't sure anyone would follow, but it was enough of a performance to convince Huxtable, who took a few steps backwards in shock until she collided with the van. It noticeably jolted her and, still stunned but recovering from the disastrous turn of events, she called the boys to get back to her.

One of them gave Ledasha a last, furious glare, then turned and ran, pushing past Logan on his way to the van. The other hastily followed. Huxtable was already in the driver's seat as they jumped into the passenger side, leaving the rear doors still swinging open as the van raced away.

Ledasha watched them, trembling at the sudden realisation it was over. Logan came up and stood in front of her. She shook her head, smiled, and they threw their arms around each other, hugging tightly.

'You did it Dash,' he said. 'I always said it, you da bomb.'

She sighed. 'We did it. But Huxtable's still out there,

and she's still got Chelsea and the others. This isn't over yet.'

But for now, they were safe. Several people were crowding them now, concern on their faces. 'Can you call the police?' she asked the first person to reach them. 'Sergeant Wilson in Barnstaple, tell him it's Logan Reeves. He'll know what to do.'

50

A week later Ledasha was relaxing in the park. Aimee sat next to her popping bubbles as she sketched the scene before them, while Tia scrolled through her phone. It was only half past nine, but the sun was up and the day was already getting warm. The world seemed normal again. Except somehow it wasn't.

Ledasha pulled her sunglasses over her eyes and lay down. She gazed up at the blue sky, enjoying the warm breeze on her skin one moment, then feeling her arms prickling with goose bumps the next. The events of the previous week felt strangely distant, as if they'd happened to someone else, but every now and then the fear would come back to her and she'd shudder. The police had arranged counselling for her, but she kept insisting she felt fine, that she'd got into worse scrapes when she was younger. That wasn't true though. She knew there'd been moments, both in the room at the farm and then in the van when she'd thought it was all over. The image of Huxtable blowing the yellow powder into her face kept haunting her. But she'd got through it, and a big part of her felt stronger because of it.

Courtney arrived with her usual aplomb, disrupting the peace. She dropped her bag on the ground, letting it land heavily against Ledasha's waist to get her attention.

'Any news?' she asked, as she plonked herself down.

Ledasha shook her head and went back to looking at the sky. 'Huxtable's still out there somewhere. Wilson said the forensics team are still poring over the farm but there's no leads yet. Most of the kids they found are doing okay though. Some are still in hospital but the rest have been allowed back home now. Once they stopped being given the drug they came round. And Logan's doing great, keeps telling everyone how he fought off the big lad chasing me so I could escape.'

'Can they remember much?' asked Tia. 'The other kids, about what they were doing there?'

'Not really. They're all weak and confused. Some of them were with her for three years apparently and they're finding it hard to adjust. Chelsea's good though, they found her locked in a barn, and Wilson thinks the others will be alright in time. With a bit of support.'

'Mental, innit,' Courtney said ruefully. 'All those hours I spent sat in her office, bored off my skull while she told me how I could be a better person, and all the time she was kidnapping them kids. I always said she was full of crap, didn't I?'

'Wilson thinks she had it in for teenage boys,' said Ledasha. 'Might be something in her past, triggered her to hate them. She wanted girls to be stronger, to be in charge. Or it could be like Huxtable said, the boys were just easier to control. We might never know.'

'You scared?' asked Tia. 'That she's still out there I mean?'

Ledasha didn't say anything immediately. She'd wondered that herself many times over the last week. 'A bit. But she's probably long gone. Wilson said there wasn't any money or paperwork at the farm so she might have already left the country. She was renting it from a local farmer in cash so there's not much of a trail. They've got a national manhunt going on, and her picture's all over the news, but I don't reckon they're holding out much hope of locating her.'

'And what, she's just gonna forget about you?' asked Courtney. 'No chance. You need to watch out Dash, she's going to come after you.'

'Courts!' exclaimed Tia. 'Don't freak her out. If Sergeant Wilson says Dash'll be safe then she'll be safe.

Right Dash?'

She shrugged. 'I guess. I'd be happier if they found her.'

'What now then?' asked Courtney. 'Exam results aren't for another month. What are we going to do until then?'

'I'm going to keep working at the cafe,' said Ledasha. 'Save up to get a bike. And Shivani's talked about us all going up to the Cotswolds for a few days to get away from it all.'

'Christ. I'd rather have Huxtable after me,' said Courtney, laying down next to Ledasha.

'Why do you need a bike?' asked Tia. 'Everything we need is round here.'

'I've applied to do a BTEC in journalism in September,' admitted Ledasha. The others all looked at her in surprise. 'Depends on GCSE results but I think I should get enough to get in. And it's at the same college as the courses you all want to do. A moped will make it easier if I need to get out to do some reporting. And I can meet up with Chelsea,' she added sheepishly.

'Aye aye,' smirked Courtney, nudging Ledasha in the ribs. 'Now the truth's coming out. You two getting along are you? 'bout time you got some action.'

'It's not like that,' Ledasha replied defensively. 'Not yet, anyway,' she added, grinning, causing the other girls to laugh and give her a friendly push.

'Well, I like her,' said Aimee. 'Even if she helped get you into danger without us there to protect you. She seemed sound though, you should ask her out.'

Ledasha checked her watch. 'It'll have to wait, I've gotta get to work. Laters, yeah?' She pushed herself up and set off for the bus stop. Marcus had been great, telling her to take as much time as she needed before coming back, but she liked the way the cafe kept her busy and stopped her from thinking about all that had gone on.

She arrived early in Lynton, and as she walked up the hill realised she hadn't been to see Jim at the railway since her abduction. With everything that had been going on she hadn't had an opportunity, but knew she ought to go to see him. He'd been part of the whole thing from the start, and deserved to know that Logan had turned up safely.

She crossed the road and walked up the lane to the cliff top. There was a spring in her step, and for the first time she was enjoying the prospect of seeing the station, now that she had good news to tell rather than the constant worry of what had happened. A few people were strolling by the wall overlooking the sea below, and more were sitting outside the cafe.

Ledasha could hear the cables on the track moving, and when she reached the railings she leaned over to see the car approaching. It didn't take long to ease into the platform, then Jim stepped out. He saw Ledasha standing there and waved hello as he let the passengers off, then he moved around to fill up the water tank before coming back to see her.

'Hello young lady,' he greeted her cheerfully. 'I saw you on the news the other day, quite the hero.'

Ledasha blushed. 'Well, they made it out to be more than it was,' she told him bashfully. 'Just glad Logan was alright.'

'And all the other kids you saved. You did well. Even managed to stay dry this time.'

Ledasha smiled. 'I didn't tell the reporters about that bit.'

'Wise move. You coming down? It's on the house, our numbers have trebled since people heard the railway's where one of the rescued kids was snatched. Everyone wants a ride in the car he was taken from.'

She still had half an hour until she was due at work, and the carriage was otherwise empty. 'Why not? It'll be good to enjoy the ride without fretting about what might have happened to Logan.'

Jim stepped to one side and held out an arm in a show of welcoming her on board. Ledasha smiled again and walked through to the front of the car, stepping outside onto the platform next to the driver's controls. She heard him greet another passenger behind her as she leaned to look at the track stretching away below. It was horribly steep and she had a momentary feeling of dizziness, the memory of her night-time exploits coming back to her. It was an insane thing to have tried. The thought briefly crossed her mind that next time she should use a rope, but then she realised what she was thinking and shook her head in exasperation. There won't be a next time, she told herself sternly. No way was she ever going near that track again.

Jim came and stood beside her and rang the bell to let the driver below know he was ready to depart. The signal came back that they were good to go, and Jim released the handle to begin the descent.

'Do you ever have to climb down on the track?' asked Ledasha. Jim didn't reply so she figured he must be concentrating and hadn't heard. 'Jim?' she asked, looking at him. He was staring straight ahead, a glazed expression in his eyes. 'Are you okay?'

'Oh, he'll be fine,' said a familiar voice behind her. 'Once he comes round.' Ledasha spun, fear flooding into her. Standing in the doorway to the cabin, hatred etched on her face, was Iris Huxtable. Ledasha froze as she noticed a gun in her hand, and a split second later saw Huxtable squeeze the trigger.

51

The dart hit her squarely in her stomach, knocking the wind out of her.

'Don't move,' commanded Huxtable, an evil sneer on her face. 'That shot might not be fatal but this one would be.' She raised her other hand and brandished a revolver. 'I'd rather not use this but don't be under any illusion, I won't hesitate.'

For a moment her vision went a little darker, then Ledasha saw they were passing beneath the first footbridge over the railway. She put a hand to her stomach and pulled out the dart, dropping it on the floor. 'What is this?'

'Something we've been working on, a new delivery system for the drug. You have about a minute before it makes its way into your system, after which you'll do anything I say.'

Ledasha was in shock. Huxtable was still here. She hadn't fled the country like Sergeant Wilson had suspected. Courtney was right, she wanted revenge.

'You probably think you've caused a lot of trouble, don't you?' Huxtable continued, her lip curled giving her a cold, hard appearance. 'But don't worry, it's nothing that can't be fixed. There are plenty of other fields, I'll be back up and running within the year. All it needs is to tidy up a few loose ends. Starting with you.'

'But, why?' Ledasha asked, eyeing the gun warily. She knew she had to do something but Huxtable was out of reach. A rumbling next to her told her the other railway car was approaching.

'Don't move,' ordered Huxtable. 'Not a word, or I promise you I'll go after your friends Logan and Chelsea next. Keep absolutely still and they'll be unharmed.'

Ledasha's head was swimming as she struggled to decide what to do. Huxtable might be lying, and go after her friends anyway. Or would they be safe if she obeyed? It was all so confusing, the effects of the drug making her disorientated. The other car trundled past and she realised too late the moment had gone.

'All I wanted was to rescue my friend,' Ledasha slurred. She grabbed the railing as she tried to stop the swaying. 'You got away. Why come after me now?'

'Because I underestimated you before. When we spoke I revealed too much about myself. Then I remembered how good your memory is, and that I'd rashly mentioned my other site. You might have led the police to me. No, you know too much, and if I can't control you then you leave me with no alternative.'

Ledasha turned to Jim for help but he was staring ahead, oblivious to what was happening right next to him. She was starting to feel a little woozy and knew she didn't have long.

'It's no use looking at him,' Huxtable remarked. 'He's completely under my control. He won't even remember seeing me when he comes round. To all intents and purposes I'm invisible to him, he'll tell everyone you were alone on here. They'll think it's tragic, that all the events last week must have been too much for you. Poor Ledasha, emotionally vulnerable, couldn't face the world anymore. Just a few more seconds, then you can end it all.'

Ledasha knew she only had seconds left before she'd lose control. Still bent double, she spotted Jim's hand resting casually on the safety bar of their viewing platform, the other holding the handle to control the brakes.

That's it, thought Ledasha in a sudden moment of clarity. The deadman's handle he'd called it. It was her last chance. Lunging for Jim's arm, she knocked it away. The car shuddered to a stop as the brakes locked on. Huxtable was thrown forwards, dropping the gun as she collided with the barrier. With a last massive effort Ledasha leaned down and heaved Huxtable's legs up, toppling her over the edge and onto the track. It must have been a good three metre drop to the track, and Huxtable landed heavily, her foot twisted nastily on one of the sleepers.

Ledasha dropped to the floor of the railway car, the clear screen keeping her safe as the drug took hold. She was aware of her surroundings but felt powerless to do anything. It was almost like an out of body experience, but her limbs and mouth failed her. She held on tightly, in a dreamlike state, waiting for someone, anyone, to tell her what to do.

Next to her, Jim had been pushed into the corner of the platform by Ledasha and the subsequent stoppage. Slowly, he moved back into his usual driver's position and put his hand back on the controls. She watched in a dazed confusion as Jim lifted the handle to release the brakes. Too late, Ledasha grasped what was happening. The car gave a small shudder then started moving, very quickly picking up speed.

'No,' Ledasha called weakly. 'Stop, she's down there.' Jim didn't react and she realised he couldn't see Huxtable, or hear her trying to warn him. He was running purely on automatic pilot. She clambered to her knees and threw herself again at him, pulling him to the ground and putting all her weight on him. The car ground to a halt again but the scream and the crunching sound from below told her she was too late. Ledasha was vaguely aware they were close to the second bridge across the tracks, and she could see people rushing up, but it took all her energy to hold Jim down away from the controls. He struggled briefly, then relaxed and fell into the same catatonic state she knew was coming for her. She closed her eyes, and let herself be swallowed up by the peace of sleep.

52

Ledasha was lying in bed in her private room at the hospital when she heard a knock. Looking up, she saw Chelsea standing in the doorway holding some yellow, bell-shaped flowers.

'Closest I could find,' she said, grinning nervously, glancing at Shivani and Ben sat by the bedside. 'Can I come in?'

'Of course,' Ledasha beamed as she propped herself up on her pillows and giggled at the flowers. The sight of Chelsea made her feel alive for the first time in ages. Ledasha quickly took in her outfit, approving of the tight fitted t-shirt over a pair of high-waisted flowery shorts.

'Are we missing something?' asked Ben.

Ledasha introduced Chelsea to her foster parents, explaining how she was the girl who'd been locked up with her at the farm.

'Are you okay now, dear?' asked Shivani, taking the flowers from her and walking to the sink.

'Yeah, I'm good thanks,' Chelsea replied. 'Bit weird being famous, the reporters and tv lot keep turning up at the house, but me mum's happy as a pig in –.' She hesitated. 'Well, she's loving the attention, she's on the phone all day long to her friends. I'll be happy when it all blows over myself.'

'Wouldn't we all,' said Shivani.

'It's been pretty mad at our place too,' Ledasha explained. 'And that was before all the excitement of yesterday. Pull up another chair, I'll fill you in.'

'Don't worry,' said Ben, getting up. 'We'll go and grab a coffee shall we, leave you two alone to catch up.'

Ledasha nodded at him gratefully. She'd had several visitors throughout the day and Ben had soon caught on that she found it easier to relax if the grown-ups weren't around. Plus he'd heard the story several times now so she knew he was probably keen to get away.

'The docs want to keep me in for a couple of days to do some tests,' Ledasha told her when they were alone. 'Make sure the after effects of the drug are all gone, but I'm fine. Really. They know that. I think they just wanna check I'm not traumatised by the whole crushing someone beneath a train thing.'

'And you're not?' asked Chelsea as she sat down next to the bed.

'Nah way man,' Ledasha replied. 'She rolled the dice, she lost. It was her or me, and after what she did to all them boys, especially Connor, I'm not losing any sleep over her getting squished. Good riddance I say.'

Chelsea reached out and held Ledasha's hand and gave it a squeeze. 'You're sure? I mean, I totes agree, so relieved to hear she's gone, but still, I wasn't there. It must have been terrifying.'

Ledasha gave a small shrug. 'Yeah, at one point I thought that was it, I'm a gonner. When she hit me with the dart it was scary at first, but the drug must have numbed it or something as it all seemed calm after that, you know? Like, I knew time was running out and all, but everything felt like it was in slow motion. I couldn't get to her, and I couldn't get away either. It was all just, I dunno, like a dream. But then I don't remember anything that happened after that. They told me she fell from the front of the car somehow and got run over, but I didn't see any of it. Or if I did the drug had kicked in enough to make me oblivious to it all. Then I woke up in the ambulance. Even that's all a blur. They must have given me something to make me sleep as the next thing I know it's today.'

'Mental,' said Chelsea, squeezing her hand again. 'But I'm so glad you're alright. You had me worried.'

Ledasha squeezed her back. There was an awkward silence as they both continued to hold hands. Ledasha didn't want her to let go, but suddenly felt more tense than she ever had when she'd been trapped by Mrs Huxtable. She could sense her face turning red and her hand started to feel clammy. She quickly pulled it away in case it was evident. This is ridiculous, she thought. She'd nearly died several times in the last week, and here she was getting all worked up about talking to someone she fancied. Sod it, she decided, I'll just get it over with and ask her out.

'Would you –'

'Did you –' said Chelsea at the same time. They both laughed. 'You first,' Chelsea said.

'No, you go,' replied Ledasha.

'I was just gonna ask, did you hear they found the second farm in Somerset?'

Ledasha felt a mixture of relief at the change of subject, and anxiousness that the moment had passed and she'd missed her chance.

'Yeah, Sergeant Wilson was here this morning,' she replied, brushing her hair back and blowing cool air onto her forehead to try to fight the blushing she knew was covering her cheeks. 'The lads on that farm started to come round this morning apparently. The drug must have begun to wear off when Huxtable didn't come back. Most were too scared to leave but a couple of them got out and raised the alarm. The police found twelve of them there, it's even bigger than the place we found.'

Chelsea shook her head. 'That's mad. And it could have been us. If you hadn't managed to escape we'd still be there now.'

'Well, not me,' said Ledasha ruefully. 'She wanted me dead. Upset her one too many times. Wouldn't have been much use to anyone then, would I? Tia was properly upset when she came to visit this morning, felt like they'd all messed up letting me go off on my own like that and get caught again.'

'So, you and Tia are, like, good friends then?' asked Chelsea.

'Yeah man, of course.' Ledasha paused then noticed Chelsea was returning her gaze nervously. 'Oh. No, not like that. She's just a friend.'

'Oh, good,' said Chelsea, who was turning red herself now. She glanced away, searching for something else to talk about.

'She's into guys,' said Ledasha before Chelsea could say anything. 'More fool her.'

Chelsea smiled and looked up. 'And you're not? And you're not seeing anyone?'

Ledasha shook her head and smiled back. 'No, I'm not. Yet,' she added.

Printed in Great Britain
by Amazon